STANDOFF

There was an angry whine from the rock face above them, and then the crack of a rifle.

As one man, the posse scattered for shelter, whipping rifles from their scabbards. Hardin swore, and Kimmel wormed his way to a better position.

Short had left the saddle in his scramble for shelter, and his horse stood in the pen, the canteen making a large lump behind the saddle. Suddenly the horse leaped to the solid thud of a striking bullet, and then followed another crack of the rifle, echoing over the mountainside.

Short swore viciously. "If he killed that horse . . ." But the horse seemed uninjured.

"Hey!" Kinsey yelled. "He shot your canteen!"

It was true enough. Water was pouring onto the ground, and Short started to get up. Sutter grabbed his arm.

"Hold it! If he could get that canteen, he could get you!"

Bantam Books by Louis L'Amour
Ask your bookseller for the books you have missed.

NOVELS

BENDIGO SHAFTER
BORDEN CHANTRY
BRIONNE
THE BROKEN GUN
THE BURNING HILLS
THE CALIFORNIOS
CALLAGHEN
CATLOW
CHANCY
THE CHEROKEE TRAIL
COMSTOCK LODE
CONAGHER
CROSSFIRE TRAIL
DARK CANYON
DOWN THE LONG HILLS
THE EMPTY LAND
FAIR BLOWS THE WIND
FALLON
THE FERGUSON RIFLE
THE FIRST FAST DRAW
FLINT
GUNS OF THE
  TIMBERLANDS
HANGING WOMAN
  CREEK
THE HAUNTED MESA
HELLER WITH A GUN
THE HIGH GRADERS
HIGH LONESOME
HONDO
HOW THE WEST WAS
  WON
THE IRON MARSHAL
THE KEY-LOCK MAN
KID RODELO
KILKENNY
KILLOE
KILRONE
KIOWA TRAIL
LAST OF THE BREED
LAST STAND AT PAPAGO
  WELLS
THE LONESOME GODS
THE MAN CALLED NOON
THE MAN FROM
  SKIBBEREEN
THE MAN FROM THE
  BROKEN HILLS
MATAGORDA
MILO TALON
THE MOUNTAIN VALLEY
  WAR
NORTH TO THE RAILS

OVER ON THE DRY SIDE
PASSIN' THROUGH
THE PROVING TRAIL
THE QUICK AND THE
  DEAD
RADIGAN
REILLY'S LUCK
THE RIDER OF LOST
  CREEK
RIVERS WEST
THE SHADOW RIDERS
SHALAKO
SHOWDOWN AT YELLOW
  BUTTE
SILVER CANYON
SON OF A WANTED MAN
TAGGART
THE TALL STRANGER
TO TAME A LAND
TUCKER
UNDER THE SWEETWATER
  RIM
UTAH BLAINE
THE WALKING DRUM
WESTWARD THE TIDE
WHERE THE LONG GRASS
  BLOWS

SHORT STORY
COLLECTIONS

BEYOND THE GREAT
  SNOW MOUNTAINS
BOWDRIE
BOWDRIE'S LAW
BUCKSKIN RUN
DUTCHMAN'S FLAT
END OF THE DRIVE
THE HILLS OF HOMICIDE
LAW OF THE DESERT
  BORN
LONG RIDE HOME
LONIGAN
MONUMENT ROCK
NIGHT OVER THE
  SOLOMONS
THE OUTLAWS OF
  MESQUITE
THE RIDER OF THE RUBY
  HILLS
RIDING FOR THE BRAND
THE STRONG SHALL LIVE
THE TRAIL TO CRAZY MAN
VALLEY OF THE SUN
WAR PARTY

WEST FROM SINGAPORE
WEST OF DODGE
YONDERING

SACKETT TITLES

SACKETT'S LAND
TO THE FAR BLUE
  MOUNTAINS
THE WARRIOR'S PATH
JUBAL SACKETT
RIDE THE RIVER
THE DAYBREAKERS
SACKETT
LANDO
MOJAVE CROSSING
MUSTANG MAN
THE LONELY MEN
GALLOWAY
TREASURE MOUNTAIN
LONELY ON THE
  MOUNTAIN
RIDE THE DARK TRAIL
THE SACKETT BRAND
THE SKY-LINERS

THE HOPALONG CASSIDY
NOVELS

THE RIDERS OF HIGH
  ROCK
THE RUSTLERS OF WEST
  FORK
THE TRAIL TO SEVEN
  PINES
TROUBLE SHOOTER

NONFICTION

EDUCATION OF A
  WANDERING MAN
FRONTIER
THE SACKETT
  COMPANION:
  A Personal Guide to
    the Sackett Novels
A TRAIL OF MEMORIES:
  The Quotations of Louis
    L'Amour, compiled by
    Angelique L'Amour

POETRY

SMOKE FROM THIS ALTAR

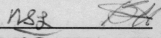

DUTCHMAN'S FLAT
Louis L'Amour

BANTAM BOOKS
NEW YORK · TORONTO · LONDON · SYDNEY · AUCKLAND

DUTCHMAN'S FLAT

*A Bantam Book / published by arrangement with
the author
Bantam edition / March 1986
Bantam reissue / July 1992*

ISBN 0-553-28111-9

Published simultaneously in the United States and Canada

Bantam Books are published by Bantam Books, a division of Bantam
Doubleday Dell Publishing Group, Inc. Its trademark, consisting of the words
"Bantam Books" and the portrayal of a rooster, is Registered in U.S. Patent
and Trademark Office and in other countries. Marca Registrada. Bantam
Books, 1540 Broadway, New York, New York 10036.

PRINTED IN THE UNITED STATES OF AMERICA

OPM   43   42   41   40   39   38   37

*Dedicated once more to
honesty in publishing.*

Contents

Foreword

The stories of the west are many, and few of them have been told. Many, of course, deal with land and cattle, with the business of simply getting from here to there, with soldiers returning from the Civil War, and of course, with the American Indian. The wagon trains, the wild boom camps, the railroads building, the adjustments, both mental and physical, to living in a different world with a different life-style, but, above all, the stories of the west are exciting because they are dealing with a selected people, selected by the circumstances.

Not everybody came west, not everybody wanted to. Those who came were the most adventurous—the hardy souls, both men and women, who were willing to risk everything to find a new life.

None of them were completely innocent as to the life into which they were entering. As always, man looked westward through rose-colored glasses, seeingly only the excitement, the chances for riches, a new life—few realized how hard it was going to be.

The frontier took care of that. Some of the newcomers turned tail and ran for shelter back home, some died of hardship and disease, by accident and warfare of one kind or another. If you were not strong you either became so or you died, it was as simple as that. Stories of the frontier are exciting because they are about dynamic people, the ones who have been through the mill. The men and women who arrived in the west were survivors, they had to be. And they had to continue to survive.

No part of it was easy, and those who survived did so because they were capable of standing alone. When you get a bunch of individualists brushing against each other, there are always possibilities for trouble, for they were proud people, secure in themselves but apt to resent any infringement of their rights or what they conceived to be so.

Most men were honest. Those who were not were soon identified and the word went along the cattle trails and the stage roads. A man with a reputation for shady deals or dishonesty of one kind or another was soon relegated to doing business with his own kind. It was simply too small a population despite the size of the country. Western men and women had no secrets except those they brought west with them. Once arrived their lives became an open book. Most of the towns were of a few hundred people only, and those which were larger were made up of known people in most instances.

Once arrived in the west a man or woman soon became known by his or her actions. Nobody asked any questions. Nobody cared what you had done or who your father and mother were. It was what you were now that mattered, it mattered that you were honest, that you had courage, that you did your job.

If a stranger rode into town people were inclined to be reserved until they knew who and what he was. He would find courtesy but not acceptance until he had shown his colors.

Because western men and women were the sort of people they were, stories grew naturally from their actions and reactions. Yet it was the land as well as the people that bred stories, a harsh land but a land of beauty and one that must forever be a consideration in whatever one planned.

In the following pages are a few stories growing out of the westward movement. Distances were great, communications difficult or delayed, and much could happen while a man was off to fight a war or drive a herd of cattle to market.

Guns were used, but not carelessly, and there were men then as now who understand nothing else.

On the back cover I've explained why this edition of *Dutchman's Flat* is coming out so closely with Bantam's recent publication of the short fiction collection I put together entitled *Riding for the Brand*. A very small number of my stories are not protected by copyright law and, without my permission, a publisher I am in no way associated with is bringing out original magazine versions of some of these works in books under the same titles with my name on them.

You'd think this publisher would remember what happened in the marketplace almost three years ago when my readers bypassed their unauthorized editions of *Law of the Desert Born* and *The Hills of Homicide* in favor of the authorized Bantam publications. Perhaps they think my readers have short memories. Or that I'd be too busy to react to what they're doing now. They're wrong.

While they may have the legal right to publish my stories contained in these two unauthorized editions, I'm now more determined than ever that my stories be published the way I see fit to best serve my readers.

I stopped work on a new novel to personally select and edit the stories that make up *Dutchman's Flat* and *Riding for the Brand* and to write the supporting historical notes that introduce each work and enhance the reading experience.

My publisher and I won't allow my readers to be shortchanged. In addition to my newly written commentaries, these authorized editions have more stories than the unauthorized ones.

Bantam Books is my official publisher and has been so for more than thirty years. They are the only publisher authorized to issue my short stories in book form. Only accept short story collections with my name on them that are published by Bantam.

It goes without saying that I'll never autograph any unauthorized editions of my books. As far as I'm concerned, they simply don't exist.

I hope you enjoy this edition of *Dutchman's Flat*.

Louis L'Amour
Los Angeles, California
February, 1986

AUTHOR'S NOTE
DUTCHMAN'S FLAT

Everything a man does is indication of his character, whether he cheats at cards or takes an unfair advantage because it is legal.

This was probably more evident in the West, where a man's actions were often starkly revealed. The population was sparse, and there was, literally, no place to hide.

Occasionally I have become so involved with the characters in a story that I hesitate to let them go, and "Dutchman's Flat" was such a story. As a result I took the same basic situation and extended the story, much later, into a novel called The Key-Lock Man. *In another such case the short story "War Party" became* Bendigo Shafter.

Characters can become very real to their author, and often it is difficult to abandon them. One wants to know more about them, about their lives after the story in question, and the only way to know is to let the story tell itself. The story of the people in "Dutchman's Flat" is as revealing of western character as any I have written.

Dutchman's Flat

The dust of Dutchman's Flat had settled in a gray film upon their faces, and Neill could see the streaks made by the sweat on their cheeks and brows and knew his own must be the same. No man of them was smiling and they rode with their rifles in their hands, six grim and purposeful men upon the trail of a single rider.

They were men shaped and tempered to the harsh ways of a harsh land, strong in their sense of justice, ruthless in their demand for punishment, relentless in pursuit. From the desert they had carved their homes, and from the desert they drew their courage and their code, and the desert knows no mercy.

"Where's he headin', you reckon?"

"Home, mostly likely. He'll need grub an' a rifle. He's been livin' on the old Sorenson place."

Kimmel spat. "He's welcome to it. That place starved out four men I know of." He stared at the hoof tracks ahead. "He's got a good horse."

"Big buckskin. Reckon we'll catch him, Hardin?"

"Sure. Not this side of his place, though. There ain't no shortcuts we can take to head him off, and he's pointin' for home straight as a horse can travel."

"Ain't tryin' to cover his trail none."

"No use tryin'." Hardin squinted his eyes against the glare of the sun. "He knows we figure he'll head for his ranch."

"He's no tenderfoot." Kesney expressed the thought that had been dawning upon them all in the last two hours. "He knows how to save a horse, an' he knows a trail."

They rode on in near silence. Hardin scratched his

unshaven jaw. The dust lifted from the hoofs of the horses as they weaved their way through the catclaw and mesquite. It was a parched and sunbaked land, with only dancing heat waves and the blue distance of the mountains to draw them on. The trail they followed led straight as a man could ride across the country. Only at draws or nests of rocks did it swerve, where they noticed the rider always gave his horse the best of it.

No rider of the desert must see a man to know him, for it is enough to follow his trail. In these things are the ways of a man made plain, his kindness or cruelty, his ignorance or cunning, his strength and his weakness. There are indications that cannot escape a man who has followed trails, and in the two hours since they had ridden out of Freedom the six had already learned much of the man they followed. And they would learn more.

"What started it?"

The words sounded empty and alone in the vast stillness of the basin.

Hardin turned his head slightly so the words could drift back. It was the manner of a man who rides much in the wind or rain. He shifted the rifle to his left hand and wiped his sweaty right palm on his coarse pants leg.

"Some loose talk. He was in the Bon Ton buyin' grub an' such. Johnny said somethin' at which he took offense an' they had some words. Johnny was wearin' a gun, but this Lock wasn't, so he gets him a gun an' goes over to the Longhorn.

"He pushes open the door an' shoots Johnny twice through the body. In the back." Hardin spat. "He fired a third shot, but that missed Johnny and busted a bottle of whiskey."

There was a moment's silence while they digested this, and then Neill looked up.

"We lynchin' him for the killin' or bustin' the whiskey?"

It was a good question, but drew no reply. The dignity of the five other riders was not to be touched by humor. They were riders on a mission. Neill let his eyes drift over the dusty copper of the desert. He had no liking for the idea of lynching any man, and he did not know the squatter from the Sorenson place. Living there should be punishment enough for any man. Besides—

"Who saw the shooting?" he asked.

"Nobody seen it, actually. Only he never gave Johnny a fair shake. Sam was behind the bar, but he was down to the other end and it happened too fast."

"What's his name? Somebody call him Lock?" Neill asked. There was something incongruous in lynching a man whose name you did not know. He shifted in the saddle, squinting his eyes toward the distant lakes dancing in the mirage of heat waves.

"What's it matter? Lock, his name is. Chat Lock."

"Funny name."

The comment drew no response. The dust was thicker now and Neill pulled his bandanna over his nose and mouth. His eyes were drawn back to the distant blue of the lakes. They were enticingly cool and beautiful, lying across the way ahead and in the basin off to the right. This was the mirage that lured many a man from his trail to pursue the always retreating shoreline of the lake. It looked like water, it really did.

Maybe there was water in the heat waves. Maybe if a man knew how, he could extract it and drink. The thought drew his hand to his canteen, but he took it away without drinking. The slosh water in the canteen was no longer enticing, for it was warm, brackish, and unsatisfying.

"You know him, Kimmel?" Kesney asked. He was a wiry little man, hard as a whipstock, with bits of sharp steel for eyes and brown muscle-corded hands. "I wouldn't know him if I saw him."

"Sure, I know him. Big feller, strong made, rusty-like hair an' maybe forty year old. Looks plumb salty, too, an' from what I hear he's no friendly sort of man. Squattin' on that Sorenson place looks plumb suspicious, for no man can make him a livin' on that dry-as-a-bone place. No fit place for man nor beast. Ever'body figures no honest man would squat on such a place."

It seemed a strange thing, to be searching out a man whom none of them really knew. Of course, they had all known Johnny Webb. He was a handsome, popular young man, a daredevil and a hellion, but a very attractive one, and a top hand to boot. They had all known him and had all liked him. Then, one of the things that made them so sure that this had been a wrong killing, even aside from the shots in the back, was the fact that Johnny Webb had been the fastest man in the Spring Valley country. Fast, and a dead shot.

Johnny had worked with all these men, and they were good men—hard men, but good. Kimmel, Hardin, and Kesney had all made something of their ranches, as had the others, only somewhat less so. They had come west when the going was rough, fought Indians and rustlers, and then battled drought, dust, and hot, hard winds. It took a strong man to survive in this country, and they had survived. He, Neill, was the youngest of them all and the newest in the country. He was still looked upon with some reserve. He had been here only five years.

Neill could see the tracks of the buckskin, and it gave him a strange feeling to realize that the man who rode that horse would soon be dead, hanging from a noose in one of those ropes attached to a saddle horn of Hardin or Kimmel. Neill had never killed a man or seen one killed by another man, and the thought made him uncomfortable.

Yet Johnny was gone, and his laughter and his jokes were a thing passed. They had brightened more than one roundup, more than one bitter day of heartbreaking labor on the range. Not that he had been an angel. He had been a proper hand with a gun and could throw one. And in his time he had had his troubles.

"He's walkin' his horse," Kesney said, "leadin' him."

"He's a heavy man," Hardin agreed, "an' he figures to give us a long chase."

"Gone lame on him maybe," Kimmel suggested.

"No, that horse isn't limpin'. This Lock is a smart one."

They had walked out of the ankle-deep dust now and were crossing a parched, dry plain of crusted earth. Hardin reined in suddenly and pointed.

"Look there." He indicated a couple of flecks on the face of the earth crust where something had spilled. "Water splashed."

"Careless," Neill said. "He'll need that water."

"No," Kesney said. "He was pourin' water in a cloth to wipe out his horse's nostrils. Bet you a dollar."

"Sure," Hardin agreed, "that's it. Horse breathes a lot better. A man runnin' could kill a good horse on this Flat. He knows that."

They rode on, and for almost a half hour no one spoke. Neill frowned at the sun. It had been on his left a few minutes ago, and now they rode straight into it.

"What's he doin'?" Kesney said wonderingly. "This ain't the way to his place!" The trail had turned again, and now the sun was on their right. Then it turned again and was at their backs. Hardin was in the lead, and he drew up and swore wickedly.

They ranged alongside him, and stared down into a draw that cracked the face of the desert alongside the trail they had followed. Below them was a place where a horse had stood, and across the bank something white fluttered from the parched clump of greasewood.

Kesney slid from the saddle and crossed the wash. When he had the slip of white, he stared at it, and then they heard him swear. He walked back and handed it to Hardin. They crowded near.

Neill took the slip from Hardin's fingers after he had read it. It was torn from some sort of book and the words were plain enough, scrawled with a flat rock for a rest.

That was a fair shutin anyways six aint nowhars
enuf, go fetch more men. Man on the gray better
titen his girth or heel have him a sorebacked hoss.

"Why that . . . !" Short swore softly. "He was lyin' within fifty yards of us when we come by. Had him a rifle, too. I seen it in a saddle scabbard on that buckskin in town. He could have got one of us, anyway!"

"Two or three most likely." Kimmel commented. The men stared at the paper and then looked back into the wash. The sand showed a trail, but cattle had walked here, too. It would make the going a little slower.

Neill, his face flushed and his ears red, was tightening his saddle girth. The others avoided his eyes. The insult to him, even if the advice was good, was an insult to them all. Their jaws tightened. The squatter was playing Indian with them, and none of them liked it.

"Fair shootin', yeah!" Sutter exploded. "Right in the back!"

The trail led down the wash now, and it was slower going. The occasional puffs of wind they had left on the desert above were gone and the heat in the bottom of the wash was ovenlike. They rode into it, almost seeming to push their way through flames that seared. Sweat dripped into their eyes until they smarted, and trickled in tiny rivulets through their dust-caked beards, making their faces itch maddeningly.

The wash spilled out into a wide, flat bed of sand left by the rains of bygone years, and the tracks were plainer now. Neill tightened his bandanna and rode on, sodden with heat and weariness. The trail seemed deliberately to lead them into the worst regions, for now he was riding straight toward an alkali lake that loomed ahead.

At the edge of the water, the trail vanished. Lock had ridden right into the lake. They drew up and stared at it, unbelieving.

"He can't cross," Hardin stated flatly. "That's deep out to the middle. Durned treacherous, too. A horse could get bogged down mighty easy."

They skirted the lake, taking it carefully, three going one way, and three the other. Finally, glancing back, Neill caught sight of Kesney's uplifted arm.

"They found it," he said. "Let's go back." Yet as he rode he was thinking what they all knew. This was a delay, for Lock knew they would have to scout the shores both ways to find his trail, and there would be a delay while the last three rejoined the first. A small thing, but in such a chase it was important.

"Why not ride right on to the ranch?" Short suggested.

"We might," Hardin speculated. "On the other hand he might fool us an' never go nigh it. Then we could lose him."

The trail became easier, for now Lock was heading straight into the mountains.

"Where's he goin'?" Kesney demanded irritably. "This don't make sense, nohow!"

There was no reply, the horsemen stretching out in single file, riding up the draw into the mountains. Suddenly Kimmel, who was now in the lead, drew up. Before him a thread of water trickled from the rock and spilled into a basin of stones.

"Huh!" Hardin stared. "I never knowed about this spring afore. Might's well have a drink." He swung down.

They all got down and Neill rolled a smoke.

"Somebody sure fixed her up nice," he said. "That wall of stone makin' that basin ain't so old."

"No, it ain't."

Short watched them drink and grinned.

"He's a fox, right enough. He's an old ladino, this one. A reg'lar mossy horn. It don't take no time for one man to drink, an' one hoss. But here we got six men an' six horses to drink an' we lose more time."

"You really think he planned it that way?" Neill was skeptical.

Hardin looked around at him. "Sure. This Lock knows his way around."

When they were riding on, Neill thought about that. Lock *was* shrewd. He was desert wise. And he was leading them a chase. If not even Hardin knew of this spring, and he had been twenty years in the Spring Valley country, then Lock must know a good deal about the country. Of course, this range of mountains was singularly desolate, and there was nothing in them to draw a man.

So they knew this about their quarry. He was a man wise in the ways of desert and trail, and one who knew the country. Also, Neill reflected, it was probable he had built that basin himself. Nobody lived over this way but Lock, for now it was not far to the Sorenson place.

Now they climbed a single horse trail across the starkly eroded foothills, sprinkled with clumps of Joshua and Spanish bayonet. It was a weird and broken land, where long fingers of black lava stretched down the hills and out into the desert as though clawing toward the alkali lake they had left behind. The trail mounted steadily and a little breeze touched their cheeks. Neill lifted his hand and wiped dust from his brow and it came away in flakes, plastered by sweat.

The trail doubled and changed, now across the rock face of the burnt red sandstone, then into the lava itself, skirting hills where the exposed ledges mounted in layers like a vast cake of many colors. Then the way dipped down, and they wound among huge boulders, smooth as so many waterworn pebbles. Neill sagged in the saddle, for the hours were growing long, and the trail showed no sign of ending.

"Lucky he ain't waitin' to shoot," Kimmel commented, voicing the first remark in over an hour. "He could pick us off like flies."

As if in reply to his comment, there was an angry whine above them and then the crack of a rifle.

As one man they scattered for shelter, whipping rifles from their scabbards, for all but two had replaced them when they reached the lake. Hardin swore, and Kimmel wormed his way to a better view of the country ahead.

Short had left the saddle in his scramble for shelter, and his horse stood in the open, the canteen making a large lump behind the saddle. Suddenly the horse leaped to the solid thud of a striking bullet, and then followed the crack of the rifle, echoing over the mountainside.

Short swore viciously. "If he killed that horse . . . !" But the horse, while shifting nervously, seemed uninjured.

"Hey!" Kesney yelled. "He shot your canteen!"

It was true enough. Water was pouring onto the ground, and swearing, Short started to get up. Sutter grabbed his arm.

"Hold it! If he could get that canteen, he could get you!"

They waited, and the trickle of water slowed, then faded to a drip. All of them stared angrily at the unrewarding rocks ahead of them. One canteen the less. Still they had all filled up at the spring and should have enough. Uncomfortably, however, they realized that the object of their chase, the man called Chat Lock, knew where he was taking them, and he had not emptied that canteen by chance. Now they understood the nature of the man they followed. He did nothing without object.

Lying on the sand or rocks they waited, peering ahead.

"He's probably ridin' off now!" Sutter barked.

Nobody showed any disposition to move. The idea appealed to none of them, for the shot into the canteen showed plainly enough the man they followed was no child with a rifle. Kimmel finally put his hat on a rifle muzzle and lifted it. There was no response. Then he tried sticking it around a corner.

Nothing happened, and he withdrew it. Almost at once, a shot hit the trail not far from where the hat had been. The indication was plain. Lock was warning them not only that he was still there, but that he was not to be fooled by so obvious a trick.

They waited, and Hardin suddenly slid over a rock and began a flanking movement. He crawled, and they waited, watching his progress. The cover he had was good, and he could crawl almost to where the hidden marksman must be. Finally, he disappeared from their sight and they waited. Neill tasted the water in his canteen and dozed.

At last they heard a long yell, and looking up, they saw Hardin standing on a rock far up the trail, waving them on. Mounting, they led Hardin's horse and rode on up the trail. He met them at the trail side, and his eyes were angry.

"Gone!" he said, thrusting out a hard palm. In it lay three brass cartridge shells. "Found 'em standing up in a line on a rock. An' look here." He pointed, and they stared down at the trail where he indicated. A neat arrow made of stones pointed down the trail ahead of them, and scratches on the face of the sandstone above it were the words: FOLLER THE SIGNS.

Kesney jerked his hat from his head and hurled it to the ground.

"Why, that dirty . . . !" He stopped, beside himself with anger. The contempt of the man they pursued was obvious. He was making fools of them, deliberately teasing them, indicating his trail as to a child or a tenderfoot.

"That ratty back-shootin' killer!" Short said. "I'll take pleasure in usin' a rope on him! Thinks he's smart!"

They started on, and the horse ahead of them left a plain trail, but a quarter of a mile further along, three dried pieces of mesquite had been laid in the trail to form another arrow.

Neill stared at it. This was becoming a personal matter now. He was deliberately playing with them, and he must know how that would set with men such as Kimmel and Hardin. It was a deliberate challenge; more, it was a sign of the utmost contempt.

The vast emptiness of the basin they skirted now was becoming lost in the misty purple light of late afternoon. On the right, the wall of the mountain grew steeper and turned a deeper red. The burnt red of the earlier hours was now a bright rust red, and here and there long fingers of quartz shot their white arrows down into the face of the cliff.

They all saw the next message, but all read and averted their eyes. It was written on a blank face of the cliff. First, there was an arrow, pointing ahead, and then the words: SHADE, SO'S YOU DON'T GIT SUNSTROK.

They rode on, and for several miles as the shadows drew down, they followed the markers their quarry left at intervals along the trail. All six of the men were tired and beaten. Their horses moved slowly, and the desert air was growing chill. It had been a long chase.

Suddenly, Kimmel and Kesney, who rode side by side, reined in. A small wall of rock was across the trail, and an arrow pointed downward into a deep cleft.

"What do you think, Hardin? He could pick us off man by man."

Hardin studied the situation with misgivings and hesitated, lighting a smoke.

"He ain't done it yet."

Neill's remark fell into the still air like a rock into a calm pool of water. As the rings of ripples spread wider into the thoughts of the other five, he waited.

Lock could have killed one or two of them, perhaps all of them by now. Why had he not? Was he waiting for darkness and an easy getaway? Or was he leading them into a trap?

"The devil with it!" Hardin exclaimed impatiently. He wheeled his horse and pistol in hand, started down into the narrow rift in the dark. One by one, they followed. The darknees closed around them, and the air was damp and chill. They rode on, and then the trail mounted steeply toward a grayness ahead of them, and they came out in a small basin. Ahead of them they heard a trickle of running water and saw the darkness of trees.

Cautiously they approached. Suddenly, they saw the light of a fire. Hardin drew up sharply and slid from his horse. The others followed. In a widening circle, they crept toward the fire. Kesney was the first to reach it, and the sound of his swearing rent the stillness and shattered it like thin glass. They swarmed in around him.

The fire was built close beside a small running stream, and nearby was a neat pile of dry sticks. On a paper, laid out carefully on a rock, was a small mound of coffee, and another of sugar. Nobody said anything for a minute, staring at the fire and the coffee. The taunt was obvious, and they were bitter men. It was bad enough to have a stranger make such fools of them on a trail, to treat them like tenderfeet, but to prepare a camp for them. . . .

"I'll be cussed if I will!" Short said violently. "I'll go sleep on the desert first!"

"Well—" Hardin was philosophical. "Might's well make the most of it. We can't trail him at night, no way."

Kimmel had dug a coffeepot out of his pack and was getting water from the stream which flowed from a basin just above their camp. Several of the others began to dig out grub, and Kesney sat down glumly, staring into the fire. He started to pick a stick off the pile left for them and then jerked his hand as though he had seen a snake. Getting up, he stalked back into the trees, and after a minute, he returned.

Sutter was looking around, and suddenly he spoke. "Boys, I know this place! Only I never knew about that crack in the wall. This here's the Mormon Well!"

Hardin sat up and looked around. "Durned if it ain't," he said. "I ain't been in here for six or seven years."

Sutter squatted on his haunches. "Look!" He was excited and eager, sketching with a stick in the sand. "Here's Mormon Well, where we are. Right over here to the northwest there's an old sawmill an' a tank just above it. I'll bet a side of beef that durned killer is holed up for the night in that sawmill!"

Kesney, who had taken most to heart the taunting of the man they pursued, was on his knees staring at the diagram drawn in the damp sand. He was nodding thoughtfully.

"He's right! He sure is. I remember that old mill! I holed up there one time in a bad storm. Spent two days in it. If that sidewinder stays there tonight, we can get him!"

As they ate, they talked over their plan. Traveling over the rugged mountains ahead of them was almost impossible in the darkness, and besides, even if Lock could go the night without stopping, his horse could not. The buckskin must have a rest. Moreover, with all the time Lock had been losing along the trail, he could not be far ahead. It stood to reason that he must have planned just this, for them to stop here, and to hole up in the sawmill himself.

"We'd better surprise him," Hardin suggested. "That sawmill is heavy timber, an' a man in there with a rifle an' plenty of ammunition could stand us off for a week."

"Has he got plenty?"

"Sure he has," Neill told them. "I was in the Bon Ton when he bought his stuff. He's got grub and he's got plenty of forty-fours. They do for either his Colt or his Winchester."

Unspoken as yet, but present in the mind of each man, was a growing respect for their quarry, a respect and an element of doubt. Would such a man as this shoot another in the back? The evidence against him was plain enough, or seemed plain enough.

Yet beyond the respect there was something else, for it was no longer simply a matter of justice to be done, but a personal thing. Each of them felt in some measure that his reputation was at stake. It had not been enough for Lock to leave an obvious trail, but he must leave markers, the sort to be used for any tenderfoot. There were men in this group who could trail a woodtick through a pine forest.

"Well," Kimmel said reluctantly and somewhat grimly, "he left us good coffee, anyway!"

They tried the coffee and agreed. Few things in this world are so comforting and so warming to the heart as hot coffee on a chilly night over a campfire when the day has been long and weary. They drank, and they relaxed. And as they relaxed the seeds of doubt began to sprout and put forth branches of speculation.

"He could have got more'n one of us today," Sutter hazarded. "This one is brush wise."

"I'll pull that rope on him!" Short stated positively. "No man makes a fool out of me!" But in his voice there was something lacking.

"You know," Kesney suggested, "if he knows these hills like he seems to, an' if he really wanted to lose us, we'd have to burn the stump and sift the ashes before we found him!"

There was no reply. Hardin drew back and eased the leg of his pants away from the skin, for the cloth had grown too hot for comfort.

Short tossed a stick from the neat pile into the fire.

"That mill ain't so far away," he suggested, "shall we give her a try?"

"Later." Hardin leaned back against a log and yawned. "She's been a hard day."

"Both them bullets go in Johnny's back?"

The question moved among them like a ghost. Short stirred uneasily, and Kesney looked up and glared around. "Sure they did! Didn't they, Hardin?"

"Sure." He paused thoughtfully. "Well, no. One of them was under his left arm. Right between the ribs. Looked like a heart shot to me. The other one went through near his spine."

"The heck with it!" Kesney declared. "No slick, rustlin' squatter can come into this country and shoot one of our boys! He was shot in the back, an' I seen both holes. Johnny got that one nigh the spine, an' he must have turned and tried to draw, then got that bullet through the heart!"

Nobody had seen it. Neill remembered that, and the thought rankled. Were they doing an injustice? He felt like a traitor at the thought, but secretly he had acquired a strong tinge of respect for the man they followed.

The fire flickered and the shadows danced a slow, rhythmic quadrille against the dark background of trees. He peeled bark from the log beside him and fed it into the fire. It caught, sparked brightly, and popped once or twice. Hardin leaned over and pushed the coffeepot nearer the coals. Kesney checked the loads in his Winchester.

"How far to that sawmill, Hardin?"

"About six miles, the way we go."

"Let's get started." Short got to his feet and brushed off the sand. "I want to get home. Got my boys buildin' fence. You either keep a close watch or they are off gal hootin' over the hills."

They tightened their saddle girths, doused the fire, and mounted up. With Hardin in the lead once more, they moved off into the darkness.

Neill brought up the rear. It was damp and chill among the cliffs and felt like the inside of a cavern. Overhead the stars were very bright. Mary was going to be worried, for he was never home so late. Nor did he like leaving her alone. He wanted to be home, eating a warm supper and going to bed in the old four-poster with the patchwork quilt Mary's grandmother made, pulled over him. What enthusiasm he had had for the chase was gone. The warm fire, the coffee, his own weariness, and the growing respect for Lock had changed him.

Now they all knew he was not the manner of man they had supposed. Justice can be a harsh taskmaster, but Western men know their kind, and the lines were strongly drawn. When you have slept beside a man on the trail, worked with him and with others like him, you come to know your kind. In the trail of the man Chat Lock, each rider of the posse was seeing the sort of man he knew, the sort he could respect. The thought was nagging and unsubstantial, but each of them felt a growing doubt, even Short and Kesney, who were most obdurate and resentful.

They knew how a backshooter lived and worked. He had his brand on everything he did. The mark of this man was the mark of a man who did things, who stood upon his own two feet, and who if he died, died facing his enemy. To the unknowing, such conclusions might seem doubtful, but the men of the desert knew their kind.

The mill was dark and silent, a great looming bulk beside the stream and the still pool of the millpond. They dismounted and eased close. Then according to a prearranged plan, they scattered and surrounded it. From behind a lodgepole pine, Hardin called out.

"We're comin' in, Lock! We want you!"

The challenge was harsh and ringing. Now that the moment had come, something of the old suspense returned. They listened to the water babbling as it trickled over the old dam, and then they moved. At their first step, they heard Lock's voice.

"Don't you come in here, boys! I don't want to kill none of you, but you come an' I will! That was a fair shootin'! You've got no call to come after me!"

Hardin hesitated, chewing his mustache. "You shot him in the back!" he yelled.

"No such thing! He was a-facin' the bar when I come in. He seen I was heeled, an' he drawed as he turned. I beat him to it. My first shot took him in the side an' he was knocked back against the bar. My second hit him in the back an' the third missed as he was a-fallin'. You hombres didn't see that right."

The sound of his voice trailed off, and the water chuckled over the stones and then sighed to a murmur among the trees. The logic of Lock's statement struck them all. It *could* have been that way.

A long moment passed, and then Hardin spoke up again.

"You come in and we'll give you a trial. Fair an' square!"

"How?" Lock's voice was a challenge. "You ain't got no witness. Neither have I. Ain't nobody to say what happened there but me, as Johnny ain't alive."

"Johnny was a mighty good man, an' he was our

friend!" Short shouted. "No murderin' squatter is goin' to move into this country an' start shootin' folks up!"

There was no reply to that, and they waited, hesitating a little. Neill leaned disconsolately against the tree where he stood. After all, Lock might be telling the truth. How did they know? There was no use hanging a man unless you were sure.

"Gab!" Short's comment was explosive. "Let's move in, Hardin! Let's get him! He's lyin'! Nobody could beat Johnny, we know that!"

"Webb was a good man in his own country!" Lock shouted in reply. The momentary silence that followed held them, and then, almost as a man they began moving in. Neill did not know exactly when or why he started. Inside he felt sick and empty. He was fed up on the whole business, and every instinct told him this man was no backshooter.

Carefully, they moved, for they knew this man was handy with a gun. Suddenly, Hardin's voice rang out.

"Hold it, men! Stay where you are until daybreak! Keep your eyes open an' your ears. If he gets out of here he'll be lucky, an' in the daylight we can get him, or fire the mill!"

Neill sank to a sitting position behind a log. Relief was a great warmth that swept over him. There wouldn't be any killing tonight. Not tonight, at least.

Yet as the hours passed, his ears grew more and more attuned to the darkness. A rabbit rustled, a pinecone dropped from a tree, the wind stirred high in the pine tops, and the few stars winked through, lonesomely peering down upon the silent men.

With daylight they moved in and they went through the doors and up to the windows of the old mill, and it was empty and still. They stared at each other, and Short swore viciously, the sound booming in the echoing, empty room.

"Let's go down to the Sorenson place," Kimmel said. "He'll be there."

And somehow they were all very sure he would be. They knew he would be because they knew him for their kind of man. He would retreat no further than his own ranch, his own hearth. There, if they were to have him and hang him, they would have to burn him out, and men would die in the process. Yet with these men there was no fear. They felt the drive of duty, the need for maintaining some law in this lonely desert and mountain land. There was only doubt which had grown until each man was shaken with it. Even short, whom the markers by the trail had angered, and Kesney, who was the best tracker among them, even better than Hardin, had been irritated by it, too.

The sun was up and warming them when they rode over the brow of the hill and looked down into the parched basin where the Sorenson place lay.

But it was no parched basin. Hardin drew up so suddenly his startled horse almost reared. It was no longer the Sorenson place.

The house had been patched and rebuilt. The roof had spots of new lumber upon it, and the old pole barn had been made watertight and strong. A new corral had been built, and to the right of the house was a fenched-in garden of vegetables, green and pretty after the desert of the day before.

Thoughtfully, and in a tight cavalcade, they rode down the hill. The stock they saw was fat and healthy, and the corral was filled with horses.

"Been a lot of work done here," Kimmel said. And he knew how much work it took to make such a place attractive.

"Don't look like no killer's place!" Neill burst out. Then he flushed and drew back, embarrassed by his statement. He was the youngest of these men and the newest in the country.

No response was forthcoming. He had but stated what they all believed. There was something stable and lasting and something real and genuine, in this place.

"I been waitin' for you."

The remark from behind them stiffened every spine. Chat Lock was here, behind them. And he would have a gun on them, and if one of them moved, he could die.

"My wife's down there fixin' breakfast. I told her I had some friends comin' in. A posse huntin' a killer. I've told her nothin' about this trouble. You ride down there now, you keep your guns. You eat your breakfast and then if you feel bound and determined to get somebody for a fair shootin', I'll come out with anyone of you or all of you, but I ain't goin' to hang.

"I ain't namin' no one man because I don't want to force no fight on anybody. You ride down there now."

They rode, and in the dooryard, they dismounted. Neill turned then, and for the first time he saw Chat Lock.

He was a big man, compact and strong. His rusty brown hair topped a brown, sun-hardened face, but with the warmth in his eyes it was a friendly sort of face. Not at all what he expected.

Hardin looked at him. "You made some changes here."

"I reckon." Lock gestured toward the well. "Dug by hand. My wife worked the windlass." He looked around at them, taking them in with one sweep of his eyes. "I've got the grandest woman in the world."

Neill felt hot tears in his eyes suddenly and busied himself loosening his saddle girth to keep the others from seeing. That was the way he felt about Mary.

The door opened suddenly, and they turned. The sight of a woman in this desert country was enough to make any many turn. What they saw was not what they expected. She was young, perhaps in her middle twenties, and she was pretty, with brown wavy hair and gray eyes and a few freckles on her nose. "Won't you come in? Chat told me he had some friends coming for breakfast, and it isn't often we have anybody in."

Heavy-footed and shamefaced they walked up on the porch. Kesney saw the care and neatness with which the hard hewn planks had been fitted. Here, too, was the same evidence of lasting, of permanence, of strength. This was the sort of man a country needed. He thought the thought before he fixed his attention on it, and then he flushed.

Inside, the room was as neat as the girl herself. How did she get the floors so clean? Before he thought, he phrased the question. She smiled.

"Oh, that was Chat's idea! He made a frame and

fastened a piece of pumice stone to a stick. It cuts into all the cracks and keeps them very clean."

The food smelled good, and when Hardin looked at his hands, Chat motioned to the door.

"There's water an' towels if you want to wash up."

Neill rolled up his sleeves and dipped his hands in the basin. The water was soft, and that was rare in this country, and the soap felt good on his hands. When he had dried his hands, he walked in. Hardin and Kesney had already seated themselves, and Lock's wife was pouring coffee.

"Men," Lock said, "this is Mary. You'll have to tell her your names. I reckon I missed them."

Mary. Neill looked up. She was Mary, too. He looked down at his plate again and ate a few bites. When he looked up, she was smiling at him.

"My wife's name is Mary," he said. "She's a fine girl!"

"She would be! But why don't you bring her over? I haven't talked with a woman in so long I wouldn't know how it seemed! Chat, why haven't you invited them over?"

Chat mumbled something, and Neill stared at his coffee. The men ate in uncomfortable silence. Hardin's eyes kept shifting around the room. That pumice stone. He'd have to fix up a deal like that for Jane. She was always fussing about the work of keeping a board floor clean. That washstand inside, too, with pipes made of hollow logs to carry the water out so she wouldn't have to be running back and forth. That was an idea, too.

They finished their meal reluctantly. One by one they trooped outside, avoiding each other's eyes. Chat Lock did not keep them waiting. He walked down among them.

"If there's to be shootin'," he said quietly, "let's get away from the house."

Hardin looked up. "Lock, was that right, what you said in the mill? Was it a fair shootin'?"

Lock nodded. "It was. Johnny Webb prodded me. I didn't want trouble, nor did I want to hide behind the fact I wasn't packin' an iron. I walked over to the saloon not aimin' for trouble. I aimed to give him a chance if he wanted it. He drawed an' I beat him. It was a fair shootin'."

"All right." Hardin nodded. "That's good enough for

me. I reckon you're a different sort of man than any of us figured."

"Let's mount up," Short said. "I got fence to build."

Chat Lock put his hand on Hardin's saddle. "You folks come over sometime. She gets right lonesome. I don't mind it so much, but you know how womenfolks are."

"Sure," Hardin said, "sure thing."

"An' you bring your Mary over." He told Neill.

Neill nodded, his throat full. As they mounted the hill, he glanced back. Mary Lock was standing in the doorway, waving to them, and the sunlight was very bright in the clean-swept dooryard.

AUTHOR'S NOTE
KEEP TRAVELIN', RIDER

Aside from the necessity of hunting game to live, to use weapons well was a necessity. The men on the frontier were not Sunday shooters, but had to be prepared to use a gun to defend themselves at any moment.

George Rutledge Gibson in his journal covering the years 1847 and 1848 says: "It is estimated that in 1847 forty-seven Americans were killed, 330 wagons destroyed, and some 6,500 head of cattle taken by Indians along the Santa Fe Trail."

James H. Cook in his Fifty Years on the Old Frontier *says,* "Everybody—except the clergy—either packed a gun or two or else kept them within mighty close reach. All disputes of any importance had to be settled by a gun or knifefight."

Frederick Law Olmstead in his A Journey Through Texas *(1850s) says,* "There are probably in Texas as many revolvers as there are male adults . . . After a little practice we could very surely chop off a snake's head from the saddle at any reasonable distance."

Keep Travelin',
Rider

When Tack Gentry sighted the weather-beaten buildings of the G Bar, he touched spurs to the buckskin and the horse broke into a fast canter that carried the cowhand down the trail and around into the ranch yard. He swung down.

"Hey!" he yelled happily, grinning. "Is that all the welcome I get?"

The door pushed open and a man stepped out on the worn porch. The man had a stubble of beard and a drooping mustache. His blue eyes were small and narrow.

"Who are yuh?" he demanded. "And what do yuh want?"

"I'm Tack Gentry!" Tack said. "Where's Uncle John?"

"I don't know yuh," the man said, "and I never heard of no Uncle John. I reckon yuh got onto the wrong spread, youngster."

"Wrong spread?" Tack laughed. "Quit your funnin'! I helped build that house there, and built the corrals by my lonesome, while Uncle John was sick. Where is everybody?"

The man looked at him carefully and then lifted his eyes to a point beyond Tack. A voice spoke from behind the cowhand. "Reckon yuh been gone a while, ain't yuh?"

Gentry turned. The man behind him was short, stocky, and blond. He had a wide, flat face, a small broken nose, and cruel eyes.

"Gone? I reckon yes! I've been gone most of a year! Went north with a trail herd to Ellsworth, then took me a job as segundo on a herd movin' to Wyoming."

* * *

Tack stared around, his eyes alert and curious. There was something wrong here, something very wrong. The neatness that had been typical of Uncle John Gentry was gone. The place looked run-down, the porch was untidy, the door hung loose on its hinges, even the horses in the corral were different.

"Where's Uncle John?" Tack demanded again. "Quit stallin'!"

The blond man smiled, his lips parting over broken teeth and a hard, cynical light coming into his eyes. "If yuh mean John Gentry, who used to live on this place, he's gone. He drawed on the wrong man and got himself killed."

"What?" Tack's stomach felt like he had been kicked. He stood there, staring. "He *drew* on somebody? *Uncle John?*"

Tack shook his head. "That's impossible! John Gentry was a Quaker. He never lifted a hand in violence against anybody or anything in his life! He never even wore a gun, never owned one."

"I only know what they tell me," the blond man said, "but we got work to do, and I reckon yuh better slope out of here. And," he added grimly, "if yuh're smart yuh'll keep right on goin', clean out of the country!"

"What do yuh mean?" Tack's thoughts were in a turmoil, trying to accustom himself to this change, wondering what could have happened, what was behind it.

"I mean yuh'll find things considerably changed around here. If yuh decide not to leave," he added, "yuh might ride into Sunbonnet and look up Van Hardin or Dick Olney and tell him I said to give yuh all yuh had comin'. Tell 'em Soderman sent yuh."

"Who's Van Hardin?" Tack asked. The name was unfamiliar.

"Yuh been away all right!" Soderman acknowledged. "Or yuh'd know who Van Hardin is. He runs this country. He's the ramrod, Hardin is. Olney's sheriff."

Tack Gentry rode away from his home ranch with his thoughts in confusion. Uncle John! Killed in a gunfight! Why, that was out of reason! The old man wouldn't fight.

He never had and never would. And this Dick Olney was sheriff! What had become of Pete Liscomb? No election was due for another year, and Pete had been a good sheriff.

There was one way to solve the problem and get the whole story, and that was to circle around and ride by the London ranch. Bill could give him the whole story, and besides, he wanted to see Betty. It had been a long time.

The six miles to the headquarters of the London ranch went by swiftly, yet as Tack rode, he scanned the grassy levels along the Maravillas. There were cattle enough, more than he had ever seen on the old G Bar, and all of them wearing the G Bar brand.

He reined in sharply. What the . . . ? Why, if Uncle John was dead, the ranch belonged to him! But if that was so, who was Soderman? And what were they doing on his ranch?

Three men were loafing on the wide veranda of the London ranch house when Tack rode up. All their faces were unfamiliar. He glanced warily from one to the other.

"Where's Bill London?" he asked.

"London?" The man in the wide brown hat shrugged. "Reckon he's to home, over in Sunbonnet Pass. He ain't never over here."

"This is his ranch, isn't it?" Tack demanded.

All three men seemed to tense. "His ranch?" The man in the brown hat shook his head. "Reckon yuh're a stranger around here. This ranch belongs to Van Hardin. London ain't got a ranch. Nothin' but a few acres back against the creek over to Sunbonnet Pass. He and that girl of his live there. I reckon though," he grinned suddenly, "she won't be there much longer. Hear tell she's goin' to work in the Longhorn Dance hall."

"Betty London? In the Longhorn?" Tack exclaimed. "Don't make me laugh, partner! Betty's too nice a girl for that! She wouldn't . . ."

"They got it advertised," the brown-hatted man said calmly.

An hour later a very thoughtful Tack Gentry rode up the dusty street of Sunbonnet. In that hour of riding he had been doing a lot of thinking, and he was remembering what Soderman had said. He was to tell Hardin or Olney that Soderman had sent him to get all that was coming to him. Suddenly, that remark took on a new significance.

Tack swung down in front of the Longhorn. Emblazoned on the front of the saloon was a huge poster announcing that Betty London was the coming attraction, that she would sing and entertain at the Longhorn. Compressing his lips, Tack walked into the saloon.

Nothing was familiar except the bar and the tables. The man behind the bar was squat and fat, and his eyes peered at Tack from folds of flesh. "What's it for yuh?" he demanded.

"Rye," Tack said. He let his eyes swing slowly around the room. Not a familiar face greeted him. Shorty Davis was gone. Nick Farmer was not around. These men were strangers, a tight-mouthed, hard-eyed crew.

Gentry glanced at the bartender. "Any ridin' jobs around here? Driftin' through, and thought I might like to tie in with one of the outfits around here."

"Keep driftin'," the bartender said, not glancing at him. "Everybody's got a full crew."

One door swung open and a tall, clean-cut man walked into the room, glancing around. He wore a neat gray suit and a dark hat. Tack saw the bartender's eyes harden and glanced thoughtfully at the newcomer. The man's face was very thin, and when he removed his hat his ash blond hair was neatly combed.

He glanced around, and his eyes lighted on Tack. "Stranger?" he asked pleasantly. "Then may I buy you a drink? I don't like to drink alone, but haven't sunk so low as to drink with these coyotes."

Tack stiffened, expecting a reaction from some of the seated men, but there was none. Puzzled, he glanced at the blond man, and seeing the cynical good humor in the man's eyes, nodded.

"Sure, I'll drink with you."

"My name," the tall man added, "is Anson Childe, by profession, a lawyer, by dint of circumstances, a gambler, and by choice, a student.

"You perhaps wonder," he added, "why these men do

not resent my reference to them as coyotes. There are three reasons, I expect. The first is that some subconscious sense of truth makes them appreciate the justice of the term. Second, they know I am gifted with considerable dexterity in expounding the gospel of Judge Colt. Third, they know that I am dying of tuberculosis and as a result have no fear of bullets.

"It is not exactly fear that keeps them from drawing on me. Let us say it is a matter of mathematics, and a problem none of them has succeeded in solving with any degree of comfort in the result. It is: how many of them would die before I did?

"You can appreciate, my friend, the quandary in which this places them, and also the disagreeable realization that bullets are no respecters of persons, nor am I. The several out there who might draw know that I know who they are. The result is that they know they would be first to die."

Childe looked at Tack thoughtfully. "I heard you ask about a riding job as I came in. You look like an honest man, and there is no place here for such."

Gentry hunted for the right words. Then he said, "This country looks like it was settled by honest men."

Anson Childe studied his glass. "Yes," he said, "but at the right moment they lacked a leader. One was too opposed to violence, another was too law abiding, and the rest lacked resolution."

If there was a friend in the community, this man was it. Tack finished his drink and strode to the door. The bartender met his eyes as he glanced back.

"Keep on driftin'," the bartender said.

Tack Gentry smiled. "I like it here," he said, "and I'm stayin'!"

He swung into the saddle and turned his buckskin toward Sunbonnet Pass. He still had no idea exactly what had happened during the year of his absence, yet Childe's remark coupled with what the others had said told him a little. Apparently, some strong, resolute men had moved in and taken over, and there had been no concerted fight against them, no organization and no leadership.

Childe had said that one was opposed to violence. That would have been his Uncle John. The one who was too law abiding would be Bill London. London had always been strong for law and order and settling things in a legal way. The others had been honest men, but small ranchers and individually unable to oppose whatever was done to them. Yet whatever had happened, the incoming elements had apparently moved with speed and finesse.

Had it been one ranch, it would have been different. But the ranches and the town seemed completely subjugated.

The buckskin took the trail at an easy canter, skirting the long red cliff of Horse Thief Mesa and wading the creek at Gunsight. Sunbonnet Pass opened before him like a gate in the mountains. To the left, in a grove of trees, was a small adobe house and a corral.

Two horses were standing at the corral as he rode up. His eyes narrowed as he saw them. Button and Blackie! Two of his uncle's favorites and two horses he had raised from colts. He swung down and started toward them, when he saw the three people on the steps.

He turned to face them, and his heart jumped. Betty London had not changed.

Her eyes widened, and her face went dead white. "Tack!" she gasped. "Tack Gentry!"

Even as she spoke, Tack saw the sudden shock with which the two men turned to stare. "That's right, Betty," he said quietly. "I just got home."

"But—but—we heard you were dead!"

"I'm not." His eyes shifted to the two men—a thick-shouldered, deep-chested man with a square, swarthy face and a lean rawboned man wearing a star. The one with the star would be Dick Olney. The other must be Van Hardin.

Tack's eyes swung to Olney. "I heard my Uncle John Gentry was killed. Did yuh investigate his death?"

Olney's eyes were careful. "Yeah," he said. "He was killed in a fair fight. Gun in his hand."

"My uncle," Tack replied, "was a Quaker. He never lifted a hand in violence in his life!"

"He was a might slow, I reckon," Olney said coolly, "but he had the gun in his hand when I found him."

"Who shot him?"

"Hombre name of Soderman. But like I say, it was a fair fight."

"Like blazes!" Tack flashed. "Yuh'll never make me believe Uncle John wore a gun! That gun was planted on him!"

"Yuh're jumpin' to conclusions," Van Hardin said smoothly. "I saw the gun myself. There were a dozen witnesses."

"Who saw the fight?" Gentry demanded.

"They saw the gun in his hand. In his right hand," Hardin said.

Tack laughed suddenly, harshly. "That does it! Uncle John's right hand has been useless ever since Shiloh, when it was shot to pieces tryin' to get to a wounded soldier. He couldn't hold a feather in those fingers, let alone a gun!"

Hardin's face tightened, and Dick Olney's eyes shifted to Hardin's face.

"You'd be better off," Hardin said quietly, "to let sleepin' dogs lie. We ain't goin' to have yuh comin' in here stirrin' up a peaceful community."

"My Uncle John was murdered," Gentry said quietly. "I mean to see his murderer punished. That ranch belongs to me. I intend to get it back!"

Van Hardin smiled. "Evidently, yuh aren't aware of what happened here," he said quietly. "Your Uncle John was in a noncombatant outfit durin' the war, was he not? Well, while he was gone, the ranch he had claimed was abandoned. Soderman and I started to run cattle on that range and the land that was claimed by Bill London. No claim to the range was asserted by anyone. We made improvements, and then durin' our temporary absence with a trail herd, John Gentry and Bill London returned and moved in. Naturally, when we returned the case was taken to court. The court ruled the ranches belonged to Soderman and myself."

"And the cattle?" Tack asked. "What of the cattle my uncle owned?"

Hardin shrugged. "The brand had been taken over by the new owners and registered in their name. As I understand it, yuh left with a trail herd immediately after yuh came back to Texas. My claim was originally asserted during yore uncle's absence. I could," he smiled, "lay claim to the money yuh got from that trail herd. Where is it?"

"Suppose yuh find out?" Tack replied. "I'm goin' to tell yuh one thing: I'm goin' to find who murdered my uncle, if it was Soderman or not. I'm also goin' to fight yuh in court. Now, if yuh'll excuse me," he turned his eyes to Betty who had stood wide-eyed and silent, "I'd like to talk to Bill London."

"He can't see yuh," Hardin said. "He's asleep."

Gentry's eyes hardened. "You runnin' this place too?"

"Betty London is going to work for me," Hardin replied. "We may be married later, so in a sense, I'm speaking for her."

"Is that right?" Tack demanded, his eyes meeting Betty's.

Her face was miserable. "I'm afraid it is, Tack."

"You've forgotten your promise, then?" he demanded.

"Things—things changed, Tack," she faltered. "I—I can't talk about it."

"I reckon, Gentry," Olney interrupted, "it's time yuh rode on. There's nothin' in this neck of the woods for yuh. You've played out your hand here. Ride on, and you'll save yourself a lot of trouble. They're hirin' hands over on the Pecos."

"I'm stayin'," Gentry said flatly.

"Remember," Olney warned, "I'm the sheriff. At the first sign of trouble, I'll come lookin' for yuh."

Gentry swung into the saddle. His eyes shifted to Betty's face, and for an instant, she seemed about to speak. Then he turned and rode away. He did not look back. It was not until after he was gone that he remembered Button and Blackie.

To think they were in the possession of Hardin and

Olney! The twin blacks he had reared and worked with, training them to do tricks, teaching them all the lore of the cow-country horses and much more.

The picture was clear now. In the year in which he had been gone these men had come in, asserted their claims, taken them to carpetbag courts, and made them stick. Backing their legal claims with guns, they had taken over the country with speed and finesse. At every turn, he was blocked. Betty had turned against him. Bill London was either a prisoner in his own house or something else was wrong. Olney was sheriff, and probably they had their own judge.

He could quit. He could pull out and go on to the Pecos. It would be the easiest way. It was even what Uncle John might have wished him to do, for John Gentry was a peace-loving man. Tack Gentry was of another breed. His father had been killed fighting Commanches, and Tack had gone to war when a mere boy. Uncle John had found a place for himself in a noncombatant outfit, but Tack had fought long and well.

His ride north with the trail herd had been rough and bloody. Twice they had fought off Indians, and once they had mixed it with rustlers. In Ellsworth, a gunman named Paris had made trouble that ended with Paris dead on the floor.

Tack had left town in a hurry, ridden to the new camp at Dodge, and then joined a trail herd headed for Wyoming. Indian fighting had been the order of the day, and once, rounding up a bunch of steers lost from the herd in a stampede, Tack had run into three rustlers after the same steers.

Tack downed two of them in the subsequent battle and then shot it out with the other in a daylong rifle battle that covered a cedar- and boulder-strewn hillside. Finally, just before sundown, they met in a hand-to-hand battle with bowie knives.

Tack remained long enough to see his old friend Major Powell, with whom he had participated in the Wagon Box Fight, and then had wandered back to Kansas. On the Platte he joined a bunch of buffalo hunters, stayed with them a couple of months, and then trailed back to Dodge.

Sunbonnet's Longhorn Saloon was ablaze with lights when he drifted into town that night. He stopped at the livery stable and put up his horse. He had taken a roundabout route, scouting the country, so he decided that Hardin and Olney were probably already in town. By now they would know of his call at the ranch and his meeting with Anson Childe.

He was laboring under no delusions about his future. Van Hardin would not hesitate to see him put out of the way if he attempted to regain his property. Hardin had brains, and Olney was no fool. There were things Gentry must know before anything could be done, and the one man in town who could and would tell him was Childe.

Leaving the livery stable, he started up the street. Turning, he glanced back to see the liveryman standing in the stable door. He dropped his hand quickly, but Gentry believed he had signaled someone across the street. Yet there was no one in sight, and the row of buildings seemed blank and empty.

Only three buildings were lighted. The Longhorn, a smaller, cheaper saloon, and the old general store. There was a light upstairs over the small saloon and several lights in the annex to the Longhorn, which passed as a hotel, the only one in Sunbonnet.

Tack walked along the street, his bootheels sounding loud in the still night air. Ahead of him was a space between the buildings, and when he drew abreast of it he did a quick sidestep off the street, flattening against the building.

He heard footsteps, hesitation, and then lightly running steps, and suddenly a man dove around the corner and grated to a stop on the gravel, staring down the alleyway between the buildings. He did not see Tack, who was flattened in the dense shadow against the building and behind a rain barrel.

The man started forward suddenly, and Tack reached out and grabbed his ankle. Caught in midstride, the fellow plunged over on his head and then lay still. For an instant, Gentry hesitated; then struck and shielded a match with his left hand. It was the brown-hatted man he had talked to on the porch of London's ranch. His head had hit a stone, and he was out cold.

Swiftly, Tack shucked the fellow's gun and emptied the shells from it and then pushed it back in his holster. A folded paper had fallen from the unconscious man's pocket, and Tack picked it up. Then, moving fast, he went down the alley until he was in back of the small saloon. By the light from a back window, he read the note.

"This," he muttered, "may help!"

Come to town quick. Trouble's brewing. We can't have anything happen now. V. H.

Van Hardin. They didn't want trouble now. Why, *now*? Folding the note, he slipped it into his pocket and flattened against the side of the saloon, studying the interior. Only two men sat in the dim interior, two men who played cards at a small table. The bartender leaned on the bar and read a newspaper. When the bartender turned his head, Tack recognized him.

Red Furness had worked for his father. He had soldiered with him. He might still be friendly. Tack lifted his knuckles and tapped lightly on the window.

At the second tap, Red looked up. Tack lighted a match and moved it past the window. Neither of the cardplayers seemed to have noticed. Red straightened, folded his paper, and then picking up a cup, walked back toward the window. When he got there, he dipped the cup into the water bucket with one hand and with the other, lifted the window a few inches.

"This is Tack Gentry. Where does Childe hang out?"

Red's whisper was low. "Got him an office and sleepin' room upstairs. There's a back stairway. Yuh watch yoreself."

Tack stepped away from his window and made his way to the stairway he had already glimpsed. It might be a trap, but he believed Red was loyal. Also, he was not sure the word was out to kill him. They probably merely wanted him out of the way and hoped he could be warned to move on. The position of the Hardin group seemed secure enough.

Reaching the top of the stairs, he walked along the

narrow catwalk to the door. He tapped softly. After an instant, there was a voice. "What do you want?"

"This is Tack Gentry. Yuh talked to me in the saloon!" The door opened to darkness, and he stepped in. When it closed, he felt a pistol barrel against his spine.

"Hold still!" Childe warned.

Behind him a match struck, and then a candle was lighted. The light still glowed in the other room, seen only by the crack under the door. Childe grinned at him. "Got to be careful," he said. "They have tried twice to dry-gulch me!

"I put flowers on their graves every Monday!" He smiled. "And keep an extra one dug. Ever since I had that new grave dug, I've been left alone. Somehow it seems to have a very sobering influence on the local roughs."

He sat down. "I tire quicker than I once did. So you're Gentry! Betty London told me about you. She thought you were dead. There was a rumor that you'd been killed by the Indians in Wyoming."

"No, I came out all right. What I want to know, rememberin' yuh said yuh were a lawyer, is what kind of a claim they have on my ranch?"

"A good one, unfortunately. While you and your uncle were gone, and most of the other men in the locality, several of these men came in and began to brand cattle. After branding a good many, they left. They returned and began working around, about the time you left, and then they ordered your uncle off.

"He wouldn't go, and they took the case to court. There were no lawyers here then, and your uncle tried to handle it himself. The judge was their man, and suddenly a half dozen witnesses appeared and were sworn in. They testified that the land had been taken and held by Soderman, Olney, and Hardin.

"They claimed their brands on the cattle asserted their claim to the land, to the home ranches of both London and Gentry. The free range was something else, but with the two big ranches in their hands and the bulk of the free range lying beyond their holdings, they were in a position to freeze out the smaller ranchers. They established a squatter's right to each of the big ranches."

"Can they do that?" Tack demanded. "It doesn't seem fair!"

"The usual thing is to allow no claim unless they have occupied the land for twenty years without hindrance, but with a carpetbag court, they do about as they please. Judge Weaver is completely in Van Hardin's hands, and your Uncle John was on the losing side in this war."

"How did Uncle John get killed?" Tack asked.

Childe shrugged. "They said he called Soderman a liar and Soderman went for his gun. Your uncle had a gun on him when they found him. It was probably a cold-blooded killing because Gentry planned on a trip to Austin and was going to appeal the case."

"Have yuh seen Bill London lately?"

"Only once since the accident."

"Accident?"

"Yes, London was headed for home, dozing along in the buckboard as he always did, when his team ran away with him. The buckboard was overturned and London's back was injured. He can't ride anymore and can't sit up very long at a time."

"Was it really an accident?" Tack wanted to know.

Childe shrugged. "I doubt it. We couldn't prove a thing. One of the horses had a bad cut on the hip. It looked as if someone with a steel-tipped bullwhip had hit the animal from beside the road."

"Thorough," Tack said. "They don't miss a bet."

Childe nodded. Leaning back in his chair he put his feet on the desk. He studied Tack Gentry thoughtfully. "You know, you'll be next. They won't stand for you messing around. I think you already have them worried."

Tack explained about the man following him, and then handed the note to Childe. The lawyer's eyes narrowed. "Hmm, sounds like they had some reason to soft-pedal the whole thing for a while. Maybe it's an idea for us. Maybe somebody is coming down here to look around, or maybe somebody has grown suspicious."

Tack looked at Childe thoughtfully. "What's your position in all this?"

The tall man shrugged, and then laughed lightly.

"I've no stake in it, Gentry. I didn't know London or your Uncle John, either. But I heard rumors, and I didn't like the attitude of the local bosses, Hardin and Olney. I'm just a burr under the saddle with which they ride this community, no more. It amuses me to needle them, and they are afraid of me."

"Got any clients?"

"Clients?" Anson Childe chuckled. "Not a one! not likely to have any, either! In a country so throttled by one man as this is, there isn't any litigation. Nobody can win against him, and they are too busy hating Hardin to want to have trouble with each other."

"Well, then," Tack said, "yuh've got a client now. Go down to Austin. Demand an investigation. Lay the facts on the table for them. Maybe yuh can't do any good, but at least yuh can stir up a lot of trouble. The main thing will be to get people talking. They evidently want quiet, so we'll give them noise.

"Find out all you can. Get some detectives started on Hardin's trail. Find out who they are, who they were, and where they came from."

Childe sat up. "I'd like it," he said ruefully, "but I don't have that kind of money." He gestured at the room. "I'm behind on my rent here. Red owns the building, so he lets me stay."

Tack grinned and unbuttoned his shirt, drawing but a money belt. "I sold some cattle up north." He counted out one thousand dollars. "Take that. Spend all or any part of it, but create a smell down there. Tell everybody about the situation here." .

Childe got up, his face flushed with enthusiasm. "Man! Nothing could please me more! I'll make it hot for them! I'll—" He went into a fit of coughing, and Tack watched him gravely.

Finally Childe straightened. "You're putting your trust in a sick man, Gentry!"

"I'm putting my trust in a fighter," Tack said drily. "Yuh'll do!" He hesitated briefly. "Also, check the title on this land."

They shook hands silently, and Tack went to the door. Softly, he opened it and stepped out into the cool night. Well, for better or worse the battle was opened. Now for the next step. He came down off the wooden stair and then walked to the street. There was no one in sight. Tack Gentry crossed the street and pushed through the swinging doors of the Longhorn.

The saloon and dance hall was crowded. A few familiar faces, but they were sullen faces, lined and hard. The faces of bitter men, defeated, but not whipped. The others were new faces, the hard, tough faces of gunhands, the weather-beaten punchers who had come in to take the new jobs. He pushed his way to the bar.

There were three bartenders now, and it wasn't until he ordered that the squat, fat man glanced down the bar and saw him. His jaw hardened and he spoke to the bartender who was getting a bottle to pour Gentry's rye.

The bartender, a lean, sallow-faced man, strolled back to him. "We're not servin' you," he said. "I got my orders!"

Tack reached across the bar, his hand shooting out so fast the bartender had no chance to withdraw. Catching the man by his stiff collar, two fingers inside the collar and their knuckles jammed hard into the man's Adam's apple, he jerked him to the bar.

"Pour!" he said.

The man tried to speak, but Tack gripped harder and shoved back on the knuckles. Weakly, desperately, his face turning blue, the man poured. He slopped out twice what he got in the glass, but he poured. Then Tack shoved hard and the man brought up violently against the backbar.

Tack lifted his glass with his left hand, his eyes sweeping the crowd, all of whom had drawn back slightly. "To honest ranchers!" he said loudly and clearly and downed his drink.

A big, hard-faced man shoved through the crowd. "Maybe yuh're meanin' some of us ain't honest?" he suggested.

"That's right!" Tack Gentry let his voice ring out in the room, and he heard the rattle of chips cease, and the shuffling of feet died away. The crowd was listening. "That's exactly right! There were honest men here, but they were murdered or crippled. My Uncle John Gentry was murdered. They tried to make it look like a fair and square killin'—they stuck a gun in his hand!"

"That's right!" A man broke in. "He had a gun! I seen it!"

Tack's eyes shifted. "What hand was it in?"

"His right hand!" the man stated positively, belligerently. "I seen it!"

"Thank you, pardner!" Tack said politely. "The gun was in John Gentry's right hand—and John Gentry's right hand had been paralyzed ever since Shiloh!"

"Huh?" The man who had seen the gun stepped back, his face whitening a little.

Somebody back in the crowd shouted out, "That's right! You're durn tootin' that's right! Never could use a rope, 'count of it!"

Tack looked around at the crowd, and his eyes halted on the big man. He was going to break the power of Hardin, Olney, and Soderman, and he was going to start right here.

"There's goin' to be an investigation," he said loudly, "and it'll begin down in Austin. Any of you fellers bought property from Hardin, or Olney better get your money back."

"Yuh're talkin' a lot!" The big man thrust toward him, his wide, heavy shoulders looking broad enough for two men. "Yuh said some of us were thieves!"

"Thieves and murderers," Tack added. "If yuh're one of the worms that crawl in Hardin's tracks, that goes for you!"

The big man lunged. "Get him, Starr!" somebody shouted loudly.

Tack Gentry suddenly felt a fierce surge of pure animal joy. He stepped back and then stepped in suddenly, and his right swung low and hard. It caught Starr as he was coming in, caught him in the pit of the stomach. He grunted and stopped dead in his tracks, but Tack set himself and swung wickedly with both hands. His left smashed into Starr's mouth, and his right split a cut over his cheekbone. Starr staggered and fell back into the crowd. He came out of the crowd, shook his head, and charged like a bull.

Tack weaved inside of the swinging fists and impaled the bigger man on a straight, hard left hand. Then he crossed a wicked right to the cut cheek, and gore cascaded down the man's face. Tack stepped in, smashing both hands to the man's body, and then as Starr stabbed a thumb at his eye, Tack jerked his head aside and butted Starr in the face.

His nose broken, his cheek laid open to the bone, Starr staggered back, and Tack Gentry walked in, swinging with both hands. This was the beginning. This man worked for Hardin and he was going to be an example. When he left this room Starr's face was going to be a sample of the crashing of Van Hardin's power. With left and right he cut and slashed at the big man's face, and Starr, overwhelmed by the attack, helpless after that first wicked body blow, crumpled under those smashing fists. He hit the floor suddenly and lay there, moaning softly.

A man shoved through the crowd, and then stopped. It was Van Hardin. He looked down at the man on the floor; then his eyes, dark with hate, lifted to meet Tack Gentry's eyes.

"Lookin' for trouble, are yuh?" he said.

"Only catchin' up with some that started while I was gone, Van!" Tack said. He felt good. He was on the balls of his feet and ready. He had liked the jarring of blows, liked the feeling of combat. He was ready. "Yuh should have made sure I was dead, Hardin, before yuh tried to steal property from a kindly old man!"

"Nothing was stolen," Van Hardin said evenly, calmly. "We took only what was ours, and in a strictly legal manner."

"There will be an investigation," Gentry replied bluntly, "from Austin. Then we'll thrash the whole thing out."

Hardin's eyes sharpened and he was suddenly wary. "An investigation? What makes you think so?"

Tack was aware that Hardin was worried. "Because I'm startin' it. I'm askin' for it, and I'll get it. There was a lot you didn't know about that land yuh stole, Hardin. Yuh were like most crooks. Yuh could only see yore side of the question and it looked very simple and easy, but there's always the thing yuh overlook, and *you* overlooked somethin'!"

The doors swung wide and Olney pushed into the room. He stopped, glancing from Hardin to Gentry. "What goes on here?" he demanded.

"Gentry is accusin' us of bein' thieves," Hardin said carelessly.

Olney turned and faced Tack. "He's in no position to accuse anybody of anything!" he said. "I'm arrestin' him for murder!"

There was a stir in the room, and Tack Gentry felt the sudden sickness of fear. "Murder? Are yuh crazy?" he demanded.

"I'm not, but you may be," the sheriff said. "I've just come from the office of Anson Childe. He's been murdered. Yuh were his last visitor. Yuh were observed sneaking into his place by the back stairs. Yuh were observed sneaking out of it. I'm arresting yuh for murder."

The room was suddenly still, and Tack Gentry felt the rise of hostility toward him. Many men had admired the courage of Anson Childe; many men had been helped by him. Frightened themselves, they had enjoyed his flouting of Hardin and Olney. Now he was dead, murdered.

"Childe was my friend!" Tack protested. "He was goin' to Austin for me!"

Hardin laughed sarcastically. "Yuh mean he knew yuh had no case and refused to go, and in a fit of rage, yuh killed him. Yuh shot him."

"Yuh'll have to come with me," Olney said grimly. "Yuh'll get a fair trial."

Silently, Tack looked at him. Swiftly, thoughts raced through his mind. There was no chance for escape. The crowd was too thick, and he had no idea if there was a horse out front, although there no doubt was, and his own horse was in the livery stable. Olney relieved him of his gun belt and they started toward the door. Starr, leaning against the doorpost, his face raw as chewed beef, glared at him evilly.

"I'll be seein' yuh!" he said softly. "Soon!"

*   *   *

Soderman and Hardin had fallen in around him, and behind them were two of Hardin's roughs.

The jail was small, just four cells and an outer office. The door of one of the cells was opened and he was shoved inside. Hardin grinned at him. "This should settle the matter for Austin," he said. "Childe had friends down there!"

Anson Childe murdered! Tack Gentry, numbed by the blow, stared at the stone wall. He had counted on Childe, counted on his stirring up an investigation. Once an investigation was started, he possessed two aces in the hole he could use to defeat Hardin in court, but it demanded a court uncontrolled by Hardin.

With Childe's death he had no friends on the outside. Betty had barely spoken to him when they met, and if she was going to work for Hardin in his dance hall, she must have changed much. Bill London was a cripple and unable to get around. Red Furness, for all his friendship, wouldn't come out in the open. Tack had no illusions about the murder. By the time the case came to trial, they would have found ample evidence. They had his guns and they could fire two or three shots from them, whatever had been used on Childe. It would be a simple thing to frame him. Hardin would have no trouble in finding witnesses.

He was standing, staring out the small window, its lower sill just on the level of his eyes, when he heard a distant rumble of thunder and a jagged streak of lightning brightened the sky, followed by more thunder. The rains came slowly, softly, and then in steadily increasing volume. The jail was still and empty. Sounds of music and occasional shouts sounded from the Longhorn; then the roar of rain drowned them out. He threw himself down on the cot in the corner of the room, and lulled by the falling rain, was soon asleep.

A long time later, he awakened. The rain was still falling, but above it was another sound. Listening, he suddenly realized what it was. The dry wash behind the town was running, probably bank full. Lying there in the darkness, he became aware of still another sound, of the nearer rushing of water. Lifting his head, he listened. Then he got to his feet and crossed the small cell.

Water was running under the corner of the jail. There had been a good deal of rain lately, and he had noted that the barrel at the corner of the jail had been full. It was overflowing, and the water had evidently washed under the corner of the building.

He walked back and sat down on the bed, and as he listened to the water, an idea came to him suddenly. Tack got up and went to the corner of the cell. Striking a match, he studied the wall and floor. Both were damp. He stamped on the stone flags of the floor, but they were solid. He kicked at the wall. It was also solid.

How thick were those walls? Judging by what he remembered of the door, the walls were all of eight inches thick, but how about the floor? Kneeling on the floor, he struck another match, studying the mortar around the corner flagstone.

Then he felt in his pockets. There was nothing there he could use to dig that mortar. His pocket knife, his bowie-knife, his keys—all were gone. Suddenly, he had an inspiration. Slipping off his wide leather belt, he began to dig at the mortar with the edge of his heavy brass belt buckle.

The mortar was damp, but he worked steadily. His hands slipped on the sweaty buckle and he skinned his fingers and knuckles on the rough stone floor, yet he persevered, scraping, scratching, digging out tiny fragments of mortar. From time to time he straightened up and stamped on the stone. It was solid as Gibraltar.

Five hours he scraped and scratched, digging until his belt buckle was no longer of use. He had scraped out almost two inches of mortar. Sweeping up the scattered grains of mortar, and digging some of the mud off his boots, he filled in the cracks as best he could. Then he walked to his bunk and sprawled out and was instantly asleep.

Early in the morning, he heard someone stirring around outside. Then Olney walked back to his cell and looked in at him. Starr followed in a few minutes, carrying a plate of food and a pot of coffee. His face was badly bruised and swollen, and his eyes were hot with hate. He put the food down, and then walked away. Olney loitered.

"Gentry," he said suddenly, "I hate to see a good hand in this spot."

Tack looked up. "I'll bet yuh do!" he said sarcastically.

"No use takin' that attitude," Olney protested, "after all, yuh made trouble for us. Why couldn't yuh leave well enough alone? Yuh were in the clear, yuh had a few dollars apparently, and yuh could do all right. Hardin took possession of those ranches legally. He can hold 'em, too."

"We'll see."

"No, I mean it. He can. Why don't yuh drop the whole thing?"

"Drop it?" Tack laughed. "How can I drop it? I'm in jail for murder now, and yuh know as well as I do I never killed Anson Childe. This trial will smoke the whole story out of its hole. I mean to see that it does."

Olney winced, and Tack could see he had touched a tender spot. That was what they were afraid of. They had him now, but they didn't want him. They wanted nothing so much as to be completely rid of him.

"Only make trouble for folks," Olney protested. "Yuh won't get nowhere. Yuh can bet that if yuh go to trial we'll have all the evidence we need."

"Sure. I know I'll be framed."

"What can yuh expect?" Olney shrugged. "Yuh're askin' for it. Why don't yuh play smart? If yuh'd leave the country we could sort of arrange maybe to turn yuh loose."

Tack looked up at him. "Yuh mean that?" Like blazes, he told himself. I can see yuh turnin' me loose! And when I walked out yuh'd have somebody there to smoke me down, shot escaping jail. Yeah, I know. "If I thought yuh'd let me go—" he hesitated, angling to get Olney's reaction.

The sheriff put his head close to the bars. "Yuh know me, Tack," he whispered. "I don't want to see you stick yore head in a noose! Sure, yuh spoke out of turn, and yuh tried to scare up trouble for us, but if yuh'd leave, I think I could arrange it."

"Just give me the chance," Tack assured him. "Once I

get out of here I'll really start movin'!" And that's no lie, he added to himself.

Olney went away, and the morning dragged slowly. They would let him go. He was praying now they would wait until the next day. Yet even if they did permit him to escape, even if they did not have him shot as he was leaving, what could he do? Childe, his best means of assistance, was dead. At every turn he was stopped. They had the law, and they had the guns.

His talk the night before would have implanted doubts. His whipping of Starr would have pleased many, and some of them would realize that his arrest for the murder of Childe was a frame. Yet none of these people would do anything about it without leadership. None of them wanted his neck in a noose.

Olney dropped in later and leaned close to the bars. "I'll have something arranged by tomorrow," he said.

Tack lay back on the bunk and fell asleep. All day the rain had continued without interruption except for a few minutes at a time. The hills would be soggy now, the trails bad. He could hear the wash running strongly, running like a river not thirty yards behind the jail.

Darkness fell, and he ate again and then returned to his bunk. With a good lawyer and a fair judge he could beat them in court. He had an ace in the hole that would help, and another that might do the job.

He waited until the jail was silent and he could hear the usual sounds from the Longhorn. Then he got up and walked over to the corner. All day water had been running under the corner of the jail and must have excavated a fair-sized hole by now. Tack knelt down and took from his pocket the fork he had secreted after his meal.

Olney, preoccupied with plans to allow Tack Gentry to escape and sure that Tack was accepting the plan, had paid little attention to the returned plate.

On his knees, Tack dug out the loosely filled in dust and dirt and then began digging frantically at the hole. He worked steadily for an hour and then crossed to the bucket for a drink of water and to stretch, and then he returned to work.

Another hour passed. He got up and stamped on the stone. It seemed to sink under his feet. He bent his knees and jumped, coming down hard on his heels. The stone gave way so suddenly he almost went through. He caught himself, withdrew his feet from the hole, and bent over, striking a match. It was no more than six inches to the surface of the water, and even a glance told him it must be much deeper than he had believed.

He took another look, waited an instant, and then lowered his feet into the water. The current jerked at them, and then he lowered his body through the hole and let go. Instantly, he was jerked away and literally thrown downstream. He caught a quick glimpse of a light from a window, and then he was whirling over and over. He grabbed frantically, hoping to get his hands on something, but they clutched only empty air. Frantically, he fought toward where there must be a bank, realizing he was in a roaring stream all of six feet deep. He struck nothing and was thrown, almost hurtled, downstream with what seemed to be overwhelming speed. Something black loomed near him, and at the same instant the water caught at him, rushing with even greater power. He grabbed again at the blob of blackness, and his hand caught a root.

Yet it was nothing secure, merely a huge cottonwood log rushing downstream. Working his way along it, he managed to get a leg over and crawled atop it. Fortunately, the log did not roll over.

Lying there in the blackness, he realized what must have happened. Behind the row of buildings that fronted on the street, of which the jail was one, was a shallow, sandy ditch. At one end of it the bluff reared up. The dry wash skirted one side of the triangle formed by the bluff, and the ditch formed the other. Water flowing off the bluff and off the roofs of the buildings and from the street of the town and the rise beyond it had flooded into the ditch, washing it deeper. Yet now he knew he was in the current of the wash itself, now running bank full, a raging torrent.

A brief flash of lightning revealed the stream down which he was shooting like a chip in a millrace. Below, he knew, was Cathedral Gorge, a narrow boulder-strewn gash in the mountain down which this wash would thunder like an express train. Tack had seen such logs go down it, smashing into boulders, hurled against the rocky walls, and then shooting at last out into the open flat below the gorge. And he knew instantly that no living thing could hope to ride a charging log through the black, roaring depths of the gorge and come out anything but a mangled, lifeless pulp.

The log he was bestriding hit a wave, and water drenched him. Then the log whirled dizzily around a bend in the wash. Before him and around another bend he could hear the roar of the gorge. The log swung, and then the driving roots ripped into a heap of debris at the bend of the wash, and the log swung wickedly across the current. Scrambling like a madman, Tack fought his way toward the roots, and then even as the log ripped loose, he hurled himself at the heap of debris.

He landed in a heap of broken boughs, and felt something gouge him, and then scrambling, he made the rocks and clambered up into their shelter, lying there on a flat rock, gasping for breath.

A long time later he got up. Something was wrong with his right leg. It felt numb and sore. He crawled over the rocks and stumbled over the muddy earth toward the partial shelter of a clump of trees.

He needed shelter, and he needed a gun. Tack Gentry knew that now that he was free they would scour the country for him. They might believe him dead, but they would want to be certain. What he needed now was shelter, rest, and food. He needed to examine himself to see how badly he was injured, yet where could he turn?

Betty? She was too far away and he had no horse. Red Furness? Possibly, but how much the man would or could help he did not know. Yet thinking of Red made him think of Childe. There was a place for him. If he could only get to Childe's quarters over the saloon!

Luckily, he had landed on the same side of the wash as the town. He was stiff and sore, and his leg was paining him grievously. Yet there was no time to be lost. What the hour was he had no idea, but he knew his progress would be slow, and he must be careful. The rain was pounding down, but he was so wet now that it made no difference.

How long it took him he never knew. He could have been no more than a mile from town, perhaps less, and he walked, crawled, and pulled himself to the edge of town and then behind the buildings until he reached the dark back stairway to Anson Childe's room. Step by step he crawled up. Luckily, the door was unlocked.

Once inside, he stood there in the darkness, listening. There was no sound. This room was windowless but for one very small and tightly curtained window at the top of the wall. Tack felt for the candle, found it, and fumbled for a match. When he had the candle alight, he started pulling off his clothes.

Naked, he dried himself with a towel, avoiding the injured leg. Then he found a bottle and poured himself a drink. He tossed it off and then sat down on the edge of the bed and looked at his leg.

It almost made him sick to look at it. Hurled against a root or something in the dark, he had torn a great, mangled wound in the calf of his leg. No artery appeared to have been injured, but in places his shinbone was visible through the ripped flesh. The wound in the calf was deeper. Cleansing it as best he could, he found a white shirt belonging to Childe and bandaged his leg.

Exhausted, he fell asleep—when, he never recalled. Only hours later he awakened suddenly to find sunlight streaming through the door into the front room. His leg was stiff and sore, and when he moved, it throbbed with pain. Using a cane he found hanging in the room, he pulled himself up and staggered to the door.

The curtains in the front room were up and sunlight streamed in. The rain seemed to be gone. From where he stood he could see into the street, and almost the first person he saw was Van Hardin. He was standing in front of the Longhorn talking to Soderman and the mustached man Tack had first seen at his own ranch.

The sight reminded him, and Tack hunted around for a gun. He found a pair of beautifully matched Colts, silver plated and ivory handled. He strapped them on with their ornate belt and holsters. Then, standing in a corner, he found a riot gun and a Henry rifle. He checked the loads in all the guns, found several boxes of ammunition for each of them, and emptied a box of .45s into the pockets of a pair of Childe's pants he pulled on. Then he put a double handful of shotgun shells into the pockets of a leather jacket he found.

He sat down then, for he was weak and trembling.

His time was short. Sooner or later someone would come to this room. Either someone would think of it, or someone would come to claim the room for himself. Red Furness had no idea he was there, so would probably not hesitate to let anyone come up.

He locked the door, and then dug around and found a stale loaf of bread and some cheese. Then he lay down to rest. His leg was throbbing with pain, and he knew it needed care, and badly.

When he awakened, he studied the street from a vantage point well inside the room and to one side of the window. Several knots of men were standing around talking, more men than should have been in town at that hour. He recognized one or two of them as being old-timers around. Twice he saw Olney ride by, and the sheriff was carrying a riot gun.

Starr and the mustached man were loafing in front of the Longhorn, and two other men Tack recognized as coming from the old London ranch were there.

He ate some more bread and cheese. He was just finishing his sandwich when a buckboard turned into the street, and his heart jumped when he saw Betty London was driving. Beside her in the seat was her father, Bill, worn and old, his hair white now, but he was wearing a gun!

Something was stirring down below. It began to look as if the lid was about to blow off. Yet Tack had no idea of his own status. He was an escaped prisoner and as such could be shot on sight legally by Olney or Starr, who seemed to be a deputy. From the wary attitude of the Van Hardin men he knew that they were disturbed by their lack of knowledge of him.

Yet the day passed without incident, and finally he returned to the bunk and lay down after checking his guns once more. The time for the payoff was near, he knew. It could come at any moment. He was lying there thinking about that and looking up at the rough plank ceiling when he heard steps on the stairs.

He arose so suddenly that a twinge of pain shot through the weight that had become his leg. The steps were on the front stairs, not the back. A quick glance from the window told him it was Betty London.

What did she want here?

Her hand fell on the knob and it turned. He eased off the bed and turned the key in the lock. She hesitated just an instant and then stepped in. When their eyes met, hers went wide, and her face went white to the lips.

"You!" she gasped. "Oh, Tack! What have you been doing! Where have you been!"

She started toward him, but he backed up and sat down on the bed. "Wait. Do they know I'm up here?" he demanded harshly.

"No, Tack. I came up to see if some papers were here, some papers I gave to Anson Childe before he was—murdered."

"Yuh think I did that?" he demanded.

"No, of course not!" Her eyes held a question. "Tack, what's the matter? Don't you like me anymore?"

"Don't I like yuh?" His lips twisted with bitterness. "Lady, yuh've got a nerve to ask that! I come back and find my girl about to go dancin' in a cheap saloon dance hall, and—"

"I needed money, Tack," Betty said quietly. "Dad needed care. We didn't have any money. Everything we had was lost when we lost the ranch. Hardin offered me the job. He said he wouldn't let anybody molest me."

"What about him?"

"I could take care of him." She looked at him, puzzled. "Tack, what's the matter? Why are you sitting down? Are you hurt?"

"My leg." He shook his head as she started forward. "Don't bother about it. There's no time. What are they saying down there? What's all the crowd in town? Give it to me, quick!"

"Some of them think you were drowned in escaping from jail. I don't think Van Hardin thinks that, nor Olney. They seem very disturbed. The crowd is in town for Childe's funeral and because some of them think you were murdered once Olney got you in jail. Some of our old friends."

"Betty!" The call came from the street below. It was Van Hardin's voice.

"Don't answer!" Tack Gentry got up. His dark green eyes were hard. "I want him to come up."

Betty waited, her eyes wide, listening. Footsteps sounded on the stairway, and then the door shoved open. "Bet—" Van Hardin's voice died out and he stood there, one hand on the doorknob, staring at Tack.

"Howdy, Hardin," Tack said, "I was hopin' yuh'd come."

Van Hardin said nothing. His powerful shoulders filled the open door, his eyes were set, and the shock was fading from them now.

"Got a few things to tell yuh, Hardin," Tack continued gently. "Before yuh go out of this feet first I want yuh to know what a sucker yuh've been."

"A sucker I've been?" Hardin laughed. "What chance have yuh got? The street down there is full of my men. Yuh've friends there, too, but they lack leadership. They don't know what to do. My men have their orders. And then I won't have any trouble with yuh, Gentry. Yore old friends around here told me all about yuh. Soft, like that uncle of yores."

"Ever hear of Black Jack Paris, Hardin?"

"The gunman? Of course, but what's he got to do with yuh?"

"Nothin', now. He did once, up in Ellsworth, Kansas. They dug a bed for him next mornin', Hardin. He was too slow. Yuh said I was soft? Well, maybe I was once. Maybe in spots I still am, but yuh see, since the folks around here have seen me I've been over the cattle trails, been doin' some Injun fightin' and rustler killin'. It makes a sight of change in a man, Hardin.

"That ain't what I wanted yuh to know. I wanted yuh to know what a fool yuh were, tryin' to steal this ranch. Yuh see, the land in our home ranch wasn't like the rest of this land, Hardin."

"What do yuh mean?" Hardin demanded suspiciously.

"Why, yuh're the smart boy," Tack drawled easily. "Yuh should have checked before takin' so much for granted. Yuh see, the Gentry ranch was a land grant. My grandmother, she was a Basque, see? The land came to us through her family, and the will she left was that it would belong to us as long as any of us lived, that it couldn't be sold or traded, and in case we all died, it was to go to the state of Texas!"

Van Hardin stared. "What?" he gasped. "What kind of fool deal is this yuh're givin' me?"

"Fool deal is right." Tack said quietly. "Yuh see, the state of Texas knows no Gentry would sell or trade, knowin' we couldn't, so if somebody else showed up with the land, they were bound to ask a sight of questions. Sooner or later they'd have got around to askin' yuh how come."

Hardin seemed stunned. From the street below, there was a sound of horses' hooves.

Then a voice said from Tack's left, "Yuh better get out, Van. There's talkin' to be done in the street. I want Tack Gentry!"

Tack's head jerked around. It was Soderman. The short, squinty-eyed man was staring at him, gun in hand. He heard Hardin turn and bolt out of the room, saw resolution in Soderman's eyes. Hurling himself toward the wall, Gentry's hand flashed for his pistol.

A gun blasted in the room with a roar like a cannon, and Gentry felt the angry whip of the bullet, and then he fired twice, low down.

Soderman fell back against the doorjamb, both hands grabbing at his stomach, just below his belt buckle. "Yuh shot me!" he gasped, round eyed. "Yuh shot—me!"

"Like you did my uncle," Tack said coolly. "Only yuh had better than an even break, and he had no break at all!"

Gentry could feel blood from the opened wound trickling down his leg. He glanced at Betty. "I've got to get down there," he said. "He's a slick talker."

Van Hardin was standing down in the street. Beside him was Olney and nearby was Starr. Other men, a half dozen of them, loitered nearby.

Slowly, Tack Gentry began stumping down the stair. All eyes looked up. Red Furness saw him and spoke out, "Tack, these three men are Rangers come down from Austin to make some inquiries."

Hardin pointed at Gentry. "He's wanted for murdering Anson Childe! Also for jailbreaking, and unless I'm much mistaken he has killed another man up there in Childe's office!"

The Rangers looked at him curiously, and then one of them glanced at Hardin. "Yuh all the hombre what lays claim to the Gentry place?"

Hardin swallowed up quickly, and then his eyes shifted. "No, that was Soderman. The man who was upstairs."

Hardin looked at Tack Gentry. With the Rangers here he knew his game was played out. He smiled suddenly. "Yuh've nothin' on me at all, gents," he said coolly. "Soderman killed John Gentry and laid claim to his ranch. I don't know nothin' about it."

"Yuh engineered it!" Bill London burst out. "Same as yuh did the stealin' of my ranch!"

"Yuh've no proof," Hardin sneered. "Not a particle. My name is on no papers, and yuh have no evidence."

Coolly, he strode across to his black horse and swung into the saddle. He was smiling gently, but there was sneering triumph behind the smile. "You've nothin' on me, not a thing!"

"Don't let him get away!" Bill London shouted. "He's the wust one of the whole kit and kaboodle of 'em!"

"But he's right!" the Ranger protested. "In all the papers we've found, there's not a single item to tie him up. If he's in it, he's been almighty smart."

"Then arrest him for horse stealin'!" Tack Gentry said. "That's my black horse he's on!"

Hardin's face went cold, and then he smiled. "Why, that's crazy! That's foolish," he said. "This is my horse. I reared him from a colt. Anybody could be mistaken, cause one black horse is like another. My brand's on him, and yuh can all see it's an old brand."

Tack Gentry stepped out in front of the black horse. "Button!" he said sharply. "Button!"

At the familiar voice, the black horse's head jerked up. "Button!" Tack called. "Hut! Hut!"

As the name and the sharp command rolled out, Button reacted like an explosion of dynamite. He jumped straight up in the air and came down hard. Then he sunfished wildly, and Van Hardin hit the dirt in a heap.

"Button!" Tack commanded. "Go get Blackie!"

Instantly, the horse wheeled and trotted to the hitching rail where Blackie stood ground hitched as Olney had left him. Button caught the reins in his teeth and led the other black horse back.

The Rangers grinned. "Reckon, mister," he said, "yuh done proved yore case. The man's a horse thief."

Hardin climbed to his feet, his face dark with fury. "Yuh think yuh'll get away with that?" His hand flashed for his gun.

Tack Gentry had been watching him, and now his own hand moved down and then up. The two guns barked as one. A chip flew from the stair post beside Tack, but Van Hardin turned slowly and went to his knees in the dust.

At almost the same instant, a sharp voice rang out. *Olney! Starr!*"

Olney's face went white and he wheeled, hand flashing for his gun. "*Anson Childe!*" he gasped.

Childe stood on the platform in front of his room and fired once, twice, three times. Sheriff Olney went down, coughing and muttering. Starr backed through the swinging doors of the saloon and sat down hard in the sawdust.

Tack stared at him. "What the—"

The tall young lawyer came down the steps. "Fooled them, didn't I? They tried to get me once too often. I got their man with a shotgun in the face. Then I changed clothes with him and lit out for Austin. I came in with the Rangers and then left them on the edge of town. They told me they'd let us have it our way unless they were needed."

"Saves the state of Texas a sight of money," one of the Rangers drawled. "Anyway, we been checkin' on this here Hardin. On Olney, too. That's why they wanted to keep things quiet around here. They knowed we was checkin' on 'em."

The Rangers moved in and with the help of a few of the townspeople rounded up Hardin's other followers.

Tack grinned at the lawyer. "Lived up to your name, pardner," he said. "Yuh sure did! All yore sheep in the fold, now!"

"What do you mean? Lived up to my name?" Anson Childe looked around.

Gentry grinned. "And a little Childe shall lead them!" he said.

TRAIL TO PIE TOWN

Billy Hamilton, mountain man, trapper, and more, tells of a shooting contest at a rendezvous at Brown's Hole. "Three posts were set in the ground about 25 yards apart. They stood six feet out of the ground and were ten inches in diameter. The top of the post was squared for a distance of about twelve inches. The arms to be used were Colt six-shooters. Horses were to be put at full speed, passing the posts not closer than ten feet and the contestant was to fire not less than two shots at each post.

"Some of our party put two bullets in each post and all at least one. I tried it twice and was somewhat surprised to find the best I could do was to place one bullet in each post."

Trail to Pie Town

Dusty Barron turned the steel-dust stallion down the slope toward the wash. He was going to have to find water soon or the horse and himself would be done for. If Emmett Fisk and Gus Mattis had shown up in the street at any other time it would have been all right.

As it was, they had appeared just as he was making a break from the saloon, and they had blocked the road to the hill country and safety. Both men had reached for their guns when they saw him, and he had wheeled his horse and hit the desert road at a dead run. With Dan Hickman dead in the saloon it was no time to argue or engage in gun pleasantries while the clan gathered.

It had been a good idea to ride to Jarilla and make peace talk, only the idea hadn't worked. Dan Hickman had called him yellow and then gone for a gun. Dan was a mite slow, a fact that had left him dead on the saloon floor.

There were nine Hickmans in Jarilla, and there were Mattis and three Fisk boys. Dusty's own tall brothers were back in the hills southwest of Jarilla, but with his road blocked he had headed the steel-dust down the trail into the basin.

The stallion had saved his bacon. No doubt about that. It was only the speed of the big desert-bred horse and its endurance, that had got him away from town before the Hickmans could catch him. The big horse had given him lead enough until night had closed in, and after that it was easier.

Dusty had turned at right angles from his original route. They would never expect that, for the turn took him down the long slope into the vast, empty expanse of

56

the alkali basin where no man of good sense would consider going.

For him it was the only route. At Jarilla they would be watching for him, expecting him to circle back to the hill country and his own people. He should have listened to Allie when she had told him it was useless to try to settle the old blood feud.

He had been riding now, with only a few breaks, for hours. Several times he had stopped to rest the stallion, wanting to conserve its splendid strength against what must lie ahead. And occasionally he had dismounted and walked ahead of the big horse.

Dusty Barron had only the vaguest idea of what he was heading into. It was thirty-eight miles across the basin, and he was heading down the basin. According to popular rumor, there was no water for over eighty miles in that direction. And he had started with his canteen only half full.

For the first hour he had taken his course from a star. Then he had sighted a peak ahead and to his left and used that for a marker. Gradually, he had worked his way toward the western side of the basin.

Somewhere over the western side was Gallo Gap, a green meadow high in the peaks off a rocky and rarely used pass. There would be water there if he could make it, yet he knew of the gap only from a story told him by a prospector he had met one day in the hills near his home.

Daybreak found him a solitary black speck in a vast wilderness of white. The sun stabbed at him with lances of fire and then rising higher bathed the great alkali basin in white radiance and blasting furnace heat. Dusty narrowed his eyes against the glare. It was at least twelve miles to the mountains.

He still had four miles to go through the puffing alkali dust when he saw the tracks. At first he couldn't believe the evidence of his eyes. A wagon—here!

While he allowed the steel-dust to take a blow, he dismounted and examined the tracks. It had been a heavy wagon pulled by four mules or horses. In the fine dust he could not find an outlined track to tell one from the other.

The tracks had come out of the white distance to the east and had turned north exactly on the route he was following. Gallo Gap, from the prospector's story, lay considerably north of him and a bit to the west.

Had the driver of the wagon known of the gap? Or had he merely turned on impulse to seek a route through the mountains. Glancing in first one and then the other direction, Dusty could see no reason why the driver should have chosen either direction. Jarilla lay southwest, but from here there was no indication of it and no trail.

Mounting again, he rode on, and when he came to the edge of the low hills fronting the mountains, he detected the wagon trail running along through the scattered rocks, parched bunch grass, and greasewood. It was still heading north. Yet when he studied the terrain before him he could see nothing but dancing heat waves and an occasional dust devil.

The problem of the wagon occupied his mind to forgetfulness of his own troubles. It had come across the alkali basin from the east. That argued it must have come from the direction of Manzano unless the wagon had turned into the trail somewhere further north on the road to Conejos.

Nothing about it made sense. This was Apache country and no place for wagon travel. A man on a fast horse, yes, but even then it was foolhardy to travel alone. Yet the driver of the wagon had the courage of recklessness to come across the dead white expanse of the basin, a trip that to say the least was miserable.

Darkness was coming again, but he rode on. The wagon interested him, and with no other goal in mind now that he had escaped the Hickmans, he was curious to see who the driver was and to learn what he had in mind. Obviously, the man was a stranger to this country.

It was then, in the fading light, that he saw the mule. The steel-dust snorted and shied sharply, but Dusty kneed it closer for a better look. It had been a big mule and a fine animal, but it was dead now. It bore evidence of that brutal crossing of the basin, and here, on the far side, the animal had finally dropped dead of heat and exhaustion.

Only then did he see the trunk. It was sitting between two rocks, partly concealed. He walked to it and looked it over. Cumbersome and heavy, it had evidently been dumped from the wagon to lighten the load. He tried to open it, but could not. It was locked tight. Beside it were a couple of chairs and a bed.

"Sheddin' his load," Dusty muttered thoughtfully. "He'd better find some water for those other mules or they'll die, too."

Then he noticed the name on the trunk. D.C. LOWE, ST. LOUIS, MO.

"You're a long way from home," Dusty remarked. He swung a leg over the saddle and rode on. He had gone almost five miles before he saw the fire.

At first, it might have been a star, but as he drew nearer he could see it was too low down, although higher than he was. The trail had been turning gradually deeper into the hills and had begun to climb a little. He rode on, using the light for a beacon.

When he was still some distance off he dismounted and tied the stallion to a clump of greasewood and walked forward on foot.

The three mules were hitched to the back of the wagon, all tied loosely and lying down. A girl was bending over a fire, and a small boy, probably no more than nine years old, was gathering sticks of dried mesquite for fuel. There was no one else in sight.

Marveling, he returned to his horse and started back. When he was still a little distance away he began to sing. His throat was dry and it was a poor job, but he didn't want to frighten them. When he walked his horse into the firelight the boy was staring up at him, wide-eyed, and the girl had an old Frontier Model Colt.

"It's all right, ma'am," he said, swinging down, "I'm just a passin' stranger an' don't mean any harm."

"Who are you?" she demanded.

"Name of Dusty Barron, ma'am. I've been followin' your trail."

"Why?" Her voice was sharp and a little frightened. She could have been no more than seventeen or eighteen.

"Mostly because I was headed thisaway an' was

wonderin' what anybody was doin' down here with a wagon, or where you might be headed."

"Doesn't this lead us anywhere?" she asked.

"Ma'am," Dusty replied, "if you're lookin' for a settlement there ain't none thisaway in less'n a hundred miles. There's a sort of town then, place they call Pie Town."

"But where did you come from?" Her eyes were wide and dark. If she was fixed up, he reflected, she would be right pretty.

"Place they call Jarilla," he said, "but I reckon this was a better way if you're travelin' alone. Jarilla's a Hickman town, an' they sure are a no-account lot."

"My father died," she told him, putting the gun in a holster hung to the wagon bed, "back there. Billy an' I buried him."

"You come across the basin alone?" He was incredulous.

"Yes. Father died in the mountains on the other side. That was three days ago."

Dusty removed his hat and began to strip the saddle and bridle from the stallion while the girl bent over her cooking. He found a hunk of bacon in his saddle pockets. "Got plenty of bacon?" he asked. "I most generally pack a mite along."

She looked up, brushing a strand of hair away from her face. She was flushed from the fire. "We haven't had any bacon for a week." She looked away quickly, and her chin quivered a little and then became stubborn. "Nor much of anything else, but you're welcome to join us."

He seated himself on the ground and leaned back on his saddle while she dished up the food. It wasn't much. A few dry beans and some corn bread. "You got some relatives out here somewheres?"

"No." She handed him a plate, but he was too thirsty to eat more than a few mouthfuls. "Father had a place out here. His lungs were bad and they told him the dry air would be good for him. My mother died when Billy was born, so there was nothing to keep us back in Missouri. We just headed west."

"You say your father had a place? Where is it?"

"I'm not sure. Father loaned some man some money, or rather, he provided him with money with which to buy stock. The man was to come west and settle on a place, stock it, and then send for Dad."

Dusty ate slowly, thinking that over. "Got anything to show for it?"

"Yes, Father had an agreement that was drawn up and notarized. It's in a leather wallet. He gave the man five thousand dollars. It was all we had."

When they had eaten, the girl and boy went to sleep in the wagon box while Dusty stretched out on the ground nearby. "What a mess!" he told himself. "Those kids comin' away out here, all by themselves now, an' the chances are that money was blowed in over a faro layout long ago!"

In the morning Dusty hitched up the mules for them. "You foller me," he advised, and turned the stallion up the trail to the north.

It was almost noon before he saw the thumblike butte that marked the entrance to Gallo Gap. He turned toward it, riding ahead to scout the best trail and at times dismounting to roll rocks aside so the wagon could get through.

Surmounting the crest of a low hill, he looked suddenly into Gallo Gap. His red-rimmed eyes stared greedily at the green grass and trees. The stallion smelled water and wanted to keep going, so waving the wagon on, he rode down into the gap.

Probably there were no more than two hundred acres here, but it was waist deep in rich green grass, and the towering yellow pines were tall and very old. It was like riding from desolation into a beautiful park. He found the spring by the sound of running water, crystal clear and beautiful, the water rippling over the rocks to fall into a clear pond at least an acre in extent. Nearby, space had been cleared for a cabin and then abandoned.

Dusty turned in the saddle as his horse stood knee deep in the water. The wagon pulled up. "This is a little bit of heaven!" he said, grinning at the girl. "Say, what's your name, anyway?"

"Ruth Grant," she said, shyly.

All the weariness seemed to have fled from her face at the sight of the water and trees. She smiled gaily, and a few minutes later as he walked toward the trees with a rifle in the crook of his elbow he heard laughter and then her voice, singing. He stopped suddenly, watching some deer feeding a short distance off, and listening to her voice. It made a lump of loneliness rise in his throat.

That night, after they had eaten steaks from a fat buck he'd killed, their first good meal in days, he looked across the fire at her. "Ruth," he said, "I think I'll locate me a home right here. I've been lookin' for a place of my own.

"I reckon what we better do is for you all to stay here with me until you get rested up. I'll build a cabin, and those mules of yours can get some meat on their bones again. Then I'll ride on down to Pie Town and locate this hombre your father had dealin's with an' see how things look."

That was the way they left it, but in the days that followed Dusty Barron had never been happier. He felled trees on the mountainside and built a cabin, and in working around he found ways of doing things he had never tried before. Ruth was full of suggestions about the house, sensible, knowing things that helped a lot. He worked the mules a little, using only one at a time and taking them turnabout.

He hunted a good deal for food. Nearby he found a salt lick and shot an occasional antelope, and several times, using a shotgun from the wagon, he killed blue grouse. In a grove of trees he found some ripe black cherries similar to those growing wild in the Guadalupe Mountains of west Texas. There was also some Mexican plum.

When the cabin was up and there was plenty of meat on hand he got his gear in shape. Then he carefully oiled and cleaned his guns.

Ruth noticed them, and her face paled a little. "You believe there will be trouble?" she asked quickly. "I don't want you to—"

"Forget it," he interrupted. "I've got troubles of my own." He explained about the killing of Dan Hickman and the long-standing feud between the families."

He left at daybreak. In his pocket he carried the leather wallet containing the agreement Roger Grant had made with Dick Lowe. It was a good day's ride from Gallo Gap to Aimless Creek, where Dusty camped the first night. The following day he rode on into Pie Town. From his talks with Ruth he knew something of Lowe and enough of the probable location of the ranch, if there was one.

A cowhand with sandy hair and crossed eyes was seated on the top rail of the corral. Dusty reined in and leaned his forearm on the saddle horn and dug for the makings. After he had rolled a smoke he pass them on to the cross-eyed rider.

"Know anything about an' hombre name of Dick Lowe?" he asked.

"Reckon so." They shared a match, and looking at each other through the smoke decided they were men of a kind. "He's up there in the Spur Saloon now."

Dusty made no move. After a few drags on the cigarette, he glanced at the fire end. "What kind of hombre is he?"

"Salty." The cowhand puffed for a moment on his cigarette. "Salty an' mean. Plumb poison with a shootin' iron, an' when you ride for him, he pays you what he wants to when you quit. If you don't think you got a square deal you can always tell him so, but when you do you better reach."

"Like that, huh?"

"Like that." He smoked quietly for a few minutes. "Four hombres haven't liked what he paid 'em. He buried all four of 'em in his own personal boothill, off to the north of the ranchhouse."

"Sounds bad. Do all his own work or does he have help?"

"He's got help. Cat McQuill an' Bugle Nose Bender. Only nobody calls him Bugle Nose to his face."

"What about the ranch? Nice place?"

"Best around here. He come in here with money, had near five thousand dollars. He bought plenty of cattle an' stocked his range well."

The cross-eyed cowhand looked at him, squinting through the smoke. "My name's Blue Riddle. I rode for him once."

"I take it you didn't argue none," Barron said, grinning.

"My maw never raised no foolish children!" Riddle

replied wryly. "They had me in a cross fire. Been Lowe alone, I'd maybe of took a chance, but as it was, they would have cut me down quick. So I come away, but I'm stickin' around, just waiting. I told him I aimed to have my money, an' he just laughed."

Dusty dropped his hand back and loosened his left-hand gun. Then he swung his leg back over the saddle and thrust his toe in the stirrup. "Well," he said, "I got papers here that say I speak for a gal that owns half his layout. I'm goin' up an' lay claim to it for her."

Riddle looked up cynically. "Why not shoot yourself and save the trouble? They'll gun you down."

Then he sized Barron up again. "What did you say your name was?"

Dusty grinned. "I didn't say, but its Dusty Barron."

Blue Riddle slid off the corral rail. "One of the Barron's from Castle Rock?" He grinned again. "This I gotta see!" . . .

Dusty was looking for a big man, but Dick Lowe, whom he spotted at once on entering the saloon, was only a bit larger than himself, and he was the only small man among the Barrons.

Lowe turned to look at him as he entered. The man's features were sharp, and his quick eyes glanced from Dusty Barron to Riddle and then back again. Dusty walked to the bar, and Riddle loitered near the door.

The man standing beside Lowe at the bar must be Cat McQuill. The reason for the nickname was obvious, for there was something feline about the man's facial appearance.

"Lowe?" Dusty inquired.

"That's right," Lowe turned toward him slowly. "Something you want?"

"Yeah," Dusty leaned nonchalantly on the bar and ordered a drink. "I'm representin' your partner."

Dick Lowe's face blanched and then turned hard as stone. His eyes glinted. However, he managed a smile with his thin lips. "Partner? I have no partner."

Dusty leaned on the bar watching his drink poured. He took his time.

*   *   *

Lowe watched him, slowly growing more and more angry. "Well," he said sharply, "if you've got something to say, say it!"

Dusty looked around, simulating surprise. "Why, I was just givin' you time to remember, Lowe! You can't tell me you can draw up an agreement with a man, have it properly notarized, and then take five thousand dollars of his money to stock a ranch and not remember it!"

Dusty was pointedly speaking loudly, and the fact angered Lowe. "You have such an agreement?" Lowe demanded.

"Sure I got it."

"Where's the party this supposed agreement belongs to? Why doesn't he speak for himself?"

"He's dead. He was a lunger an' died on his way west."

Lowe's relief was evident. "I'm afraid," he said, "that this is all too obvious an attempt to get some money out of me. It won't work."

"It's nothing of the kind. Grant's dead, but he left a daughter and a son. I aim to see they get what belongs to 'em, Mr. Lowe. I hope we can do it right peaceable."

Lowe's face tightened, but he forced a smile. He was aware he had enemies in Pie town and did not relish their overhearing this conversation. He was also aware that it was pretty generally known that he had come into Pie Town with five thousand in cash and bought cattle when everyone on the range was impoverished.

"I reckon this'll be easy settled," he said. "You bring the agreement to the ranch, an' if it's all legal I reckon we can make a deal."

"Sure!" Dusty agreed. "See you tomorrow!"

On the plank steps of the hotel he waited until Riddle caught up with him. "You ain't actually goin' out there, are you?" Blue demanded. "That's just askin' for trouble!"

"I'm goin' out," Dusty agreed. "I want a look at the ranch myself. If I can ride out there I can get an idea what kind of stock he's got and what shape the ranch is in. I've got a hunch if we make a cash settlement Lowe isn't goin' to give us much more chance to look around if he can help it.

"Besides, I've talked in front o' the folks here in town, and rough as some of them may be they ain't goin' to see no orphans get gypped. No Western crowd would stand for that unless it's some outlaws like Lowe and his two pals."

Riddle walked slowly away shaking his head with doubt. Dusty watched him go and then went on inside.

He was throwing a saddle on the steel-dust next morning when he heard a low groan. Gun in hand he walked around the corner of the corral. Beyond a pile of poles he saw Blue Riddle pulling himself off the ground. "What happened?" Dusty demanded.

"Bender an' McQuill. They gave me my walkin' papers. Said I'd been in town too long, which didn't bother Lowe none till I took up with you. They gave me till daybreak to pull my freight."

He staggered erect, holding a hand to his head. "Then Bender bent a gun over my noggin."

Barron's eyes narrowed. "Play rough, don't they?" He looked at Riddle. "What are you goin' to do?"

"You don't see me out there runnin' down the road, do you?" Riddle said. "I'm sittin' tight!"

"Wash your face off, then," Dusty suggested, "an' we'll eat!"

"You go ahead," Riddle replied. "I'll be along."

Dusty glanced back over his shoulder as he left and saw Blue Riddle hiking toward the Indian huts that clustered outside of Pie Town.

When he rode out of town an hour later Dusty Barron was not feeling overly optimistic. Riddle had stayed behind only at Dusty's insistence, but now that Dusty was headed toward Lowe's ranch he no longer felt so confident. Dick Lowe was not a man to give up easily, nor to yield his ranch or any part of it without a fight. The pistol-whipping of Riddle had been ample evidence of the lengths to which he was prepared to go.

The range through which Dusty rode was good. This was what he had wanted to see. How they might have bargained in town he was not sure. He doubted if anyone there would interfere if a deal was made by him. It was his own problem to see that Ruth and Billy Grant got a fair deal, and that could not be done unless he knew something, at least, of the ranch and the stock.

Dusty was quite sure now that Lowe had never expected the consumptive Roger Grant to come west and claim his piece of the ranch. Nor had he planned to give it to him if he had. He knew very well that he himself was riding into the lion's mouth, but felt he could depend on his own abilities and that Lowe would not go too far after his talk before the bystanders who had been in the saloon. By now Lowe would know that the story would be known to all his enemies in Pie Town.

Cat McQuill was loafing on the steps when Dusty rode up, and the gunman's eyes gleamed with triumph at seeing him. "Howdy!" he said affably. "Come on in! The boss is waitin' for you!"

Bugle Nose Bender was leaning against the fireplace and Lowe was seated at his desk. "Here he is, Boss!" McQuill said as they entered.

Lowe glanced up sharply. "Where's the agreement?" he asked, holding out his hand.

Barron handed it to him, and the rancher opened it, took a quick look, and then glanced up. "This is it, Cat!"

Too late Dusty heard the slide of gun on leather and whirled to face McQuill, but the pistol barrel crashed down over the side of his head and he hit the floor. Even as he fell he realized what a fool he had been, yet he had been so sure they would talk a little, at least, try to run a blazer or to buy him off cheap.

Bender lunged toward him and kicked him in the ribs. Then Lowe reached over and jerking him to his knees, struck him three times in the face. The pistol barrel descended again and drove him down into a sea of blackness.

How long they had pounded him he had no idea. When he opened his eyes, he struggled, fighting his way to a realization of where he was. It took him several minutes to understand that he was almost standing on his head in the road, one foot caught in the stallion's stirrup!

The steel-dust, true to his training, was standing rigid in the road, his head turned to look at his master. "Easy boy!" Dusty groaned. "Easy does it!" Twisting his foot in the stirrup, he tried to free it, but to no avail.

He realized what they had planned. After beating him they had brought him out here, wedged his foot in the stirrup, struck the horse, and when he started to move, ridden hastily away before they could be seen. Most horses, frightened by the unfamiliar burden in the stirrup, would have raced away over the desert and dragged him to death. It had happened to more than one unwary cowhand.

They had reckoned without the steel-dust. The stallion had been reared by Dusty Barron from a tiny colt, and the two had never been long apart. The big horse had known instantly that something was radically wrong and had gone only a little way and then stopped. His long training told him to stand, and he stood stock still.

Dusty twisted his foot again but couldn't get loose. Nor could he pull himself up and get hold of the stirrup and so into the saddle. He was still trying this when hoofbeats sounded on the road.

He looked around wildly, fearful of Lowe's return. Then a wave of relief went over him. It was Blue Riddle!

"Hey!" Blue exclaimed. "What the heck happened?" He swung down from his horse and hastily extricated Dusty from his predicament.

Barron explained. "They wanted me killed so it would look like I was dragged to death! Lucky they got away from here in a hurry, afraid they might be seen!"

"But they got the agreement!" Riddle protested.

"Uh-uh." Barron grinned and then gasped as his bruised face twinged with pain. "That was a copy. I put the agreement down an' traced over it. He took a quick look and thought it was the real thing. Now we got to get to town before he realizes what happened."

Despite his battered and bruised body and the throbbing of his face, Dusty crawled into the saddle and they raced up the road to Pie Town.

Two men were standing on the hotel porch as they rode up. One of them glanced at Dusty Barron. "Howdy. Young woman inside wants to see you."

Dusty rushed into the lobby and stopped in surprise. Facing him was Ruth Grant, holding Billy by the hand, but her smile fled when she saw his face. "Oh!" she cried. "What's happened to you?"

Briefly, he explained. Then he demanded, "How'd you get here?"

"After you left," Ruth told him. "I was worried. After Father's death and the trouble we had before you came, there was no time to think of anything, and I had to always be thinking of where we would go and what we would do. Then I remembered a comment Father made once.

"You see, Mr. Lowe left a trunk with us to bring west or send to him later. It wasn't quite full, so Father opened it to pack some other things in it. He found something there that worried him a great deal, and he told me several times that he was afraid he might have trouble when we got out here.

"From all he said I had an idea what he found, so after you were gone we searched through the trunk and found some letters and a handbill offering a five-thousand-dollar reward for Lowe. Why he kept them I can't imagine, but the sheriff says some criminals are very vain and often keep such things about themselves."

"And then you rode on here?"

She nodded. "We met two men who were trailing you, and as they had extra horses with them so they could travel fast, we joined them."

Dusty's face tightened. "Men looking for me?"

Riddle interrupted. "Dick Lowe's ridin' into town now!"

Dusty Barron turned, loosening his guns. He started for the door.

"I'm in on this, too!" Riddle said, trailing him.

They walked out on the porch and stepped down into the street, spreading apart. Dick Lowe and his two henchmen had dismounted and were starting into the saloon when something made them glance up the street.

"Lowe!" Dusty yelled. "You tried to kill me, an' I'm comin' for you!"

Dick Lowe's hard face twisted with fury as he wheeled, stepping down into the dust.

He stopped in the street, and Cat McQuill and Bender moved out to either side.

Dusty Barron walked steadily down the street, his eyes on Dick Lowe. All three men were dangerous, but Lowe was the man he wanted, and Lowe was the man he intended to get first.

"This man's an outlaw!" he said, speaking to Bender and McQuill. "He's wanted for murder in St. Louis! If you want out, get out now!"

"You're lying!" Bender snarled.

Dusty Barron walked on. The sun was bright in the street, and little puffs of dust arose at every step. There were five horses tied to the hitch rail behind the three men. He found himself hoping none of them would be hit by a stray shot. To his right was Blue Riddle, walking even with him, his big hands hovering over his guns.

His eyes clung to Dick Lowe, riveted there as though he alone lived in the world. He could see the man drop into a half crouch, noticed the bulge of the tobacco sack in his breast pocket, the buttons down the two sides of his shirt. Under the brim of the hat he could see the straight bar of the man's eyebrows and the hard gleam of the eyes beneath, and then suddenly the whole tableau dissolved into flaming, shattering action.

Lowe's hand flashed for his gun and Dusty's beat him by a hair breadth, but Dusty held his fire, lifting the gun slowly. Lowe's quick shot flamed by his ear, and he winced inwardly at the proximity of death. Then the gunman fired again and the bullet tugged impatiently at his vest. He drew a long breath and squeezed off a shot, then another.

Lowe rose on tiptoes, opened his mouth wide as if to gasp for breath, seemed to hold himself there for a long moment, and then pitched over into the street.

Dusty's gun swung with his eyes and he saw Bender was down on his knees, and so he opened up on McQuill. The Cat man jerked convulsively and then began to back away, his mouth working and his gun hammering. The man's gun stopped firing, and he stared at it, pulled the trigger again, and then reached for a cartridge from his belt.

Barron stood spraddle-legged in the street and saw

Cat's hand fumble at his belt. The fingers came out with a cartridge and moved toward the gun, and then his eyes glazed and he dropped his iron. Turning, as though the whole affair had slipped his mind, he started for the saloon. He made three steps and then lifted his foot, seemed to feel for the saloon step, and fell like a log across the rough board porch.

Blue Riddle was on his knees, blood staining a trouser leg. Bender was sprawled out in the dust, a darkening pool forming beneath him.

Suddenly the street was filled with people. Ruth ran up to Dusty and he slid his arm around her. With a shock, he remembered. "You said two men were looking for me. Who?"

"Only us."

He turned, staring. Two big men were facing him, grinning. "Buck and Ben! How in tarnation did you two find me?"

Buck Barron grinned. "We was wonderin' what happened to you. We come to town and had a mite of a ruckus with the Hickmans. What was left of them headed for El Paso in a mighty hurry—both of 'em.

"Then an Injun kid come ridin' up on a beat-up hoss and said you all was in a sight of trouble, so we figgered we'd come along and see how you made out."

"An Injun?" Dusty was puzzled.

"Yeah," Riddle told him, "that was my doin'. I figgered you was headed for trouble, so I sent an Injun kid off after your brothers. Heck, if I'd knowed what you was like with a six-gun I'd never have sent for 'em!"

Ben Barron grinned and rubbed at the stubble of whiskers. "An' if we'd knowed there was on'y three, we'd never have come!" He looked from Dusty to Ruth. "Don't look like you'd be comin' home right soon with that place at Gallo Gap an' what you've got your arm around. But what'll we tell Allie?"

"Allie?" Ruth drew away from him, eyes wide. "Who's Allie? You didn't tell me you had a girl!"

Dusty winked at his brothers. "Allie? She's war chief of the Barron tribe! Allie's my ma!"

He turned to Riddle. "Blue, how's about you sort of

keepin' an eye on that gap place for me for a week or so? I reckon I'd better take Ruth home for a spell. Allie, she sure sets a sight of store by weddin's!"

Ruth's answering pressure on his arm was all the answer he needed.

AUTHOR'S NOTE
MISTAKES CAN KILL YOU

The guns of the West were many, most of them manufactured in this country, some imported from abroad. To many Westerners any rifle was a Winchester, any pistol a Colt. Both brands were so common that they were accepted names for the type of weapon in question, just as today to many people any camera is a Kodak. Guns were in great demand, so many manufacturers opened their shops. Some lasted for years, some only for months. Pistols were made with multiple barrels, with two cylinders, with knives attached, with knuckle dusters (so-called brass knuckles), with about every kind of contrivance one can imagine.

The Walch twelve-shot pistol mentioned in this story was also made in a ten-shot version. Their manufacture began in the winter of 1859–60. Their size and weight were approximately that of other pistols of the time, and a casual glance would discern no differences.

Among the most-used pistols on the frontier were various versions of the Remington, but there were also Sharps, Marlin, and Stevens pistols, as well as J. B. Driscoll, Forehand & Wadsworth, Lindsay, Marston, Starr, Merwin Hulbert, and dozens of others, including the Charles Sneider two-cylinder revolver, carrying fourteen shots.

On the frontier, mistakes could kill you, and it did not pay to take anything for granted.

Mistakes Can Kill You

Ma Redlin looked up from the stove. "Where's Sam? He still out yonder?"

Johnny rubbed his palms on his chaps. "He ain't comin' to supper, Ma. He done rode off."

Pa and Else were watching him, and Johnny saw the hard lines of temper around Pa's mouth and eyes. Ma glanced at him apprehensively, but when Pa did not speak, she looked to her cooking. Johnny walked around the table and sat down across from Else.

When Pa reached for the coffeepot he looked over at Johnny. "Was he alone, boy? Or did he ride off with that no-account Albie Bower?"

It was in Johnny neither to lie nor to carry tales. Reluctantly, he replied. "He was with somebody. I reckon I couldn't be sure who it was."

Redlin snorted and put down his cup. It was a sore point with Joe Redlin that his son and only child should take up with the likes of Albie Bower. Back in Pennsylvania and Ohio the Redlins had been good God-fearing folk, while Bower was no good, and came from a no-good outfit. Lately, he had been flashing money around, but he claimed to have won it gambling at Degner's Four Star Saloon.

"Once more I'll tell him," Redlin said harshly. "I'll have no son of mine traipsin' with that Four Star outfit. Pack of thieves, that's what they are."

Ma looked up worriedly. She was a buxom woman with a round apple-cheeked face. Good humor was her normal manner. "Don't you be sayin' that away from home,

Joe Redlin. That Loss Degner is a gunslinger, and he'd like nothin' so much as to shoot you after you takin' Else from him."

"I ain't afeerd of him." Redlin's voice was flat. Johnny knew that what he said was true. Joe Redlin was not afraid of Degner, but he avoided him, for Redlin was a small rancher, a one-time farmer, and not a fighting man. Loss Degner was bad all through and made no secret of it. His Four Star was the hangout for all the tough element, and Degner had killed two men since Johnny had been in the country, as well as pistol whipping a half dozen more.

It was not Johnny's place to comment, but secretly he knew the older Redlin was right. Once he had even gone so far as to warn Sam, but it only made the older boy angry.

Sam was almost twenty-one and Johnny but seventeen, but Sam's family had protected him and he had lived always close to the competence of Pa Redlin. Johnny had been doing a man's work since he was thirteen, fighting a man's battles, and making his own way in a hard world.

Johnny also knew what only Else seemed to guess, that it was Hazel, Degner's red-haired singer, who drew Sam Redlin to the Four Star. It was rumored that she was Degner's woman, and Johnny had said as much to Sam. The younger Redlin had flown into a rage and whirling on Johnny had drawn back his fist. Something in Johnny's eyes stopped him, and although Sam would never have admitted it, he was suddenly afraid.

Like Else, Johnny had been adrift when he came to the R Bar. Half dead with pneumonia, he had come up to the door on his black gelding, and the Redlin's hospitality had given him a bed and the best care the frontier could provide, and when Johnny was well, he went to work to repay them. Then he stayed on for the spring roundup as a forty-a-month hand.

He volunteered no information, and they asked him no questions. He was slightly built and below medium height, but broad shouldered and wiry. His shock of chestnut hair always needed cutting, and his green eyes held a lurking humor. He moved with deceptive slowness, for he was quick at work, and skillful with his hands. Nor did he wait to be told about things, for even before he began riding he had mended the buckboard, cleaned out and shored up the spring, repaired the door hinges, and cleaned all the guns.

"We collect from Walters tomorrow," Redlin said suddenly. "Then I'm goin' to make a payment on that Sprague place and put Sam on it. With his own place he'll straighten up and go to work."

Johnny stared at his plate, his appetite gone. He knew what that meant, for it had been in Joe Redlin's mind that Sam should marry Else and settle on that place. Johnny looked up suddenly, and his throat tightened as he looked at her. The gray eyes caught his, searched them for an instant, and then moved away, and Johnny watched the lamplight in her ash blonde hair, turning it to old gold.

He pushed back from the table and excused himself, going out into the moonlit yard. He lived in a room he had built into a corner of the barn. They had objected at first, wanting him to stay at the house, but he could not bear being close to Else, and then he had the lonely man's feeling for seclusion. Actually, it had other advantages, for it kept him near his horse, and he never knew when he might want to ride on.

That black gelding and his new .44 Winchester had been the only incongruous notes in his getup when he arrived at the R Bar, for he had hidden his guns and his best clothes in a cave up the mountain, riding down to the ranch in shabby range clothes with only the .44 Winchester for safety.

He had watched the ranch for several hours despite his illness before venturing down to the door. It paid to be careful, and there were men about who might know him.

Later, when securely in his own room, he had returned to his cache and dug out the guns and brought his outfit down to the ranch. Yet nobody had ever seen him with guns on, nor would they, if he was lucky.

The gelding turned its head and nickered at him, rolling its eyes at him. Johnny walked into the stall and stood there, one hand on the horse's neck. "Little bit longer, boy, then we'll go. You sit tight now."

There was another reason why he should leave now, for he had learned from Sam that Flitch was in town. Flitch had been on the Gila during the fight, and he had been a friend of Card Wells, whom Johnny had killed at Picacho. Moreover, Flitch had been in Cimarron a year before that when Johnny, only fifteen then, had evened the score with the men who had killed his father and stolen their outfit. Johnny had gunned two of them down and put the third into the hospital.

Johnny was already on the range when Sam Redlin rode away the next morning to make his collection. Pa Redlin rode out with Else and found Johnny branding a yearling. Pa waved and rode on, but Else sat on her horse and watched him. "You're a good hand, Johnny," she said when he released the calf. "You should have your own outfit."

"That's what I want most," he admitted. "But I reckon I'll never have it."

"You can if you want it enough. Is it because of what's behind you?"

He looked up quickly then. "What do you know of me?"

"Nothing, Johnny, but what you've told us. But once, when I started into the barn for eggs, you had your shirt off and I saw those bullet scars. I know bullet scars because my own father had them. And you've never told us anything, which usually means there's something you aren't anxious to tell."

"I guess you're right." He tightened the girth on his saddle. "There ain't much to tell, though. I come west with my pa, and he was a lunger. I drove the wagon myself after we left Independence. Clean to Caldwell, then on to Santa Fe. We got us a little outfit with what Pa had left, and some mean fellers stole it off us, and they killed Pa."

Joe Redlin rode back to join them as Johnny was swinging into the saddle. He turned and glanced down at the valley. "Reckon that range won't get much use, Johnny," he said anxiously, "and the stock sure need it. Fair to middlin' grass, but too far to water."

"That draw, now," Johnny suggested. "I been thinkin' about that draw. It would take a sight of work, but a couple of good men with teams and some elbow grease could build them a dam across that draw. There's a sight of water comes down when it rains, enough to last most of the summer if it was dammed. Maybe even the whole year."

The three horses started walking toward the draw, and Johnny pointed out what he meant. "A feller over to Mobeetie did that one time," he said, "and it washed his dam out twice, but the third time she held, and he had him a little lake, all the year around."

"That's a good idea, Johnny." Redlin studied the setup and then nodded. "A right good idea."

"Sam and me could do it," Johnny suggested, avoiding Pa Redlin's eyes.

Pa Redlin said nothing, but both Johnny and Else knew that Sam was not exactly ambitious about extra work. He was a good hand, Sam was, strong and capable, but he was bigheaded about things and was little inclined to sticking with a job.

"Reminds me," Pa said, glancing at the sun. "Sam should be back soon."

"He might stop in town," Else suggested, and was immediately sorry she had said it for she could see the instant worry on Redlin's face. The idea of Sam Redlin stopping at the Four Star with seven thousand dollars on him was scarcely a pleasant one. Murder had been done there for much, much less. And then Sam was overconfident. He was even cocky.

"I reckon I'd better ride in and meet him," Redlin said, genuinely worried now. "Sam's a good boy, but he sets too much store by himself. He figures he can take care of himself anywhere, but that pack of wolves . . ." His voice trailed off to silence.

Johnny turned in his saddle. "Why, I could just as well ride in, Pa," he said casually, "I ain't been to town for a spell, and if anything happened, I could lend a hand."

Pa Redlin was about to refuse, but Else spoke up quickly. "Let him go, Pa. He could do some things for me, too, and Johnny's got a way with folks. Chances are he could get Sam back without trouble."

That's right! Johnny's thoughts were grim. Send me along to save your boy. You don't care if I get shot, just so's he's been saved. Well, all right, I'll go. When I come back I'll climb my gelding and light out. Up to Oregon. I never been to Oregon.

Flitch was in town. His mouth tightened a little, but at that, it would be better than Pa going. Pa always said the wrong thing, being outspoken like. He was a man who spoke his mind, and to speak one's mind to Flitch or Loss Degner would mean a shooting. It might be he could get Sam out of town all right. If he was drinking it would be hard. Especially if that redhead had her hands on him.

"You reckon you could handle it?" Pa asked doubtfully.

"Sure," Johnny said, his voice a shade hard, "I can handle it. I doubt if Sam's in any trouble. Later, maybe. All he'd need is somebody to side him."

"Well," Pa was reluctant, "better take your Winchester. My six-gun, too."

"You hang onto it. I'll make out."

Johnny turned the gelding and started back toward the ranch, his eyes cold. Seventeen he might be, but four years on the frontier on your own make pretty much of a man out of you. He didn't want any more shooting, but he had six men dead on his back trail now, not counting Comanches and Kiowas. Six, and he was seventeen. Next thing, they would be comparing him to the Kid or to Wes Hardin.

He wanted no gunfighter's name, only a little spread of his own where he could run a few cows and raise horses, good stock, like some he had seen in East Texas. No range ponies for him, but good blood. That Sprague place now . . . but that was Sam's place, or as good as his. Well, why not? Sam was getting Else, and it was little enough he could do for Pa and Ma, to bring Sam home safe.

He left the gelding at the water trough and walked into the barn. In his room he dug some saddle gear away from a corner and, out of a hiding place in the corner, he took his guns. After a moment's thought, he took but one of them, leaving the .44 Russian behind. He didn't want to go parading into town with two guns on him, looking like a sure-enough shooter. Besides, with only one gun and the change in him, Flitch might not spot him at all.

Johnny was at the gate riding out when Else and Pa rode up. Else looked at him, her eyes falling to the gun on his hip. Her face was pale and her eyes large. "Be careful, Johnny. I had to say that because you know how hot-headed Pa is. He'd get killed, and he might get Sam killed."

That was true enough, but Johnny was aggrieved. He looked her in the eyes. "Sure, that's true, but you didn't think of Sam, now, did you? You were just thinking of Pa."

Her lips parted to protest, but then her face seemed to stiffen. "No, Johnny, it wasn't only Pa I thought of. I did think of Sam. Why shouldn't I?"

That was plain enough. Why shouldn't she? Wasn't she going to marry him? Wasn't Sam getting the Sprague place when they got that money back safe?

He touched his horse lightly with a spur and moved on past her. All right, he would send Sam back to her, if he could. It was time he was moving on, anyway.

The gelding liked the feel of the trail and moved out fast. Ten miles was all, and he could do that easy enough, and so he did it, and Johnny turned the black horse into the street and stopped before the livery stable, swinging down. Sam's horse was tied at the Four Star's hitchrail. The saddlebags were gone.

Johnny studied the street and then crossed it and walked down along the buildings on the same side as the Four Star. He turned quickly into the door.

Sam Redlin was sitting at a table with the redhead, the saddlebags on the table before him, and he was drunk. He was very drunk. Johnny's eyes swept the room. The bartender and Loss Degner were standing together, talking. Neither of them paid any attention to Johnny, for neither knew him. But Flitch did.

Flitch was standing down the bar with Albie Bower, but none of the old Gila River outfit. Both of them looked up, and Flitch kept looking, never taking his eyes from Johnny. Something bothered him, and maybe it was the one gun.

Johnny moved over to Sam's table. They had to get out of here fast, before Flitch remembered. "Hi, Sam," he said. "Just happened to be in town, and Pa said if I saw you, to side you on the way home."

Sam stared at him sullenly. "Side me? You?" He snorted his contempt. "I need no man to side me. You can tell Pa I'll be home later tonight." He glanced at the redhead. "Much later."

"Want I should carry this stuff home for you?" Johnny put his hand on the saddlebags.

"Leave him be!" Hazel protested angrily. "Can't you see he don't want to be bothered? He's capable of takin' care of himself, an' he don't need no kid for gardeen!"

"Beat it," Sam said. "You go on home. I'll come along later."

"Better come now, Sam." Johnny was getting worried, for Loss Degner had started for the table.

"Here, you!" Degner was sharp. "Leave that man alone! He's a friend of mine, and I'll have no saddle tramp annoying my customers!"

Johnny turned on him. "I'm no saddle tramp. I ride for his pa. He asked me to ride home with him—now. That's what I aim to do."

As he spoke he was not thinking of Degner, but of Flitch. The gunman was behind him now, and neither Flitch, fast as he was, nor Albie Bower was above shooting a man in the back.

"I said to beat it." Sam stared at him drunkenly. "Saddle tramp's what you are. Folks never should have took you in."

"That's it," Degner said. "Now get out! He don't want you nor your company."

There was a movement behind him, and he heard Flitch say, "Loss, let me have him. I know this hombre. This is that kid gunfighter, Johnny O'Day, from the Gila."

Johnny turned slowly, his green eyes flat and cold. "Hello, Flitch. I heard you were around." Carefully, he moved away from the table, aware of the startled look on Hazel's face, the suddenly tight awareness on the face of Loss Degner. "You lookin' for me, Flitch?" It was a chance he had to take. His best chance now. If shooting started, he might grab the saddlebags and break for the door and then the ranch. They would be through with Sam Redlin once the money was gone.

"Yeah." Flitch stared at him, his unshaven face hard with the lines of evil and shadowed by the intent that rode him hard. "I'm lookin' for you. Always figured you got off easy, made you a fast rep gunnin' down your betters."

Bower had moved up beside him, but Loss Degner had drawn back to one side. Johnny's eyes never left Flitch. "You in this, Loss?"

Degner shrugged. "Why should I be? I was no Gila River gunman. This is your quarrel. Finish it between you."

"All right, Flitch," Johnny said. "You want it. I'm givin' you your chance to start the play."

The stillness of a hot midafternoon lay on the Four Star. A fly buzzed against the dusty, cobwebbed back window. Somewhere in the street a horse stamped restlessly, and a distant pump creaked. Flitch stared at him, his little eyes hard and bright. His sweat-stained shirt was torn at the shoulder, and there was dust ingrained in the pores of his face.

His hands dropped in a flashing draw, but he had only cleared leather when Johnny's first bullet hit him, puncturing the Bull Durham tag that hung from his shirt pocket. The second shot cut the edge of it, and the third, fourth, and fifth slammed Albie Bower back, knocking him back step by step, but Albie's gun was hammering, and it took the sixth shot to put him down.

Johnny stood over them, staring down at their bodies, and then he turned to face Loss Degner.

Degner was smiling, and he held a gun in his hand from which a thin tendril of smoke lifted. Startled, Johnny's eyes flickered to Sam Redlin.

Sam lay across the saddlebags, blood trickling from his temples. He had been shot through the head by Degner under cover of the gun battle, murdered without a chance!

Johnny O'Day's eyes lifted to Loss Degner's. The saloonkeeper was still smiling. "Yes, he's dead, and I've killed him. He had it coming, the fool! Thinking we cared to listen to his bragging! All we wanted was that money, and now we've got it. Me—Hazel and I! We've got it."

"Not yet." Johnny's lips were stiff and his heart was cold. He was thinking of Pa, Ma, and Else. "I'm still here."

"You?" Degner laughed. "With an empty gun? I counted your shots, boy. Even Johnny O'Day is cold turkey with an empty gun. Six shots—two for Flitch, and beautiful shooting, too, but four shots for Albie, who was moving and shooting, not so easy a target. But now I've got you. With you dead, I'll just say Sam came here without any money, that he got shot during the fight. Sound good to you?"

Johnny still faced him, his gun in his hand. "Not bad," he said, "but you still have me here, Loss. And this gun ain't empty!"

Degner's face tightened and then relaxed. "Not empty? I counted the shots, kid, so don't try bluffing me. Now I'm killing you." He tilted his gun toward Johnny O'Day, and Johnny fired once, twice . . . a third time. As each bullet hit him, Loss Degner jerked and twisted, but the shock of the wounds, and death wounds they were, was nothing to the shock of the bullets from that empty gun.

He sagged against the bar and then slipped floorward. Johnny moved in on him. "You can hear me, Loss?" The killer's eyes lifted to his. "This ain't a six-shooter. It's a Walch twelve-shot Navy gun, thirty-six caliber. She's right handy, Loss, and it only goes to show you shouldn't jump to conclusions."

Hazel sat at the table, staring at the dying Degner. "You better go to him, Red," Johnny said quietly. "He's only got a minute."

She stared at him as he picked up the saddlebags and backed to the door.

Russell, the storekeeper, was on the steps with a half dozen others, none of whom he knew. "Degner killed Sam Redlin," he said. "Take care of Sam, will you?"

At Russell's nod, Johnny swung to the saddle and turned the gelding toward home.

He wouldn't leave now. He couldn't leave now. They would be all alone there, without Sam. Besides, Pa was going to need help on that dam. "Boy," he touched the gelding's neck, "I reckon we got to stick around for a while."

AUTHOR'S NOTE
BIG MEDICINE

There is more than one way to skin a cat, and in this story old Billy Dunbar finds an unexpected way, based upon knowledge and experience.

The term "medicine" in Indian frontier language is perhaps best translated by the word "magic." However, it implied something more than that and often implied something awesome or powerful. In this case, of course, it implies magic, and old Billy Dunbar knew when and how to use it.

A knowledge of Indian ways and beliefs was often more essential to survival than a gun, for frontiersmen were ruled as we are by beliefs and superstitions. One did not survive in Indian country on muscle and firepower alone, but by what the frontiersman was inclined to call "savvy," something that was gained only by eating the dust, drinking the water, and crossing a lot of horizons.

Big Medicine

Old Billy Dunbar was down flat on his face in a dry wash swearing into his beard. The best gold-bearing gravel he had found in a year, and then the Apaches would have to show up!

It was like them, the mean, ornery critters. He hugged the ground for dear life and hoped they would not see him, tucked away as he was between some stones where an eddy of the water that once ran through the wash had dug a trench between the stones.

There were nine of them. Not many, but enough to take his scalp if they found him, and it would be just as bad if they saw his burros or any of the prospect holes he had been sinking.

He was sweating like a stuck hog bleeds, lying there with his beard in the sand and the old Sharps .50 ready beside him. He wouldn't have much of a chance if they found him, slithery fighters like they were, but if that old Sharps threw down on them he'd take at least one along to the happy hunting ground with him.

He could hear them now, moving along the desert above the wash. Where in tarnation were they going? He wouldn't be safe as long as they were in the country, and this was country where not many white men came. Those few who did come were just as miserable to run into as the Apaches.

The Apache leader was a lean muscled man with a hawk nose. All of them slim and brown without much meat on them, the way Apaches were, and wearing nothing but breechclouts and headbands.

He lay perfectly still. Old Billy was too knowing in Indian ways to start moving until he was sure they were

gone. He lay right there for almost a half hour after he had
last heard them, and then he came out of it cautious as a
bear reaching for a honey tree.

When he got on his feet, he hightailed it for the edge
of the wash and took a look. The Apaches had vanished.
He turned and went down the wash, taking his time and
keeping the old Sharps handy. It was a mile to his burros
and to the place where his prospect holes were. Luckily,
he had them back in a draw where there wasn't much
chance of them being found.

Billy Dunbar pulled his old gray felt hat down a little
tighter and hurried on. Jennie and Julie were waiting for
him, standing head to tail so they could brush flies off each
other's noses.

When he got to them he gathered up his tools and
took them back up the draw to the rocks at the end. His
canteens were full, and he had plenty of grub and ammunition. He was lucky that he hadn't shot that rabbit when
he saw it. The Apaches would have heard the bellow of
the old Sharps and come for him, sure. He was going to
have to be careful.

If they would just kill a man it wouldn't be so bad,
but these Apaches liked to stake a man out on an anthill
and let the hot sun and ants do for him, or maybe the
buzzards—if they got there soon enough.

This wash looked good, too. Not only because water
had run there, but because it was actually cutting into the
edge of an old riverbed. If he could sink a couple of holes
down to bedrock, he'd bet there'd be gold and gold aplenty.

When he awakened in the morning he took a careful
look around his hiding place. One thing, the way he was
located, if they caught him in camp they couldn't get at
him to do much. The hollow was perhaps sixty feet across,
but over half of it was covered by shelving rock from
above, the cliff ran straight up from there for an easy fifty
feet. There was water in a spring and enough grass to last
the burros for quite some time.

After a careful scouting around, he made a fire of
dead mesquite, which made almost no smoke, and fixed
some coffee. When he had eaten, Dunbar gathered up his

pan, pick, shovel, and rifle and moved out. He was loaded more than he liked, but it couldn't be helped.

The place he had selected to work was the inside of the little desert stream. The stream took a bend and left a gravel bank on the inside of the elbow. That gravel looked good. Putting his Sharps down within easy reach, Old Billy got busy.

Before sundown he had moved a lot of dirt and tried several pans, loading them up and going over to the stream. Holding the pan under the water, he began to stir the gravel, breaking up the lumps of clay and stirring until every piece was wet. Then he picked out the larger stones and pebbles and threw them to one side. He put his hands on opposite sides of the pan and began to oscillate it vigorously under water, moving it in a circular motion so the contents were shaken from side to side.

With a quick glance to make sure there were no Apaches in sight, he tipped the pan slightly, to an angle of about thirty degrees so the lighter sands, already buoyed up by the water, could slip out over the side.

He struck the pan several good blows to help settle the gold, if any, and then dipped for more water and continued the process. He worked steadily at the pan, with occasional glances around until all the refuse had washed over the side but the heavier particles. Then with a little clean water, he washed the black sand and gold into another pan, which he took from the brush where it had been concealed the day before.

For some time he worked steadily. Then, as the light was getting bad, he gathered up his tools and concealing the empty pan, carried the other with him back up the wash to his hideout.

He took his Sharps and crept out of the hideout and up the wall of the canyon. The desert was still and empty on every side.

"Too empty, durn it!" he grumbled. "Them Injuns'll be back. Yuh can't fool an Apache."

Rolling out of his blankets at sunup, he prepared a quick breakfast and then went over his takings of the day with a magnet. This black sand was mostly particles of magnetite, ilmenite, and black magnetic iron oxide. What he couldn't draw off, he next eliminated by using a blow box.

"Too slow, with them Apaches around," he grumbled. "A man workin' down there could mebbe do sixty, seventy pans a day in that sort of gravel, but watchin' for Injuns ain't goin' t' help much!"

Yet he worked steadily, and by nightfall, despite interruptions he had handled more than fifty pans. When the second day was over, he grinned at the gold he had. It was sufficient color to show he was on the right track. Right here, by using a rocker, he could have made it pay, but he wasn't looking for peanuts.

He had cached his tools along with the empty pan in the brush at the edge of the wash. When morning came, he rolled out and was just coming out of the hideout when he saw the Apache. He was squatted in the sand staring at something, and despite his efforts to keep his trail covered, Dunbar had a good idea what that something would be. He drew back into the hideout.

Lying on his middle, he watched the Indian get to his feet and start working downstream. When he got down there a little further, he was going to see those prospect holes. There would be nothing Dunbar could do then. Nor was there anything he could do now. So far as he could see, only one Apache had found him. If he fired to kill the Indian, the others would be aware of the situation and come running.

Old Billy squinted his eyes and pondered the question. He had a hunch that Indian wasn't going to go for help. He was going to try to get Dunbar by himself, so he could take his weapons and whatever else he had of value.

The Indian went downstream further and slipped out of sight. Billy instantly ducked out into the open and scooted down the canyon into the mesquite. He dropped flat there and inched along in the direction the Indian had gone.

He was creeping along, getting nearer and nearer to his prospect holes, when suddenly instinct or the subconscious hearing of a sound warned him. Like a flash, he rolled over, just in time to see the Indian leap at him, knife in hand!

Billy Dunbar was no longer a youngster, but he had lived a life in the desert, and he was as hard and tough as whalebone. As the Apache leaped, he caught the knife wrist in his left hand, and stabbed at the Indian's ribs with his own knife. The Apache twisted away, and Billy gave a heave. The Indian lost balance. They rolled over and then fell over the eight-foot bank into the wash!

Luck was with Billy. The Indian hit first, and Billy's knife arm was around him, with the point gouging at the Indian's back. When they landed, the knife went in to the hilt.

Billy rolled off, gasping for breath. Hurriedly, he glanced around. There was no one in sight. Swiftly, he clawed at the bank, causing the loosened gravel to cave down, and in a few minutes of hot, sweating work the Indian was buried.

Turning, Billy lit out for his hideaway, and when he made it, he lay there gasping for breath, his Sharps ready. There would be no work this day. He was going to lie low and watch. The other Indians would come looking, he knew.

After dark he slipped out and covered the Indian better, and then he used a mesquite bush to wipe out as well as possible the signs of their fighting. Then he cat-footed it back to the hollow and tied a rawhide string across the entrance with a can of loose pebbles at the end to warn him if Indians found him. Then he went to sleep.

At dawn he was up. He checked the Sharps and then cleaned his .44 again. He loaded his pockets with cartridges just in case and settled down for a day of it.

Luckily, he had shade. It was hot out there, plenty hot. You could fry an egg on those rocks by ten in the morning—not that he had any eggs. He hadn't even seen an egg since the last time he was in Fremont, and that had been four months ago.

He bit off a chew of tobacco and rolled it in his jaws. Then he studied the banks of the draw. An Apache could move like a ghost and look like part of the landscape. He had known them to come within fifteen feet of a man in grassy country without being seen, and not tall grass at that.

It wouldn't be so bad if his time hadn't been so short. When he left Fremont, Sally had six months to go to pay off the loan on her ranch, or out she would go. Sally's husband had been killed by a bronc down on the Sandy. She was alone with the kids, and that loan about to take their home away.

When the situation became serious, Old Billy thought of this wash. Once, several years before, he had washed out some color here, and it looked rich. He had left the country about two jumps ahead of the Apaches and swore he'd never come back. Nobody else was coming out of here with gold, either, so he knew it was still like he remembered. Several optimistic prospectors had tried it and were never heard of again. However, Old Billy had decided to take a chance. After all, Sally was all he had, and those two grandchildren of his deserved a better chance than they'd get if she lost the place.

The day moved along, a story told by the shadows on the sides of the wash. You could almost tell the time by those shadows. It wasn't long before Dunbar knew every bush, every clump of greasewood and mesquite along its length, and every rock.

He wiped the sweat from his brow and waited. Sally was a good girl. Pretty, too, too pretty to be a widow at twenty-two. It was almost midafternoon when his questing eye halted suddenly on the bank of the wash. He lay perfectly still, eyes studying the bank intently. Yet his eyes had moved past the spot before they detected something amiss. He scowled, trying to remember. Then it came to him.

There had been a torn place there, as though somebody had started to pull up a clump of greasewood and then abandonded it. The earth had been exposed and a handful of roots. Now it was blotted out. Straining his eyes he could see nothing, distinguish no contours that seemed human, only that the spot was no longer visible. The spot was mottled by shadows and sunlight through the leaves of the bush.

Then there was a movement, so slight that his eye

scarcely detected it, and suddenly the earth and torn roots were visible again. They had come back. Their stealth told him they knew he was somewhere nearby, and the logical place for him would be right where he was.

Now he was in for it. Luckily, he had food, water, and ammunition. There should be just eight of them unless more had come. Probably they had found his prospect holes and trailed him back this way.

There was no way they could see into his hollow, no way they could shoot into it except through the narrow entrance, which was rock and brush. There was no concealed approach to it. He dug into the bank a little to get more earth in front of himself.

No one needed to warn him of the gravity of the situation. It was one hundred and fifty miles to Fremont and sixty miles to the nearest white man, young Sid Barton, a cowhand turned rancher who had started running some cattle on the edge of the Apache country.

Nor could he expect help. Nobody ever came into this country, and nobody knew where he was but Sally, and she only knew in a general way. Prospectors did not reveal locations where they had found color.

Well, he wasn't one of these restless young coots who'd have to be out there tangling with the Apaches. He could wait. And he would wait in the shade while they were in the sun. Night didn't worry him much. Apaches had never cared much for night fighting, and he wouldn't have much trouble with them.

One of them showed himself suddenly—only one arm and a rifle. But he fired, the bullet striking the rock overhead. Old Billy chuckled. "Tryin' t' draw fire," he said, "get me located."

Billy Dunbar waited, grinning through his beard. There was another shot and then more stillness. He lay absolutely still. A hand showed and then a foot. He rolled his quid in his jaws and spat. An Indian suddenly showed himself and then vanished as though he had never been there. Old Billy watched the banks cynically. An Indian showed again and hesitated briefly this time, but Dunbar waited.

Suddenly, within twenty feet of the spot where Dunbar lay, an Indian slid down the bank and with a shrill whoop, darted for the entrance to the hideaway. It was point-blank, even though a moving target. Billy let him have it!

The old Sharps bellowed like a stricken bull and leaped in his hands. The Apache screamed wildly and toppled over backwards, carried off his feet by the sheer force of the heavy-caliber bullet. Yells of rage greeted the shot.

Dunbar could see the Indian's body sprawled under the sun. He picked up an edged pieced of white stone and made a straight mark on the rack wall beside him, then seven more. He drew a diagonal line through the first one. "Seven t' go," he said.

A hail of bullets began kicking sand and dirt up around the opening. One shot hit overhead and showered dirt down almost in his face. "Durn you!" he mumbled. He took his hat off and laid it beside him, his six-shooter atop of it, ready to hand.

No more Indians showed themselves, and the day drew on. It was hot out there. In the vast brassy vault of the sky a lone buzzard wheeled.

He tried no more shots, just waiting. They were trying to tire him out. Doggone it—in this place he could outwait all the Apaches in the Southwest—not that he wanted to!

Keeping well below the bank, he got hold of a stone about the size of his head and rolled it into the entrance. Instantly, a shot smacked the dirt below it and kicked dirt into his eyes. He wiped them and swore viciously. Then he got another stone and rolled that in place, pushing dirt up behind them. He scooped his hollow deeper and peered thoughtfully at the banks of the draw.

Jennie and Julie were eating grass, undisturbed and unworried. They had been with Old Billy too long to be disturbed by these—to them meaningless—fusses and fights. The shadow from the west bank reached farther toward the east, and Old Billy waited, watching.

He detected an almost indiscernible movement atop the bank, in the same spot where he had first seen an

Indian. Taking careful aim, he drew a bead on the exposed roots and waited.

He saw no movement, nothing, yet suddenly he focused his eyes more sharply and saw the roots were no longer exposed. Nestling the stock against his shoulder, his finger eased back on the trigger. The old Sharps wavered, and he waited. The rifle steadied, and he squeezed again.

The gun jumped suddenly and there was a shrill yell from the Apache, who lunged to full height and rose on his tiptoes, both hands clasping his chest. The stricken redskin then plunged face forward down the bank in a shower of gravel. Billy reloaded and waited. The Apache lay still, lying in the shadow below the bank. After watching him for a few minutes, alternating between the still form and the banks of the draw, Dunbar picked up his white stone and marked another diagonal white mark, across the second straight line.

He stared at the figures with satisfaction. "Six left," he said. He was growing hungry. Jennie and Julie had both decided to lie down and call it a day.

As luck would have it, his shovel and pick were concealed in the brush at the point where the draw opened into the wider wash. He scanned the banks suddenly and then drew back. Grasping a bush, he pulled it from the earth under the huge rocks. He then took the brush and some stones and added to his parapet. With some lumps of earth and rock he gradually built it stronger.

Always he returned to the parapet, but the Apaches were cautious and he saw nothing of them. Yet his instinct told him they were there, somewhere. And that, he knew, was the trouble. It was the fact he had been avoiding ever since he had holed up for the fight. They would always be around somewhere now. Three of their braves were missing— dead. They would never let him leave the country alive.

If he had patience, so had they, and they could afford to wait. He could not. It was not merely a matter of getting home before the six-month period was up—and less than two months remained of that—it was a matter of getting home with enough money to pay off the loan. And with the best of luck it would require weeks upon weeks of hard, uninterrupted work.

And then he saw the wolf.

It was no more than a glimpse, and a fleeting glimpse. Billy Dunbar saw the sharply pointed nose and bright eyes and then the swish of a tail! The wolf vanished somewhere at the base of the shelf of rock that shaded the pocket. It vanished in proximity to the spring.

Old Billy frowned and studied the spot. He wasn't the only one holed up here! The wolf evidently had a hole somewhere in the back of the pocket, and perhaps some young, as the time of year was right. His stillness after he had finished work on the entrance had evidently fooled the wolf into believing the white man was gone.

Obviously, the wolf had been lying there, waiting for him to leave so it could come out and hunt. The cubs would be getting hungry. If there were cubs.

The idea came to him then. An idea utterly fantastic, yet one that suddenly made him chuckle. It might work! It could work! At least, it was a chance, and somehow, some way, he had to be rid of those Apaches!

He knew something of their superstitions and beliefs. It was a gamble, but as suddenly as he conceived the idea, he knew it was a chance he was going to take.

Digging his change of clothes out of the saddlebags, he got into them. Then he took his own clothing and laid it out on the ground in plain sight—the pants, then the coat, the boots, and nearby, the hat.

Taking some sticks he went to the entrance of the wolf den and built a small fire close by. Then he hastily went back and took a quick look around. The draw was empty, but he knew the place was watched. He went back and got out of line of the wolf den, and waited.

The smoke was slight, but it was going into the den. It wouldn't take long. The wolf came out with a rush, ran to the middle of the pocket, took a quick, snarling look around, and then went over the parapet and down the draw!

Working swiftly, he moved the fire and scattered the few sticks and coals in his other fireplace. Then he brushed the ground with a branch. It would be a few minutes before they moved, and perhaps longer.

Crawling into the wolf den he next got some wolf hair, which he took back to his clothing. He put some of the hair in his shirt and some near his pants. A quick look down the draw showed no sign of an Indian, but that they had seen the wolf, he knew, and he could picture their surprise and puzzlement.

Hurrying to the spring, he dug from the bank near the water a large quantity of mud. This was an added touch, but one that might help. From the mud, he formed two roughly human figures. About the head of each he tied a blade of grass.

Hurrying to the parapet for a stolen look down the draw, he worked until six such figures were made. Then, using thorns and some old porcupine quills he found near a rock, he thrust one or more through each of the mud figures.

They stood in a neat row facing the parapet. Quickly, he hurried for one last look into the draw. An Indian had emerged. He stood there in plain sight, staring toward the place!

They would be cautious, Billy knew, and he chuckled to himself as he thought of what was to follow. Gathering up his rifle, the ammunition, a canteen, and a little food, he hurried to the wolf den and crawled back inside.

On his first trip he had ascertained that there were no cubs. At the end of the den there was room to sit up, topped by the stone of the shelving rock itself. To his right, a lighted match told him there was a smaller hole of some sort.

Cautiously, Billy crawled back to the entrance, and careful to avoid the wolf tracks in the dust outside, he brushed out his own tracks and then retreated into the depths of the cave. From where he lay he could see the parapet.

Almost a half hour passed before the first head lifted above the poorly made wall. Black straight hair, a red headband, and the sharp, hard features of their leader.

Then other heads lifted beside him, and one by one

the six Apaches stepped over the wall and into the pocket. They did not rush, but looked cautiously about, and their eyes were large, frightened. They looked all around, then at the clothing and then at the images. One of the Indians grunted and pointed.

They drew closer and then stopped in an awed line, staring at the mud figures. They knew too well what they meant. Those figures meant a witch doctor had put a death spell on each one of them.

One of the Indians drew back and looked at the clothing. Suddenly he gave a startled cry and pointed—at the wolf hair!

They gathered around, talking excitedly and then glancing over their shoulders fearfully.

They had trapped what they believed to be a white man, and knowing Apaches, Old Billy would have guessed they knew his height, weight, and approximate age. Those things they could tell from the length of his stride, the way he worked, the pressure of a footprint in softer ground.

They had trapped a white man, and a wolf had escaped! Now they found his clothing lying here, and on the clothing, the hair of a wolf!

All Indians knew of wolf-men, those weird creatures who changed at will from wolf to man and back again, creatures that could tear the throat from a man while he slept and could mark his children with the wolf blood.

The day had waned, and as he lay there, Old Billy Dunbar could see that while he had worked the sun had neared the horizon. The Indians looked around uneasily. This was the den of a wolf-man, a powerful spirit who had put the death spell on each of them, who came as a man and went as a wolf.

Suddenly, out on the desert, a wolf howled!

The Apaches started as if struck, and then as a man they began to draw back. By the time they reached the parapet they were hurrying.

Old Billy stayed the night in the wolf hole, lying at its mouth, waiting for dawn. He saw the wolf come back, stare about uneasily, and then go away. When light came he crawled from the hole.

The burros were cropping grass and they looked at

him. He started to pick up a pack saddle and then dropped it. "I'll be durned if I will!" he said.

Taking the old Sharps and the extra pan, he walked down to the wash and went to work. He kept a careful eye out, but saw no Apaches. The gold was panning out even better than he had dreamed would be possible. A few more days—suddenly, he looked up.

Two Indians stood in plain sight, facing him. The nearest one walked forward and placed something on a rock and then drew away. Crouched, waiting, Old Billy watched them go. Then he went to the rock. Wrapped in a piece of tanned buckskin was a haunch of venison!

He chuckled suddenly. He was big medicine now. He was a wolf-man. The venison was a peace offering, and he would take it. He knew now he could come and pan as much gold as he liked in Apache country.

A few days later he killed a wolf, skinned it, and then buried the carcass, but the head he made a cap to fit over the crown of his old felt hat, and wherever he went, he wore it.

A month later, walking into Fremont behind the switching tails of Jennie and Julie, he met Sally at the gate. She was talking with young Sid Barton.

"Hi," Sid said, grinning at him. Then he looked quizzically at the wolfskin cap. "Better not wear that around here! Somebody might take you for a wolf!"

Old Billy chuckled. "I am!" he said. "Yuh're durned right, I am! Ask them Apaches!"

MAN FROM BATTLE FLAT

One of the unfortunate aspects of Western history is that too many people who have not taken the trouble to ascertain the facts are continually expressing themselves with assumed authority on what did or did not happen.

Often I hear the comment that Western men could not shoot accurately, that their guns were no good, and so on. Well, I know of several thousand men who are now dead who wish that were true.

Men did carry weapons as an habitual thing over most of the West, and they could shoot not only with skill but often with exceptional skill. For this there is unlimited documentary and eyewitness evidence. Here and there in the following historical notes I shall quote from various sources.

From the journal of William H. Brewer, of the Whitney Geological Survey of California: "Southern California is still unsettled. We all continually wear arms, each wears both a Bowie knife and a pistol [Navy Revolver] while we always have for game or otherwise, a Sharp's rifle, Sharp's carbine, and two double-barreled shotguns. Fifty or sixty murders a year have been common here in Los Angeles and some think it odd there has been no violent death in the two weeks we have been here . . . as I write this there are at least six heavy loaded revolvers in the tent, besides Bowie knives and other weapons, so we anticipate no danger."

The time was 1860, the population of Los Angeles about 3,500 people.

The Man from Battle Flat

At half-past four Krag Moran rode in from the canyon trail, and within ten minutes half the town knew that Ryerson's top gunhand was sitting in front of the Palace.

Nobody needed to ask why he was there. It was to be a showdown between Ryerson and the Squaw Creek nesters, and the showdown was to begin with Bush Leason.

The Squaw Creek matter had divided the town, yet there was no division where Bush Leason was concerned. The big nester had brought his trouble on himself and if he got what was coming to him nobody would be sorry. That he had killed five or six men was a known fact.

Krag Moran was a lean, wide-shouldered young man with smoky eyes and a still, Indian-dark face. Some said he had been a Texas Ranger, but all the town knew about him for sure was that he had got back some of Ryerson's horses that had been run off. How he would stack up against a sure-thing killer like Bush Leason was anybody's guess.

Bush Leason was sitting on a cot in his shack when they brought him the news that Moran was in town. Leason was a huge man, thick through the waist and with a wide, flat, cruel face. When they told him he said nothing at all, just continued to clean his double-barreled shotgun. It was the gun that had killed Shorty Grimes.

Short Grimes had ridden for Tim Ryerson, and between them cattleman Ryerson and rancher Chet Lee had sewed up all the range on Battle Flat. Neither of them drifted cattle on Squaw Creek, but for four years they had been cutting hay from its grass-rich meadows, until the nesters had moved in.

Ryerson and Lee ordered them to leave. They replied the land was government land open to filing. Hedrow talked for the nesters, but it was Bush Leason who wanted to talk, and Bush was a troublemaker. Ryerson gave them a week and, when they didn't move, tore down fences and burned a barn or two.

In all of this Shorty Grimes and Krag Moran had no part. They had been repping on Carol Duchin's place at the time. Grimes had ridden into town alone and stopped at the Palace for a drink. Leason started trouble, but the other nesters stopped him. Then Leason turned at the door. "Ryerson gave us a week to leave the country. I'm giving you just thirty minutes to get out of town! Then I come a-shooting!"

Shorty Grimes had been ready to leave, but after that he had decided to stay. A half hour later there was a challenging yell from the dark street out front. Grimes put down his glass and started for the door, gun in hand. He had just reached the street door when Bush Leason stepped through the back door and ran forward, three light, quick steps.

Bush Leason stopped them, still unseen. "Shorty!" he called softly.

Pistol lowered, unsuspecting, Shorty Grimes had turned, and Bush Leason had emptied both barrels of the shotgun into his chest.

One of the first men into the saloon after the shooting was Dan Riggs, editor of *The Bradshaw Journal*. He knew what this meant, knew it and did not like it, for he was a man who hated violence and felt that no good could come of it. Nor had he any liking for Bush Leason. He had warned the nester leader, Hedrow, about him only a few days before.

Nobody liked the killing but everybody was afraid of Bush. They had all heard Bush make his brags and the way to win was to stay alive. . . .

Now Dan Riggs heard that Krag Moran was in town, and he got up from his desk and took off his eye-shade. It was no more than ninety feet from the front of the print shop to the Palace and Dan walked over. He stopped there in front of Krag. Dan was a slender, middle-aged man with thin hands and a quiet face. He said:

"Don't do it, son. You mount up and ride home. If you kill Leason that will just be the beginning."

"There's been a beginning. Leason started it."

"Now, look here—" Riggs protested, but Krag interrupted him.

"You better move," he said, in that slow Texas drawl of his. "Leason might show up any time."

"We've got a town here," Riggs replied determinedly. "We've got women and homes and decent folks. We don't want the town shot up and we don't want a lot of drunken killings. If you riders can't behave yourselves, stay away from town! Those farmers have a right to live, and they are good, God-fearing people!"

Krag Moran just sat there. "I haven't killed anybody," he said reasonably, his face a little solemn. "I'm just a-sittin' here."

Riggs started to speak, then with a wave of exasperated hands he turned and hurried off. And then he saw Carol Duchin.

Carol Duchin was several things. By inheritance, from her father, she owned a ranch that would make two of Ryerson's. She was twenty-two years old, single, and she knew cattle as well as any man. Chet Lee had proposed to her three times and had been flatly refused three times. She both knew and liked Dan Riggs and his wife, and she often stopped over night at the Riggs' home when in town. Despite that, she was cattle, all the way.

Dan Riggs went at once to Carol Duchin and spoke his piece. Right away she shook her head. "I won't interfere," she replied. "I knew Shorty Grimes and he was a good man."

"That he was," Riggs agreed sincerely, "I only wish they were all as good. That was a dastardly murder and I mean to say so in the next issue of my paper. But another killing won't help things any, no matter who gets killed."

Carol asked him: "Have you talked to Bush Leason?"

Riggs nodded. "He won't listen either. I tried to get him to ride over to Flagg until things cooled off a little. He laughed at me."

She eyed him curiously.

"What do you want me to do?"

"Talk to Krag. For you, he'll leave."

"I scarcely know him." Carol Duchin was not planning to tell anyone how much she did know about Krag Moran, nor how interested in the tall rider she had become. During his period of repping with her roundup he had not spoken three words to her, but she had noticed him, watched him, and listened to her riders talk about him among themselves.

"Talk to him. He respects you. All of them do."

Yes, Carol reflected bitterly, he probably does. And he probably never thinks of me as a woman.

She should have known better. She was the sort of girl no man could ever think of in any other way. Her figure was superb, and she very narrowly escaped genuine beauty. Only her very coolness and her position as owner had kept more than one cowhand from speaking to her. So far only Chet Lee had found the courage. But Chet never lacked for that.

She walked across the street toward the Palace, her heart pounding, her mouth suddenly dry. Now that she was going to speak to Krag, face to face, she was suddenly frightened as a child. He got to his feet as she came up to him. She was tall for a girl, but he was still taller. His mouth was firm, his jaw strong and clean boned. She met his eyes and found them smoky green and her heart fluttered.

"Krag," her voice was natural, at least, "don't stay here. You'll either be killed or you'll kill Bush. In either case it will be just one more step and will just lead to more killing."

His voice sounded amused, yet respectful, too. "You've been talking to Dan Riggs. He's an old woman."

"No," suddenly she was sure of herself, "no, he's telling the truth, Krag. Those people have a right to that grass, and this isn't just a feud between you and Leason. It means good men are going to be killed, homes destroyed, crops ruined, and the work of months wiped out. You can't do this thing."

"You want me to quit?" He was incredulous. "You know this country. I couldn't live in it, nor anywhere the story traveled."

She looked straight into his eyes. "It often takes a braver man not to fight."

He thought about that, his smoky eyes growing somber. Then he nodded. "I never gave it any thought," he said seriously, "but I reckon you're right. Only I'm not that brave."

"Listen to Dan!" she pleaded. "He's an intelligent man! He's an editor! His newspaper means something in this country and will mean more. What he says is important."

"Him?" Krag chuckled. "Why, ma'am, that little varmint's just a-fussin'. He don't mean nothing, and nobody pays much attention to him. He's just a little man with ink on his fingers!"

"You don't understand!" Carol protested.

Bush Leason was across the street. During the time Krag Moran had been seated in front of the Palace Bush had been doing considerable serious thinking. How good Krag was, Bush had no idea, nor did he intend to find out, yet a showdown was coming and from Krag's lack of action he evidently intended for Bush to force the issue.

Bush was not hesitant to begin it, but the more he considered the situation the less he liked it. The wall of the Palace was stone, so he could not shoot through it. There was no chance to approach Krag from right or left without being seen for some time before his shotgun would be within range. Krag had chosen his position well, and the only approach was from behind the building across the street.

This building was empty, and Bush had gotten inside and was lying there watching the street when the girl came up. Instantly, he perceived his advantage. As the girl left, Krag's eyes would involuntarily follow her. In that instant he would step from the door and shoot Krag down. It was simple and it was foolproof.

"You'd better go, ma'am," Krag said. "It ain't safe here. I'm staying right where I am until Leason shows."

She dropped her hands helplessly and turned away from him. In that instant, Bush Leason stepped from the door across the street and jerked his shotgun to his shoulder. As he did so, he yelled.

Carol Duchin was too close. Krag shoved her hard with his left hand and stepped quickly right, drawing as he stepped and firing as his right foot touched the walk.

Afterward, men who saw it said there had never been anything like it before. Leason whipped up his shotgun and yelled, and in the incredibly brief instant, as the butt settled against Leason's shoulder, Krag pushed the girl, stepped away from her, and drew. And he fired as his gun came level.

It was split-second timing and the fastest draw that anybody had ever seen in Bradshaw; the .45 slug slammed into Bush Leason's chest just as he squeezed off his shot, and the buckshot *whapped* through the air, only beginning to scatter and at least a foot and a half over Krag Moran's head. And Krag stood there flatfooted and shot Bush again as he stood leaning back against the building. The big man turned sideways and fell into the dust off the edge of the walk.

As suddenly as that it was done. And then Carol Duchin got to her feet, her face and clothes dusty. She brushed her clothes with quick, impatient hands, and then turned sharply and looked at Krag Moran. "I never want to see you again!" she flared. "Don't put a foot on my place! Not for any reason whatever!"

Krag Moran looked after her helplessly, took an involuntary step after her, and then stopped. He glanced once at the body of Bush Leason and the men gathered around it. Then he walked to his horse. Dan Riggs was standing there, his face shadowed with worry. "You've played hell!" he said.

"What about Grimes?"

"I know, I know! Bush was vicious. He deserved killing, and if ever I saw murder it was his killing of

Grimes, but that doesn't change this. He had friends, and all of the nesters will be sore. They'll never let it alone."

"Then they'll be mighty foolish." Krag swung into the saddle, staring gloomily at Carol Duchin. "Why did she get mad?"

He headed out of town. He had no regrets about the killing. Leason was a type of man that Krag had met before, and they kept on killing and making trouble until somebody shot too fast for them. Yet he found himself upset by the worries of Riggs as well as the attitude of Carol Duchin. Why was she so angry? What was the matter with everybody?

Moran had the usual dislike for nesters possessed by all cattlemen, yet Riggs had interposed an element of doubt, and he studied it as he rode back to the ranch. Maybe the nesters had an argument, at that. This idea was surprising to him, and he shied away from it.

As the days passed and the tension grew, he found himself more and more turning to thoughts of Carol. The memory of her face when she came across the street toward him and when she pleaded with him, and then her flashing and angry eyes when she got up out of the dust.

No use thinking about her, Moran decided. Even had she not been angry at him, what could a girl who owned the cattle she owned want with a drifting cowhand like himself. Yet he did think about her. He thought about her too much. And then the whole Bradshaw country exploded with a bang. Chet Lee's riders, with several hotheads from the Ryerson outfit, hit the nesters and hit them hard. They ran off several head of cattle, burned haystacks and two barns, killed one man, and shot up several houses. One child was cut by flying glass. And the following morning a special edition of *The Bradshaw Journal* appeared.

ARMED MURDERERS RAID SLEEPING VALLEY

Blazing barns, ruined crops and death remained behind last night after another vicious, criminal raid by the murderers, masquerading as

cattlemen, who raided the peaceful, sleeping settlement on Squaw Creek.

Ephraim Hershman, 52 years old, was shot
down in defense of his home by gunmen from
the Chet Lee and Ryerson ranches when they
raided Squaw Valley last night. Two other men
were wounded, while young Billy Hedrow, 3
years old, was severely cut by flying glass when
the night-riders shot out the windows. . . .

Dan Riggs was angry and it showed all the way through
the news and in the editorial adjoining. In a scathing
attack he named names and bitterly assailed the ranchers
for their tactics, demanding intervention by the territorial
governor.

Ryerson came stamping out to the bunkhouse, his
eyes hard and angry. "Come on!" he yelled. "We're going
in and show that durned printer where he gets off! Come
on! Mount up!"

Chet Lee was just arriving in town when the cavalcade from the Ryerson place hit the outskirts of Bradshaw.
It was broad daylight, but the streets of the town were
empty and deserted.

Chet Lee was thirty-five, tough as a boot, and with
skin like a sunbaked hide. His eyes were cruel, his lips
thin and ugly. He shoved Riggs aside and his men went
into the print shop, wrecked the hand press, threw the
type out into the street, and smashed all the windows out
of the shop. Nobody made a move to harm Dan Riggs,
who stood pale and quiet at one side. He said nothing to
any of them until the end, and then it was to Ryerson.

"What good do you think this will do?" he asked
quietly. "You can't stop people from thinking. You can't
throttle the truth. In the end it always comes out. Grimes
and Leason were shot in fights, but that last night was
wanton murder and destruction of property."

"Oh, shut up!" Ryerson flared. "You're getting off
lucky!"

Lee's little eyes brightened suddenly. "Maybe," he
said, "a rope is what this feller needs!"

Dan Riggs looked at Lee without shifting an inch. "It

would be like you to think of that," he said, and Lee struck him across the mouth.

Riggs got slowly to his feet, blood running down his lips. "You're fools," he said quietly, "you don't seem to realize that if you can destroy the property of others, they can destroy it for you. Or do you realize that when any freedom is destroyed for others, it is destroyed for you, too.

"You've wrecked my shop, ruined my press. Tyrants and bullies have always tried that sort of thing, especially when they are in the wrong."

Nobody said anything, Ryerson's face was white and stiff, and Krag felt suddenly uneasy. Riggs might be a fool but he had courage. It had been a rotten thing for Chet Lee to hit him when he couldn't fight back.

"We fought for the right of a free press and free speech back in seventy-six," Dan Riggs persisted. "Now you would try to destroy the free press because it prints the truth about you. I tell you now, you'll not succeed."

They left him standing there among the ruins of his printing shop and all he owned in the world, and then they walked to the Palace for a drink. Ryerson waved them to the bar.

"Drinks are on me!" he said. "Drink up!"

Krag Moran edged around the crowd and stopped at Ryerson's elbow. "Got my money, boss?" he asked quietly. "I've had enough."

Ryerson's eyes hardened. "What kind of talk is that?" Chet Lee had turned his head and was starting hard at Moran. "Don't be a fool!"

"I'm not a fool. I'm quitting. I want my money. I'll have no part in that sort of thing this morning. It was a mean, low trick."

"You pointing any part of that remark at me?" Lee turned carefully, his flat, wicked eyes on Krag. "I want to know."

"I'm not hunting trouble." Krag spoke flatly. "I spoke my piece. You owe me forty bucks, Ryerson."

Ryerson dug his hand into his pocket and slapped two gold eagles on the bar. "That pays you off! Now get out of the country! I want no part of turncoats! If you're around here after twenty-four hours, I'll hunt you down like a dog!"

Krag had turned away. Now he smiled faintly. "Why, sure! I reckon you would! Well, for your information, Ryerson. I'll be here!"

Before they could reply, he strode from the room. Chet Lee stared after him. "I never had no use for that saddle tramp, anyway!"

Ryerson bit the end off his cigar. His anger was cooling and he was disturbed. Krag was a solid man. Despite Lee, he knew that. Suddenly he was disturbed—or had it been ever since he saw Dan Riggs's white, strained face? Gloomily, he stared down at his whiskey. What was wrong with him? Was he getting old? He glanced at the harsh face of Chet Lee—why wasn't he as sure of himself as Lee? Weren't they here first? Hadn't they cut hay in the valley for four years? What right had the nesters to move in on them?

Krag Moran walked outside and shoved his hat back on his head. Slowly, he built a smoke. Why, he was a damned fool! He had put himself right in the middle by quitting. Now he would be fair game for Leason's friends, with nobody to stand beside him. Well, that would not be new. He had stood alone before he came here, and he could again.

He looked down the street. Dan Riggs was squatted in the street, picking up his type. Slowly, Krag drew on his cigarette; then he took it from his lips and snapped it into the gutter. Riggs looked up as his shadow fell across him. His face was still dark with bitterness.

Krag nodded at it. "Can you make that thing work again? The press, I mean."

Riggs stared at the wrecked machine. "I doubt it," he said quietly. "It was all I had, too. They think nothing of wrecking a man's life."

Krag squatted beside him and picked up a piece of the type and carefully wiped off the sand. "You made a mistake," he said quietly. "You should have had a gun on your desk."

"Would that have stopped them?"

"No."

"Then I'm glad I didn't have it. Although," there was a flicker of ironic humor in his eyes, "sometimes I don't feel peaceful. There was a time this afternoon when if I'd had a gun—"

Krag chuckled. "Yeah," he said, "I see what you mean. Now let's get this stuff picked up. If we can get that press started, we'll do a better job—and this time I'll be standing beside you."

Two days later the paper hit the street, and copies of it swiftly covered the country.

BIG RANCHERS WRECK JOURNAL PRESS
Efforts of the big ranchers of the Squaw Creek Valley range to stifle the free press have proved futile. . . .

There followed the complete story of the wrecking of the press and the threats to Dan Riggs. Following that was a rehash of the two raids on the nesters, the accounts of the killings of Grimes and Leason, and the warning to the state at large that a full-scale cattle war was in the making unless steps were taken to prevent it.

Krag Moran walked across the street to the saloon, and the bartender shook his head at him. "You've played hob," he said. "They'll lynch both of you now."

"No, they wont. Make mine rye."

The bartender shook his head. "No deal. The boss says no selling to you or Riggs."

Krag Moran's smile was not pleasant. "Don't make any mistakes, Pat," he said quietly. "Riggs might take that—I won't. You set that bottle out here on the bar or I'm going back after it. And don't reach for that shotgun! If you do, I'll part your hair with a bullet."

The bartender hesitated and then reached carefully for the bottle. "It ain't me, Krag," he objected. "It's the boss."

"Then you tell the boss to tell me." Krag poured a drink, tossed it off, and walked from the saloon.

*   *   *

When Moran crossed the street, there was a sorrel mare tied in front of the shop. He glanced at the brand and felt his mouth go dry. He pushed open the door and saw her standing there in the half shadow—and Dan Riggs was gone.

"He needed coffee," Carol said quietly. "I told him I'd stay until you came back."

He looked at her and felt something moving deep within him, an old feeling that he had known only in the lonesome hours when he had found himself wanting someone, something . . . and this was it.

"I'm back." She still stood there. "But I don't want you to go."

She started to speak, and then they heard the rattle of hoofs in the street and suddenly he turned and watched the sweeping band of riders come up the street and stop before the shop. Chet Lee was there, and he had a rope.

Krag Moran glanced at Carol. "Better get out of here," he said. "This will be rough." And then he stepped outside.

They were surprised and looked it. Krag stood there with his thumbs hooked in his belt, his eyes running over them. "Hi!" he said easily. "You boys figure on using that rope?"

"We figure on hanging an editor," Ryerson said harshly.

Krag's eyes rested on the old man for an instant. "Ryerson," he said evenly, "you keep out of this. I have an idea if Chet wasn't egging you on, you'd not be in this. I've also an idea that all this trouble centers around one man, and that man is Chet Lee."

Lee sat his horse with his eyes studying Krag carefully. "And what of it?" he asked.

Riggs came back across the street. In his hand he held a borrowed rifle, and his very manner of holding it proved he knew nothing about handling it. As he stepped out in front of the cattlemen, Carol Duchin stepped from the print shop. "As long as you're picking on unarmed men and helpless children," she said clearly, "you might as well fight a woman, too!"

Lee was shocked. "Carol! What are you doin' here? You're *cattle!*"

"That's right, Chet. I run some cows. I'm also a

woman. I know what a home means to a woman. I know what it meant to Mrs. Hershman to lose her husband. I'm standing beside Riggs and Moran in this—all the way."

"Carol!" Lee protested angrily. "Get out of there! This is man's work! I won't have it!"

"She does what she wants to, Chet," Krag said, "but you're going to fight me."

Chet Lee's eyes came back to Krag Moran. Suddenly he saw it there, plain as day. This man had done what he had failed to do; he had won. It all boiled down to Moran. If he was out of the way. . . . "Boss," it was one of Ryerson's men, "look out."

Ryerson turned his head. Three men from the nester outfit stood ranged at even spaces across the street. Two of them held shotguns, one a Spencer rifle. "There's six more of us on the roofs," Hedrow called down. "Anytime you want to start your play, Krag, just open the ball."

Ryerson shifted in his saddle. He was suddenly sweating, and Krag Moran could see it. Nevertheless, Moran's attention centered itself on Chet Lee. The younger man's face showed his irritation and his rage at the futility of his position. Stopped by the presence of Carol, he was now trapped by the presence of the nesters.

"There'll be another day!" He was coldly furious. "This isn't the end!"

Krag Moran looked at him carefully. He knew all he needed to know about the man he faced. Chet Lee was a man driven by a passion for power. Now it was the nesters, later it would be Ryerson, and then, unless she married him, Carol Duchin. He could not be one among many; he could not be one of two. He had to stand alone.

"You're mistaken, Chet," Moran said. "It ends here."

Chet Lee's eyes swung back to Krag. For the first time he seemed to see him clearly. A slow minute passed before he spoke. "So that's the way it is?" he said softly.

"That's the way it is. Right now you can offer your holdings to Ryerson. I know he has the money to buy them. Or you can sell out to Carol, if she's interested. But you sell out, Chet. You're the troublemaker here. With you gone I think Ryerson and Hedrow could talk out a sensible deal."

"I'll talk," Hedrow said quietly, "and I'll listen."

Ryerson nodded. "That's good for me. And I'll buy, Chet. Name a price."

Chet Lee sat perfectly still. "So that's the way it is?" he repeated. "And if I don't figure to sell?"

"Then we take your gun and start you out of town," Krag said quietly.

Lee nodded. "Yeah, I see. You and Ryerson must have had this all figured out. A nice way to do me out of my ranch. And your quitting was all a fake."

"There was no plan," Moran said calmly. "You've heard what we have to say. Make your price. You've got ten minutes to close a deal or ride out without a dime."

Chet Lee's face did not alter its expression. "I see," he said. "But suppose something happens to you, Krag? Then what? Who here could make me toe the line? Or gamble I'd not come back?"

"Nothing's going to happen to me." Krag spoke quietly. "You see, Chet, I know your kind."

"Well," Chet shrugged, glancing around, "I guess you've got me." He looked at Ryerson. "Fifty thousand?"

"There's not that much in town. I'll give you twelve, and that's just ten thousand more than you hit town with."

"Guess I've no choice," Chet said. "I'll take it." He looked at Krag. "All right if we go to the bank?"

"All right."

Chet swung his horse to the right, but as he swung the horse he suddenly slammed his right spur into the gelding's ribs. The bay sprang sharply left, smashing into Riggs and knocking him down. Only Krag's quick leap backwards against the print shop saved him from going down, too. As he slammed home his spur, Chet grabbed for his gun. It came up fast and he threw a quick shot that splashed Krag Moran's face with splinters; then he swung his horse and shot, almost point blank, into Krag's face!

But Moran was moving as the horse swung, and as the horse swung left, Moran moved away. The second shot blasted past his face and then his own guns came up and he fired, two quick shots. So close was Chet Lee that

Krag heard the slap of the bullets as they thudded into his ribs below the heart.

Lee lost hold of his gun and slid from the saddle, and the horse, springing away, narrowly missed stepping on his face.

Krag Moran stood over him, looking down. Riggs was climbing shakily to his feet, and Chet was alive yet, staring at Krag.

"I told you I knew your kind, Chet," Krag said quietly. "You shouldn't have tried it."

Carol Duchin was in the cafe when Krag Moran crossed the street. He had two drinks under his belt and he was feeling them, which was rare for him. Yet he hadn't eaten and he could not remember when he had.

She looked up when he came through the door and smiled at him. "Come over and sit down," she said. "Where's Dan?"

Krag smiled with hard amusement. "Getting money from Ryerson to buy him a new printing outfit."

"Hedrow?"

"Him and the nesters signed a contract to supply Ryerson with hay. They'd have made a deal in the beginning of it hadn't been for Chet. Hedrow tried to talk business once before. I heard him."

"And you?"

He placed his hat carefully on the hook and sat down. He was suddenly tired. He ran his fingers through his crisp, dark hair. "Me?" he blinked his eyes and reached for the coffeepot. "I am going to shave and take a bath. Then I'm going to sleep for twenty hours about, and then I'm going to throw the leather on my horse and hit the trail."

"I told you over there," Carol said quietly, "that I didn't want you to go."

"Uh-uh. If I don't go now," he looked at her somberly, "I'd never want to go again."

"Then don't go," she said.

And he didn't.

AUTHOR'S NOTE
WEST OF THE TULAROSAS

The Tularosa Mountains lie west of the Plains of St. Augustine in New Mexico and just west of the Continental Divide. This was an area haunted by many of the old Apache chiefs, such as Mangas Colorado, Cochise, Geronimo, and Chato, and few settlers escaped their attentions.

Gold was discovered by soldiers, but the first attempts at mining were discouraged by the Apache. Stories of lost mines and buried gold are common, and somewhere about here or off to the north and west was the supposed site of the Lost Adams Diggings, subject of one of the most famous of lost-mine stories.

Off to the south lay Alma. Now the town is gone, as so many others are, without anything left but a name on a map. Alma was a hangout for Butch Cassidy, Elza Lay, Harvey Logan, and their friends.

One story has it that French, a local cattleman, was having trouble with rustlers, and one of his hands, a pretty tough lad himself, suggested to French that if he were to hire some friends of his who were passing through he would have no more trouble with rustlers. French did as advised, and the rustling promptly stopped. The rustlers were small fry and they wanted no trouble with the likes of Logan or Cassidy. Supposedly French had no idea who his new hands were, but it was obvious the rustlers did.

As a result, French's ranch near Alma became a regular stopping place for the Wild Bunch, a place where using false names they could conveniently disappear for a few weeks or months, as necessity demanded.

West of the Tularosas

The dead man had gone out fighting. Scarcely more than a boy, and a dandy in dress, he had been man enough when the showdown came.

Propped against the fireplace stones, legs stretched before him, loose fingers still touching the butt of his .45 Colt, he had smoked it out to a bloody, battle-stained finish. Evidence of it lay all about him. Whoever killed him had spent time, effort, and blood to do it.

As they closed in for the payoff at least one man had died on the threshold.

The fight that ended here had begun elsewhere. From the looks of it this cabin had been long deserted, and the dead man's spurs were bloodstained. At least one of his wounds showed evidence of being much older than the others. A crude attempt had been made to stop the bleeding.

Baldy Jackson, one of the Tumbling K riders who found the body, dropped to his knees and picked up the dead man's Colt.

"Empty!" he said. "He fought 'em until his guns were empty, an' then they killed him."

"Is he still warm?" McQueen asked. "I think I can smell powder smoke."

"He ain't been an hour dead, I'd guess. Wonder what the fuss was about?"

"Worries me," McQueen looked around, "considering our situation." He glanced at Bud Fox and Kim Sartain, who appeared in the doorway. "What's out there?"

"At least one of their boys rode away still losing blood. By the look of things this lad didn't go out alone, he took somebody with him." Sartain was rolling a smoke. "No feed in the shed, but that horse out there carries a mighty fine saddle."

"Isn't this the place we're headed for?" Fox asked. "It looks like the place described."

Sartain's head came up. "Somebody comin'!" he said. "Riders, an' quite a passel of them."

Sartain flattened against the end of the fireplace and Fox knelt behind a windowsill. Ward McQueen planted his stalwart frame in the doorway, waiting. "This isn't so good. We're goin' to be found with a dead man, just killed."

There were a half dozen riders in the approaching group, led by a stocky man on a gray horse and a tall, oldish man wearing a badge.

They drew up sharply on seeing the horses and McQueen. The short man stared at McQueen, visibly upset by his presence. "Who're you? And what are you doin' here?"

"I'll ask the same question," McQueen spoke casually. "This is Firebox range, isn't it?"

"I know that." The stocky man's tone was testy. "I ought to. I own the Firebox."

"Do you now?" Ward McQueen's reply was gentle, inquiring. "Might be a question about that. Ever hear of Tom McCracken?"

"Of course! He used to own the Firebox."

"That's right, and he sold it to Ruth Kermitt of the Tumbling K. I'm Ward McQueen, her foreman. I've come to take possession."

His reply was totally unexpected, and the stocky man was obviously astonished. His surprise held him momentarily speechless, and then he burst out angrily.

"That's impossible! I'm holdin' notes against young Jimmy McCracken! He was the old man's heir, an' Jimmy signed the place over to me to pay up."

"As of when?" Ward asked.

His thoughts were already leaping ahead, reading sign along the trail they must follow. Obviously something was very wrong, but he was sure that Ruth's deed, a copy of which he carried with him, would be dated earlier than whatever this man had. Moreover, he now had a hunch that the dead man lying behind him was that same Jimmy McCracken.

"That's neither here nor there! Get off my land or be drove off!"

"Take it easy, Webb!" The sheriff spoke for the first time. "This man may have a just claim. If Tom McCracken sold out before he died, your paper isn't worth two hoots."

That this had occurred to Webb was obvious, and that he did not like it was apparent. Had the sheriff not been present, Ward was sure, there would have been a shooting. As yet, they did not know he was not alone, as none of the Tumbling K men had shown themselves.

"Sheriff," McQueen said, "my outfit rode in here about fifteen minutes ago, and we found a dead man in this cabin. Looks like he lost a runnin' fight with several men, and when his ammunition gave out, they killed him."

"Or you shot him," Webb said.

Ward did not move from the door. He was a big man, brown from sun and wind, lean and muscular. He wore two guns.

"I shot nobody." His tone was level, even. "Sheriff, I'm Ward McQueen. My boss bought this place from McCracken for cash money. The deed was delivered to her, and the whole transaction was recorded in the courts. All that remained was for us to take possession, which we have done."

He paused. "The man who is dead inside is unknown to me, but I'm making a guess he's Jimmy McCracken. Whoever killed him wanted him dead mighty bad. There was quite a few of them, and Jimmy did some good shootin'. One thing you might look for is a couple of wounded men, or somebody else who turns up dead."

The sheriff dismounted. "I'll look around, McQueen. My name's Foster, Bill Foster." He waved a hand to the stocky cattleman. "This is Neal Webb, owner of the Runnin' W."

Ward McQueen stepped aside to admit the sheriff,

and as he did so Kim Sartain showed up at the corner of the house, having stepped through a window to the outside. Kim Sartain was said to be as good with his guns as McQueen.

Foster squatted beside the body. "Yeah, this is young Jimmy, all right. Looks like he put up quite a scrap."

"He was game," McQueen said. He indicated the older wound. "He'd been shot somewhere and rode in here, ridin' for his life. Look at the spurs. He tried to get where there was help but didn't make it."

Foster studied the several wounds and the empty cartridge cases. McQueen told him of the hard-ridden mustang, but the sheriff wanted to see for himself. Watching the old man, McQueen felt renewed confidence. The lawman was careful and shrewd, taking nothing for granted, accepting no man's unsupported word. That McQueen and his men were in a bad position was obvious.

Neal Webb was obviously a cattleman of some local importance. The Tumbling K riders were not only strangers but they had been found with the body.

Webb was alert and aware. He had swiftly catalogued the Tumbling K riders as a tough lot, if pushed. McQueen he did not know, but the K foreman wore his guns with the ease of long practice. Few men carried two guns, most of them from the Texas border country. Nobody he knew of used both at once; the second gun was insurance, but it spoke of a man prepared for trouble.

Webb scowled irritably. The setup had been so perfect! The old man dead, the gambling debts, and the bill of sale. All that remained was to . . . and then this outfit appeared with what was apparently a legitimate claim. Who would ever dream the old man would sell out? But how had the sale been arranged? There might still be a way, short of violence.

What would Silas Hutch say? And Ren Oliver? It angered Webb to realize he had failed, after all his promises. Yet who could have foreseen this? It had all appeared so simple, but who could have believed that youngster would put up a fight like he did? He had been a laughing, friendly youngster, showing no sense of responsibility, no steadiness of purpose. He had been inclined to sidestep trouble rather than face it, so the whole affair had looked simple enough.

One thing after another had gone wrong. First, the ambush failed. The kid got through it alive and then made a running fight of it. Why he headed for this place Webb could not guess, unless he had known the Tumbling K outfit was to be here.

Two of Webb's best men were dead and three wounded, and he would have to keep them out of sight until they were well again. Quickly, he decided the line cabin on Dry Legget would be the best hideout.

Foster came from the woods, his face serious.

"McQueen, you'd better ride along to town with me. I found sign that six or seven men were in this fight, and several were killed or hurt. This requires investigation."

"You mean I'm under arrest?"

"No such thing. Only you'll be asked questions. We'll check your deed an' prob'ly have to get your boss up here. We're goin' to get to the bottom of this."

"One thing, Foster, before we go. I'd like you to check our guns. Nobody among us has fired a shot for days. I'd like you to know that."

"You could have switched guns," Webb suggested.

McQueen ignored him. "Kim, why don't you fork your bronc an' ride along with us? Baldy, you an' Bud stay here and let nobody come around unless its the sheriff or one of us. Got it?"

"You bet!" Jackson spat a stream of tobacco juice at an ant. "Nobody'll come around, believe me."

Neal Webb kept his mouth shut but he watched irritably. McQueen was thinking of everything, but as Webb watched the body of young McCracken tied over the saddle he had an idea. Jimmy had been well liked around town, so if the story got around that McQueen was his killer, there might be no need for a trial or even a preliminary hearing. It was too bad Foster was so stiff-necked.

Kim Sartain did not ride with the group. With his Winchester across his saddle bows he kept off to the flank or well back in the rear where the whole group could be watched. Sheriff Foster noted this, and his frosty old eyes glinted with amused appreciation.

"What's he doin' back there?" Webb demanded. "Make him ride up front, Sheriff!"

Foster smiled. "He can ride where he wants. He don't make me nervous, Webb. What's eatin' you?"

The town of Pelona for which they were riding faced the wide plains from the mouth of Cottonwood Canyon, and faced them without pretensions. The settlement, dwarfed by the bulk of the mountain behind it, was a supply point for cattlemen, a stage stop, and a source of attraction for cowhands to whom Santa Fe and El Paso were faraway dream cities.

In Pelona, with its four saloons, livery stable, and five stores, Si Hutch, who owned Hutch's Emporium, was king.

He was a little old man, grizzled, with a stubble of beard and a continually cranky mood. Beneath that superficial aspect he was utterly vicious, without an iota of mercy for anything human or animal.

Gifted in squeezing the last drop of money or labor from those who owed him, he thirsted for wealth with the same lust that others reserved for whiskey or women. Moreover, although few realized it, he was cruel as an apache and completely depraved. One of the few who realized the depth of his depracity was his strong right hand, Ren Oliver.

Oliver was an educated man and for the first twenty-five years of his life had lived in the east. Twice, once in New York and again in Philadelphia, he had been guilty of killing. In neither case had it been proved, and in only one case had he been questioned. In both cases he had killed to cover his thieving, but finally he got in too deep and realizing his guilt could be proved, he skipped town.

In St. Louis he shot a man over a card game. Two months later he knifed a man in New Orleans, then drifted west, acquiring gun skills as he traveled. Since boyhood his career had been a combination of cruelty and dishonesty, but not until he met Si Hutch had he made it pay. Behind his cool, somewhat cynical expression few people saw the killer.

He was not liked in Pelona. Neither was he disliked. He had killed two men in gun battles since arriving in town, but both seemed to have been fair, standup matches. He was rarely seen with Si Hutch, for despite the small population they had been able to keep their cooperation a secret. Only Neal Webb, another string to Hutch's bow, understood the connection. One of the factors that aided Hutch in ruling the Pelona area was that his control was exercised without being obvious. Certain of his enemies had died by means unknown to either Ren Oliver or Neal Webb.

The instrument of these deaths was unknown, and for that reason Si Hutch was doubly feared.

When Sheriff Foster rode into town with Webb and McQueen, Si Hutch was among the first to know. His eyes tightened with vindictive fury. That damned Webb! Couldn't he do anything right? His own connection with the crimes well covered, he could afford to sit back and await developments.

Ward McQueen had been doing some serious thinking on the ride into town. The negotiations between Ruth Kermitt and old Tom McCracken had been completed almost four months ago. McCracken had stayed on at the Firebox even after the title was transferred and was to have managed it for another six months. His sudden death ended all that.

Webb had said he owned the ranch by virtue of young Jimmy signing it over to pay a gambling debt. This was impossible, for Jimmy had known of the sale and had been present during the negotiations. That, then, was an obvious falsehood. Neal Webb had made an effort to obtain control of the ranch, and Jimmy McCracken had been killed to prevent his doing anything about it.

The attempt to seize control of the ranch argued a sure and careful mind, and a ruthless one. Somehow he did not see Webb in that role, although Webb was undoubtedly a part of the operation. Still, what did he know? Pelona was a strange town and he was a stranger. Such towns were apt to be loyal to their own against any outsider. He must walk on cat feet, careful to see where he stepped. Whoever was in charge did not hesitate to kill, or hesitate to lose his own men in the process.

Sheriff Foster seemed like an honest man, but how independent was he? In such towns there were always factions who controlled, and elected officials were often only tools to be used.

Faced with trickery and double-dealing as well as such violence, what could he do? When Ruth arrived from the Tumbling K in Nevada there would be no doubt that she owned the Firebox and that Jimmy had known of it. That would place the killing of young Jimmy McCracken at Neal Webb's door.

Red Oliver was on the walk in front of the Bat Cave Saloon when they tied up before the sheriff's office. He had never seen either McQueen or Sartain before but knew them instantly for what they were, gunfighters, and probably good.

McQueen saw the tall man in the gray suit standing on the boardwalk. Something in the way he carried himself seemed to speak of what he was. As he watched, Oliver turned in at the Emporium. Ward finished tying his roan and went into the sheriff's office.

Nothing new developed from the talk in the office of the sheriff, nor in the hearing that followed. Young Jimmy McCracken had been slain by persons unknown after a considerable chase. The evidence seemed to establish that several men had been involved in the chase, some of whom had been killed or wounded by McCracken.

Ward McQueen gave his own evidence and listened as the others told what they knew or what tracks seemed to indicate. As he listened he heard whispering behind him, and he was well aware that talk was going around. After all, he and the Tumbling K riders were strangers. What talk he could overhear was suspicion of his whole outfit.

Neal Webb had a bunch of tough men around him and he was belligerent. When telling what he knew he did all he could to throw suspicion on the Tumbling K. However, from what he could gather, all of Webb's riders were present and accounted for. If Webb had been one of those involved in the killing of McCracken it must have been with other men than his own.

After the inquest McQueen found himself standing beside the sheriff. "What kind of a country is this, Sheriff? Do you have much trouble?"

"Less than you'd expect. Webb's outfit is the biggest, but his boys don't come in often. When they want to have a blowout they ride down to Alma. They do some drinkin' now an' again but they don't r'ar up lookin' for trouble."

"Many small outfits?"

"Dozen or so. The Firebox will be the largest if you run cows on all of it." Foster studied him. "Do you know the range limits of the Firebox?"

"We figure to run stock from the Apache to Rip-Roaring Mesa and Crosby Creek, south to Dillon Mountain and up to a line due east from there to the Apache."

"That's a big piece of country but it is all Firebox range. There are a few nesters squatted in Bear Canyon, and they look like a tough outfit, but they've given me no trouble."

"Miss Kermitt holds deeds on twelve pieces of land," Ward explained. "Those twelve pieces control most of the water on that range, and most of the easy passes. We want no trouble, but we'll run cattle on range we're entitled to."

"That's fair enough. Watch your step around Bear Canyon. Those boys are a mean lot."

Kim Sartain was somewhere around town but McQueen was not worried. The gunslinging segundo of the Tumbling K was perfectly capable of taking care of himself, and in the meanwhile Ward had business of his own to take care of. He glanced up and down the street, studying the stores. Two of them appeared better stocked than the others. One was Hutch's Emporium, a large store apparently stocked to the doors with everything a rancher could want. The other stores were smaller but were freshly painted and looked neat.

McQueen walked along to the Emporium. A small man with a graying beard looked up at him as he came to the counter. It was an old-fashioned counter, curved in-

ward on the front to accommodate women shoppers who
wore hoopshirts.

"Howdy there! Stranger in town?"

"Tumbling K. We've taken over the Firebox, and
we'll need supplies."

Hutch nodded agreeably. "Glad to help! The Firebox,
hey? Had a ruckus out there, I hear."

"Nothin' much." Ward walked along, studying the
goods on the shelves and stacked on tables. He was also
curious about the man behind the counter. He seemed
genial enough, but his eyes were steel bright and glassy.
He was quick-moving and obviously energetic.

"Troublin' place, the Firebox. Old McCracken seemed
to make it pay but nobody else ever done it. You reckon
you'll stay?"

"We'll stay."

McQueen ordered swiftly and surely, but not all they
would need. There were other stores in town, and he preferred to test the water before he got in too deep. The
Firebox would need to spend a lot of money locally and he
wanted to scatter it around. Hutch made no comment
until he ordered a quantity of .44-caliber ammunition.

"That's a lot of shootin'. You expectin' a war?"

"War? Nothing like that, but we're used to wars.
Jimmy McCracken was killed for some reason by some
right vicious folks. If they come back we wouldn't want
them to feel unwelcome."

The door opened and Neal Webb walked in. He
strode swiftly to the counter and was about to speak when
he recognized McQueen. He gulped back his words, whatever they might have been.

"Howdy. Reckon you got off pretty easy."

McQueen took his time about replying. "Webb, the
Tumblin' K is in this country to stay. You might as well
get used to us and accept the situation. Then we can have
peace between us and get on with raising and marketing
cattle. We want no trouble, but we're ready if it comes.

"We did business with McCracken and I couldn't
have found a finer man. His son seemed cut from the
same pattern.

"They didn't belong to my outfit, so I'm droppin' this

right here. If it had been one of my men I'd backtrail the killers until I found where they came from. Then I'd hunt their boss and I'd stay with him until he was hanged, which is what he deserves."

Behind McQueen's back Hutch gestured, and the hot remarks Webb might have made were stifled. Puzzled, McQueen noticed the change and the sudden shift of Webb's eyes. Finishing his order he stepped into the street.

As he left a gray-haired, impatient-seeming man brushed by him. "Neal," he burst out, "where's that no-account Bemis? He was due over to my place with that horse he borried. I need that paint the worst way!"

"Forget it," Webb said. "I'll see he gets back to you."

"But I want to see Bemis! He owes me money!"

Ward McQueen let the door close behind him and glanced across the street. A girl with red-gold hair was sweeping the boardwalk there. She made a pretty picture and he crossed the street.

As he stepped up on the walk, she glanced up. Her expression changed as she saw him. Her glance was the swiftly measuring one of a pretty girl who sees a stranger, attractive and possibly unmarried. She smiled.

"You must be one of that new outfit the town's talking about. The Tumbling K, isn't it?"

"It is." He shoved his hat back on his head. Kim should see this girl, he thought. She's lovely. "I'm the foreman."

She glanced across the street toward Hutch's store. "Started buying from Hutch? Like him?"

"I don't know him. Do you run this store?"

"I do, and I like it. What's more I almost make money with it. Of course Hutch gets most of the business. I've had no trouble with him, so far."

He glanced at her. Did that mean she expected trouble? Or that Hutch was inclined to cause trouble for competitors?

"I'm new here so I thought I'd scatter my business until I find out where I get the best service." He smiled. "I want to order a few things."

A big man was coming up the walk, a very big man,

and Ward McQueen sensed trouble in the man's purposeful stride. He was taking in the whole walk, and he was
bareheaded. His worn boots were run down at the heels
and his faded shirt was open halfway down his chest for
lack of buttons. His ponderous fists swung at the ends of
powerfully muscled arms, and his eyes darkened savagely
as he saw Ward McQueen.

"Watch yourself!" The girl warned. "That's Flagg
Warneke!"

The big man towered above McQueen. When he
came to a stop in front of Ward his chin was on a level
with Ward's eyebrows and he seemed as wide as a barn
door.

"Are you McQueen? Well, I'm Flagg Warneke, from
Bear Canyon! I hear you aim to run us nesters off your
range! Is that right?"

"I haven't made up my mind yet," Ward replied.
"When I do I'll come to see you."

"Oh! You haven't made up your mind yet? Well, see
that you don't! And stay away from Bear Canyon! That
place belongs to us, an' if you come huntin' trouble, you'll
get it!"

Coolly, Ward McQueen turned his back on the giant.
"Why not show me what stock you have?" he suggested to
the girl. "I—"

A huge hand clamped on his shoulder and spun him
around. "When I talk to you, *face me!*" Warneke roared.

As the big hand spun him around Ward McQueen
threw a roundhouse right to the chin that knocked the big
man floundering against the post of the overhang. Instantly, Ward moved in, driving a wicked right to the
body and then swinging both hands to the head.

The man went to his knees and McQueen stepped
back. Then, as if realizing for the first time that he had
been struck, Warneke came off the walk with a lunge. He
swung his right but Ward went inside, punching with both
hands. The big man soaked up punishment like a sponge
takes water, and he came back, punching with remarkable
speed for such a big man.

A blow caught McQueen on the jaw and he crashed
against the side of the store, his head ringing. Warneke

followed up on the punch, but he was too eager for the kill and missed.

Ward stepped in, smashing his head against the big man's chin and then punching with both hands to the body. His head buzzed and his mouth had a taste of blood. The big man clubbed at his kidneys and tried to knee him, but Ward slid away and looped a punch that split Warneke's ear and showered Ward with blood.

Warneke staggered but recovering came back, his eyes blazing with fury. When Warneke threw a punch Ward went under it and grabbed the big man by the knees, upending him. The big man hit the walk on his shoulder blades with a crash that raised dust, but he came up fast, landing a staggering right to Ward's head. Ward countered with a left and then crossed a right to the jaw. The big man went to his haunches.

A crowd had gathered and the air was filled with shouted encouragement to one or the other. Ward's shirt was torn and when he stepped back to let Warneke get up again his breath was coming in great gasps. The sheer power and strength of the big man was amazing. He had never hit a man so hard and had him still coming.

McQueen, no stranger to rough and tumble fighting, moved in, circling a little. Warneke, cautious now, was aware he was in a fight. Before, his battles had always ended quickly, this was different. McQueen stabbed a left to the mouth, feinted, and did it again. He feinted again, but this time he whipped a looping uppercut to the body that made Warneke's mouth fall open. The big man swung a ponderous blow that fell short and McQueen circled him warily. The speed was gone from the Bear Canyon man now, and McQueen only sought a quick way to end it.

McQueen, oblivious of the crowd, moved in warily. Warneke, hurt though he was, was as dangerous as a cornered grizzly. McQueen's greatest advantage had been that Warneke had been used to quick victories and had not expected anything like what had happened. Also, McQueen had landed the first blow and followed it up before the bigger man could get set. He stalked him now, and then feinted suddenly and threw a high hard one to the chin. Warneke was coming in when the blow landed.

For an instant he stiffened, and then fell forward to the walk and lay still.

McQueen stepped back to the wall and let his eyes sweep the faces of the crowd. For the first time he saw Sartain standing in front of the store, his thumbs hooked in his belt, watching the people gathered about.

Nearest the porch was a tall man in a gray suit, a man he had observed before when he first rode into town.

"That was quite a scrap," said the man in gray. "My congratulations. If there is ever anything I can do, just come to me. My name is Ren Oliver."

"Thanks."

Ward McQueen picked up his fallen hat and then tentatively he worked his fingers. Nothing was broken but his hands were stiff and sore from the pounding. He gave Sartain a half smile. "Looks like we've picked a tough job. That was a Bear Canyon nester!"

"Yeah." Kim gave him a wry look. "Wonder who put him up to it?"

"You think it was planned?"

"Think about it. You've made no decision on Bear Canyon. You ain't even seen the place or its people, but he had the idea you were going to run them off. And how did he know where you were and who you were? I think somebody pointed you out."

"That's only if somebody has it in for him, or for us."

Sartain's smile was cynical. "You don't think they have? You should have seen how green Webb turned when you said you had title to the Firebox. If the sheriff hadn't been there he'd have tried to kill you."

"And why was the sheriff there? That's another thing we'd better find out."

McQueen nodded. "You're right, Kim. While you're around, keep your eyes and ears open for a man named Bemis. You won't see him, I think, but find out what you can about him."

"Bemis? What do you know about him?"

"Darned little." McQueen touched his cheek with gentle fingers where a large red, raw spot had resulted from Warneke's fist. "Only he ain't around, and he should be."

Sartain walked off down the street and the crowd drifted slowly away, reluctant to leave the scene. McQueen hitched his guns into place and straightened his clothes. He glanced around and saw a sign, Clarity's Store.

The girl had come back into her doorway, and he glanced at her. "Are you Clarity?"

"I am. The first name is Sharon and I'm Irish. Did they call you McQueen?"

"They did. And the first name is Ward."

He stepped into the store, anxious to get away from the curious eyes. The store was more sparsely stocked than Hutch's much larger store, but the stock gave evidence of careful selection and a discriminating taste. There were many things a western store did not normally stock.

"I have a washbasin," she suggested. "I think you'd better take a look at yourself in a mirror."

"I will," he said, grinning a little, "but I'd rather not." He glanced around again. "Do you stock shirts by any chance? Man-size shirts?"

She looked at him critically. "I do, and I believe I have one that would fit you."

She indicated the door to the washbasin and then went among the stacks of goods on the shelves behind the counter.

A glance in the mirror and he saw what she meant. His face was battered and bloody, his hair mussed. He could do little about the battered but the blood he could wash away, and he did so. The back door opened on a small area surrounded by a high fence. It was shaded by several old elms and a cottonwood or two, and in the less shaded part there were flowers. He washed his face, holding compresses on his swollen cheekbones and lip. Then he combed his hair.

Sharon Clarity came with a shirt. It was a dark blue shirt with two pockets. He stripped off the rags of his other shirt and donned the new one and dusted off his hat.

She gave him a quick look and a smile when he emerged, saying "It's an improvement, anyway." She folded some other shirts and returned them to the shelves.

He paid for the shirt she had provided, and she said, "You know what you've done, don't you? You've whipped the toughest man in Bear Canyon. Whipped him in a standup fight. Nobody has ever done that, and nobody has even come close. Nobody has even tried for a long time."

She paused, frowning a little. "It puzzles me a little. Warneke isn't usually quarrelsome. That's the first time I ever saw him start a fight."

"Somebody may have given him an idea. I hadn't had time to even think about Bear Canyon. I haven't even ridden over the ranch, and yet he had the idea we were about to run them off."

She looked at him appraisingly, at the wide shoulders, the narrow hips. There was power in every line of him, a power she had just seen unleashed with utter savagery. Having grown up with four brawling brothers she knew something about men. This one had fought coolly, skillfully. "You've started something you know. That Bear Canyon outfit is tough. Even Neal Webb's boys fight shy of them."

"Webb has a tough outfit?"

"You've seen some of them. There are two or three known killers in the bunch. Why he keeps them, I couldn't say."

"Like Bemis, for example?"

"You know Harve Bemis? He's one of them, but not the worst by a long shot. The worst ones are Overlin and Bine."

These were names he knew. Bine he had never seen, but he knew a good deal about him, as did any cattleman along the border country of Texas. An occasional outlaw and suspected rustler, he had run with the Youngers in Missouri before riding south to Texas.

Overlin was a Montana gunhand known around Bannock and Alder Gulch, but he had ridden the cattle trails from Texas several times and was a skilled cowhand, as well. McQueen had seen him in Abilene and at Doan's Crossing. On that occasion he himself had killed an outlaw who was trying to cut the herd with which McQueen was riding. The fact that such men rode with Webb made the situation serious.

He purchased several items and then hired a man with a wagon to freight the stuff to the Firebox. Kim

Sartain was loitering in front of the saloon when McQueen came down to get his horse.

"Bemis ain't around," he confided, "an' it's got folks wonderin' because he usually plays poker at the Bat Cave Saloon. Nobody's seen him around for several days." He paused, "I didn't ask. I just listened."

For three days the Firebox was unmolested, and in those three days much was accomplished. The shake roof needed fixing, and some fences had to be repaired. Baldy had that job and when he finished he stood back and looked it over with satisfaction. "Bud, that there's an elephant-proof fence."

"Elephant proof? You mean an elephant couldn't get past that fence? You're off your trail!"

"Of course it's elephant proof. You don't see any elephant's in there, do you?"

Bud Fox just looked at him and rode away.

All hands were in the saddle from ten to twelve hours a day. The cattle were more numerous than expected, especially the younger stuff. Several times McQueen cut trails made by groups of riders, most of them several days old. Late on the afternoon of the third day he rode down the steep slope to the bottom of a small canyon near the eastern end of the Dillons and found blood on the grass.

The stain was old and dark but unmistakably blood. He walked his horse around, looking for sign. He found a leaf with blood on it, then another. The blood had come from someone riding a horse, a horse that toed in slightly. Following the trail he came to where several other horsemen had joined the wounded man. One of the other horses was obviously a led horse.

Men had been wounded in the fight with McCracken. Could these be the same? If so, where were they going? He rode on over the Dillons and off what was accepted as Firebox range. He had crossed a saddle to get into this narrow canyon, but further along it seemed to open into a wider one. He pushed on, his Winchester in his hands.

The buckskin he rode was a mountain horse accustomed to rough travel. Moreover, it was fast and had stamina, the sort of horse a man needed when riding into trouble. The country into which he now ventured was unknown to him, wild and rough. The canyon down which he rode opened into a wider valley that tightened up into another deep, narrow canyon.

Before him was a small stream. The riders had turned down canyon.

It was dusk and shadows gathered in the canyons, only a faint red glow from the setting sun crested the rim of the canyon. Towering black walls lifted about him, and on the rocky edge across the way a dead, lightning-blasted pine pointed a warning finger from the cliff. The narrow valley was deep in the mystery of darkness, and the only sound that from the stream was a faint rustling. Then wind sighed in the junipers and the buckskin stopped, head up, ears pricked.

"Ssh!" he whispered, putting a warning hand on the buckskin's neck. "Take it easy, boy. Take it easy now."

The horse stepped forward, seeming almost to walk on tiptoe. This was the Box, one of the deepest canyons in the area. McCracken had spoken of it during their discussions that led to his sale of the ranch.

Suddenly he glimpsed a faint light on the rock wall. Speaking softly to the buckskin he slid from the saddle, leaving his rifle in the scabbard.

Careful to allow no jingle of spurs he felt his way along the sandy bottom. Rounding a shoulder of rock he saw a small campfire and the moving shadow of a man in a wide hat. Crouching near a bush he saw that shadow replaced by another, a man with a bald head.

In the silence of the canyon, where sounds were magnified, he heard a voice. "Feelin' better, Bemis? We'll make it to Dry Leggett tomorrow."

The reply was huskier, the tone complaining. "What's the boss keepin' us so far away for? Why didn't he have us to the Runnin' W? This hole I got in me is no joke."

"You got to stay under cover. We're not even suspected, an' we won't be if we play it smart."

His eyes picked out three men lying near the fire, covered with blankets, one with a bandaged head. One of those who was on his feet was preparing a meal. From the distance he could just make out their faces, the shape of their shoulders, and of the two on their feet, the way they moved. Soon he might be fighting these men, and he wanted to know them on sight. The man in the wide hat turned suddenly toward him.

Hansen Bine!

Never before had he seen the man but the grapevine of the trails carried accurate descriptions of such men and of places as well. Gunfighters were much discussed, more than prizefighters or baseball players, even more than racehorses or buckers.

Bine was known for his lean, wiry body, the white scar on his chin, and his unnaturally long, thin fingers.

"What's the matter, Bine?" Bemis asked.

"Somethin' around. I can feel it."

"Cat, maybe. Lots of big ones in these canyons. I saw one fightin' a bear, one time. A black bear. No lion in his right mind would tackle a grizzly."

Bine looked again into the night and then crossed to the fire and seated himself. "Who d'you reckon those riders were who went to the cabin after we left? I saw them headed right for it."

"The boss, maybe. He was supposed to show up with the sheriff."

There was silence except for the crackling of the fire, only barely discernible at the distance. The flames played shadow games on the rock wall. Then Bemis spoke, "I don't like it, Hans. I don't like it at all. I been shot before, but this one's bad. I need some care. I need a doctor."

"Take it easy, Bemis. You'll get there, all in good time."

"I don't like it. Sure, he doesn't want nobody to know, but I don't want to die, either."

Talk died down as the men sat up to eat, and Ward drew carefully back and walked across the sand to his horse. He swung into the saddle and turned the animal, but as the buckskin lined out to go back along the canyon its hoof clicked on stone!

He had believed himself far enough away not to be heard, but from behind him he heard a startled exclamation, and Ward put the horse into a lope in the darkness. From behind him there was a challenge and then a rifle shot, but he was not worried. The shot would have been fired on chance, as Ward knew he could not be seen and there was no straight shot possible in the canyon.

He rode swiftly, so swiftly that he realized he had missed his turn and was following a route up a canyon strange to him. The bulk of the Dillons arose on his right instead of ahead or on his left as they should be. By the stars he could see that the canyon up which he now rode was running east and west and he was headed west. Behind him he heard sounds of pursuit but doubted they would follow far.

The riding was dangerous, as the canyon was a litter of boulders and the trunks of dead trees. A branch canyon opened and he rode into it, his face into a light wind. He heard no further sounds of pursuit and was pleased, wanting no gun battle in these narrow, rock-filled canyons where a ricochet could so easily kill or wound a man. He saw the vague gleam of water and rode his horse into a small mountain stream. Following the stream for what he guessed was close to a mile, he found his way out of the stream to a rocky shelf. A long time later he came upon a trail and the shape of some mountains he recognized.

As he rode he considered what he had heard. Harve Bemis, as he suspected, had been one of those who attacked Jimmy McCracken. More than likely Bine had been there as well. That, even without what else he knew of Neal Webb, placed the attack squarely on Webb's shoulders.

With Jimmy McCracken slain and a forged bill of sale, Webb would have been sure nothing could block his claim to the Firebox range.

So what should he do now? Relinquish his attempt to seize the Firebox and let the killing go for nothing? All McQueen's experience told him otherwise. Webb would seek some other way to advance his claim, and he would seek every opportunity to blacken the reputation of the Tumbling K riders.

The men he had seen in the canyon were headed for Dry Leggett. Where was that? What was it? That he must find out, also he must have a talk with Sheriff Bill Foster.

Ruth Kermitt would not like this. She did not like trouble, and yet those who worked for her always seemed to be fighting to protect her interests. Of late she had refused to admit there might be occasions when fighting could not be avoided. She had yet to learn that in order to have peace both sides must want it equally. One side cannot make peace; they can only surrender. Ward McQueen knew of a dozen cases where one side had agreed to lay down their arms if allowed to leave peacefully. In every case of which he knew, the ones who surrendered their arms were promptly massacred.

He had been in love with Ruth since their first meeting, and they had talked of marriage. Several times they had been on the verge of it but something always intervened. Was it altogether accident? Or was one or both of them hesitating? Marriage would be new for each, yet he had always been a freely roving man, going where he willed, living as he wished.

He shook such thoughts from his head. This was no time for personal considerations. He was a ranch foreman with a job to do, a job that might prove both difficult and dangerous. He must put the Firebox on a paying basis.

Their Nevada ranch was still the home ranch, but Ruth had bought land in other states, in Arizona and New Mexico as well as Utah, and she had traded profitably in cattle. One of the reasons for his hesitation, if he was hesitating, was because Ruth Kermitt was so wealthy. He himself had done much to create that wealth and to keep what she had gained. From the time when he had saved her herd in Nevada he had worked untiringly. He knew cattle, horses, and men. He also knew range conditions. The Tumbling K range fattened hundreds of white-faced cattle. The Firebox, further south and subject to different weather conditions, could provide a cushion against disaster on the northern range. She had bought, on his advice, for a bargain price. Old Tom and young Jimmy had planned to return to a property they owned in Wyoming. As Tom had known Ruth's father, he offered her a first chance.

On Ward's advice she had purchased land around water holes, insuring her of water so they would control much more land than they owned.

It was almost daybreak when McQueen rolled into his bunk in the Firebox bunkhouse. Sartain opened an eye and glanced at him curiously. Then he went back to sleep. Kim asked no questions and offered no comments but missed little.

Baldy Jackson was putting breakfast together when McQueen awakened. He sat up on his bunk and called out to Baldy in the next room. "Better get busy and muck this place out," Ward suggested. "Ruth—Miss Kermitt—may be down before long."

"Ain't I got enough to do? Cookin' for you hungry coyotes, buildin' fence, an' mixin' 'dobe? This place is good enough for a bunch of thistle-chinned cowhands."

"You heard me," McQueen said cheerfully. "And while you're at it, pick out a cabin site for the boss. One with a view. She will want a place of her own."

"Better set up an' eat. You missed your supper."

"Where's the boys? Aren't they eating?"

"They et an' cleared out hours ago." Baldy glanced at him. "What happened last night? Run into somethin'?"

"Yes, I did." He splashed water on his face and hands. "I came upon a camp of five men, three of them wounded. They were headed for a place called Dry Leggett."

"Canyon west of the Plaza."

"Plaza?"

"Kind of settlement, mostly Mexicans. Good people. A few 'dobes, a couple of stores, and a saloon or two."

"How well do you know this country, Baldy?"

Jackson gave him a wry look. "Pretty well. I punched cows for the S U south of here, and rode into the Plaza more times than I can recall. Been over around Socorro. Back in the old days I used to hole up back in the hills from time to time."

Baldy was a good cowhand and a good cook, but in his younger years he had ridden the outlaw trail until time brought wisdom. Too many of his old pals had wound up at the end of a rope.

"Maybe you can tell me where I was last night. I think I was over around that they used to call the Box. He described the country and Baldy listened, sipping coffee. "Uh-huh," he said finally, "that canyon you hit after crossing the Dillons must have been Devil. You probably found them holed up in the Box or right below it. Leavin', you must have missed Devil Canyon and wound up on the south fork of the 'Frisco. Then you come up the trail along the Centerfire and home."

Racing hoofs interrupted. McQueen put down his cup as Bud Fox came through the door.

"Ward, that herd we gathered in Turkey Park is gone! Sartain trailed 'em toward Apache Mountain!"

"Wait'll I get my horse." Baldy jerked off his apron.

"You stay here!" McQueen told him. "Get down that Sharps an' be ready. Somebody may have done this just to get us away from the cabin. Anyway, I've a good idea who is responsible."

Riding swiftly, Fox led him to the tracks. Kim Sartain had followed after the herd. The trail skirted a deep canyon, following an intermittent stream into the bed of the Apache, and then crossed the creek into the rough country beyond.

Suddenly McQueen drew up, listening. Ahead of them they heard cattle lowing. Kim came down from the rocks.

"Right up ahead. Four of the wildest, roughest lookin' hands I've seen in years."

"Let's go," McQueen said. Touching spurs to his horse as he plunged through the brush and hit the flat land at a dead run with the other two riders spreading wide behind him. The movements of the cattle killed the sound of their charge until they were almost up to the herd. Then one of the rustlers turned and slapped a hand for his six-shooter. McQueen's gun leaped to his hand and he chopped it down, firing as it came level. The rush of his horse was too fast for accurate shooting and his bullet clipped the outlaw's horse across the back of the neck. It dropped in its cracks, spilling its rider. Ward charged into him, knocking him sprawling, almost under the hoofs of the buckskin.

Swinging wide McQueen saw that Sartain had downed his man, but the other two were converging on Bud Fox. Both swung away when they saw Kim and McQueen closing in. One of them swung a gun on Kim and Kim's gun roared. The man toppled from the saddle and the last man quickly lifted his hands.

He was a thin, hard-featured man with narrow, cruel eyes. His hair was uncut, his jaws unshaved. His clothing was ragged. There was nothing wrong with his gun, it was new and well kept.

Now his face, despite its hardness, wore a look of shock. His eyes went from McQueen to Sartain to Fox. "You boys shoot mighty straight but you'll wish you never seen the day!"

Fox took his rope from the saddle tree. "He's a rustler, Ward, caught in the act, an' there's plenty of good trees."

"Now, look!" The man protested, suddenly frightened.

"What gave you the idea you could run off our stock?" Ward asked.

"Nothin'. The stock was in good shape." He looked suddenly at McQueen who still wore the marks of battle. "You're the gent who whipped Flagg! He'll kill you for that, if not for this. You won't live a week."

"Bud, tie this man to his saddle an' tie him tight. We'll take him into town for the law to handle. Then we'll visit Bear Canyon."

"You'll do *what*?" their prisoner sneered. "Why, you fool! Flagg will kill you! The whole bunch will!"

"No," Ward assured him, "they will not. If they'd left my stock alone they could have stayed. Now they will get out or be burned out. That's the message I'm taking to them."

"Wait a minute." The man's eyes were restless. Suddenly his arrogance was gone and he was almost pleading. "Lay off Bear Canyon! This was none o' their doin', anyway."

"You're talking," Ward said, and waited.

"Neal Webb put us up to it. Promised us fifteen bucks a head for every bit of your stock we throwed into the Sand Flats beyond Apache."

"Will you say that to a judge?"

His face paled. "If you'll protect me. That Webb outfit, they kill too easy to suit me."

When they rode down the street of Pelona to the sheriff's office the town sprawled lazy in the sunshine. By the time they reached the sheriff's office nearly fifty men had crowded around. Foster met them at the door, his shrewd old eyes going from McQueen to the rustler.

"Well, Chalk," he spat, "looks like you run into the wrong crowd." His eyes shifted to McQueen. "What's he done?"

"Rustled a herd of Firebox stock."

"Him alone?"

"There were four of them. The other three were in no shape to bring back. They won't be talkin'. This one will."

A man at the edge of the crowd turned swiftly and hurried away. McQueen's eyes followed him. He went up the walk to the Emporium. A moment later Ren Oliver emerged and started toward them.

"Who were the others, Chalk? Were they from Bear Canyon?"

"Only me," Chalk's eyes were haunted. "Let's get inside!"

"Hang him!" Somebody yelled. "Hang the rustler!"

The voice was loud. Another took it up, then still another. McQueen turned to see who was shouting. Somebody else shouted, "Why waste time? *Shoot him!*"

The shot came simultaneously with the words, and Ward McQueen saw the prisoner fall, a hole between his eyes.

"Who did that?" Ward's contempt and anger were obvious. "Anybody who would shoot an unarmed man with his hands tied is too low-down to live."

The crowd stirred but nobody even looked around. Those who might know were too frightened to speak. On the edge of the crowd Ren Oliver stood with several others who had drawn together. "I didn't see anybody fire, McQueen, but wasn't the man a rustler? Hasn't the state been saved a trial?"

"He was also a witness who was ready to testify that Neal Webb put him up to the rustlin' and was payin' for the cattle!"

Startled, people in the crowd began to back away, and from the fringes of the crowd they began to disappear into stores or up and down the street. There seemed to be no Webb riders present, but Kim Sartain, sitting his horse back from the crowd, a hand on his gun butt, was watching. He had come up too late to see the shooting.

"Webb won't like that, McQueen," Ren Oliver said. "I speak only from friendship."

"Webb knows where to find me. And tell him this time it won't be a kid he's killing!"

Sheriff Foster chewed on the stub of his cigar. His blue eyes had been watchful. "That's some charge you've made, McQueen. Can you back it up?"

Ward indicated the dead man. "There's my witness. He told me Webb put him up to it, and that Bear Canyon wasn't involved. As for the rest of it—"

He repeated the story of the tracks he had followed, of the men holed up in the Box.

"You think they went on to Dry Leggett?" Foster asked.

"That was what I heard them say, but they might have changed their minds. Bemis was among the wounded and he was worried. He had a bad wound and wanted care." Then he added, "Bine did most of the talking."

Ward McQueen tied his horse in front of Sharon Clarity's store, where there was shade. With Sartain at his side he crossed to the Bat Cave.

The saloon was a long, rather narrow room with a potbellied stove at either end and a bar that extended two-thirds the room's length. There were a roulette table and several card tables.

A hard-eyed, baldheaded bartender leaned thick forearms on the bar, and three men loafed there, each with a drink. At the tables several men played cards. They glanced up as the Tumbling K men entered, then resumed their game.

McQueen ordered two beers and glanced at Ren Oliver, who sat in one of the card games. Had Oliver been only a bystander? Or had he fired the shot that killed Chalk?

Oliver glanced up and smiled. "Care to join our game?"

McQueen shook his head. He would have enjoyed playing cards with Oliver, for there are few better ways to study a man than to play cards with him. Yet he was in no mood for cards, and he hadn't the time. He had started something with his comments about Webb. Now he had to prove his case.

He finished his beer and then, followed by Sartain, he returned to the street. Ren Oliver watched them go, then cashed in and left the game. When he entered the Emporium, Hutch glared at him.

"Get rid of him!" Hutch said. "Get rid of him now!"

Oliver nodded. "Got any ideas?"

Hutch's eyes were mean. "You'd botch the job. Leave it to me!"

"You?" Oliver was incredulous.

Hutch looked at him over his steel-rimmed glasses. Ren Oliver, who had known many hard men, remembered only one such pair of eyes. They were the eyes of a big swamp rattler he had killed as a boy. He remembered how those eyes had stared into his. He felt a chill.

"To me," Hutch repeated.

It was dark when Ward McQueen, trailed by Kim and Bud Fox, reached the scattered, makeshift cabins in Bear Canyon. It was a small settlement, and he had heard much about it in the short time he had been around. The few women were hard-eyed slatterns as tough as their men. Rumor had it they lived by rustling and horse thieving or worse.

"Bud," McQueen said, "stay with the horses. When we leave we may have to leave fast. Be ready, and when you hear me yell, come a-runnin'!"

Followed by Kim he walked toward the long bunkhouse that housed most of the men. Peering through a window he saw but two men, one playing solitaire, the other mending a belt. The room was lighted by lanterns. Nearby was another house, and peering in they saw a short bar and a half dozen men sitting around. One of them was Flagg Warneke.

Ward McQueen stepped to the door and opened it. He stepped in, Kim following, moving quickly left against the log wall.

Flagg saw them first. He was tipped back in his chair and he let the legs down carefully, poised for trouble.

"What d' you want?" he demanded. "What're you doin' here?"

All eyes were on them. Two men, four guns, against six men and eight guns. There were others around town.

"This mornin' Chalk and some other riders ran off some of our cows. We had trouble and three men got killed. I told Chalk if he told me who was involved I'd not ride down here. He didn't much want me to come to Bear Canyon, and to tell you the truth, I hadn't been plannin' on coming down here."

"Chalk started to talk, and somebody killed him."

"*Killed* him? Killed Chalk? Who did it?"

"You make your own guess. Who was afraid of what he might say? Who stood to lose if he did talk?"

They absorbed this in silence and then a fat-faced man at the end of the table. "Those fellers with Chalk? You say you killed them?"

"They chose to fight."

"How many did you lose?"

"We lost nobody. There were three of us, four of them. They just didn't make out so good."

"What're you here for?" Flagg demanded.

"Two things. To see if you have any idea about who killed Chalk and to give you some advice. *Stay away from Firebox cattle!*"

Silence hung heavy in the room. Flagg's face was still swollen from the beating he had taken and the cuts had only begun to heal. His eyes were hard as he stared at McQueen.

"We'll figure out our own answers to the first question. As to the second, we've no use for Firebox cows. As for you and that feller with you—*get out!*"

McQueen made no move, "Remember, friend, Bear Canyon is on Firebox range. What you may not know is that Firebox *owns* that land, every inch of it. You stay if Firebox lets you, and right now the Firebox is *me!* Behave yourselves and you'll not be bothered, but next time there will be no warning. We'll come with guns and fire!"

He reached for the latch with his left hand, and as the door opened, Flagg said, "I put my mark on you, anyway!"

McQueen laughed. "And you're wearing some of mine. Regardless of how things work out, Flagg, it was a good fight and you're a tough man to whip!"

He opened the door and Kim Sartain stepped out and quickly away. He followed.

Yet they had taken no more than three steps when the door burst open and the fat-faced man lunged out, holding a shotgun in both hands. He threw the shotgun to his shoulder. As one man, Ward and Kim drew and fired. The fat-faced man's shotgun sagged in his hands and he backed up slowly and sat down.

Men rushed from the bunkhouse and Kim shot a man with a buffalo gun. Ward shot through the open door at the hanging lantern. It fell, spewing oil and flame. In an instant the room was afire.

Men and women rushed from the other buildings and the two backed to their horses, where Bud awaited them on the rim of the firelight.

Several men grabbed a heavy wagon by the tongue and wheeled it away from the fire. Others got behind to shove. Of Flagg, McQueen saw nothing.

As the three rode away, they glanced back at the mounting flames. The saloon was on fire, as well as the bunkhouse.

"Think this will move them out?" Kim asked.

"I've no idea. I'm no hand for ths sort of thing. Not burning folks out. They'd no right there, and that's deeded land, as I told him. They may have believed it to be government land. If they'd acted half decent I'd have paid them no mind."

"There's no good in that crowd," Kim said.

"Maybe not, but Flagg fought a good fight. He had me worried there, for a spell."

"He didn't get into this fight."

"No, and I think he'd have acted all right. I think he has judgment, which I can't say for that fat-faced gent. He just went hog-wild."

Baldy Jackson was pacing the yard and muttering when they rode in. "Durn it all! You fellers ride away with your shootin' irons on.. Then we hear nothin' of you! Where've you been?"

"What do you mean 'we'?" Kim said. "Since when have you become more than one?"

"He was including me, I think." Sharon Clarity got

up from the chair where she had been sitting, but I've only been here a few minutes. I came to warn you."

"To warn us?"

"To warn you, Mr. McQueen. Sheriff Foster is coming for you. He will arrest you for killing Neal Webb."

"For *what*?" Ward swung down from his horse and trailed the reins. "What happened to Webb?"

"He was found dead on the trail not fifteen minutes after you left town. He had been shot in the back."

Neal Webb killed! Ward McQueen sat down in one of the porch chairs. By whom, and for what?

Ward McQueen knew what western men thought of a back shooter. That was a hanging offense before any jury one could get, but more often a lynch mob would handle such cases before the law got around to it.

Kim Sartain had been with him, but he would be considered a prejudiced witness.

"Pour me some coffee, Baldy," he suggested. He glanced over at Sharon Clarity. "And thanks." He hesitated. "I hope your riding to warn me won't make enemies for you."

"Nobody knew," she replied cheerfully. "Anyway, I think you and the Tumbling K are good for this country. Things were getting kind of one-sided around here."

"Neal Webb killed?" Ward mused. "I wonder what that means? I'd sort of thought he was behind all the trouble, but this makes me wonder."

"It does, doesn't it?" Sharon said. "Almost as if he was killed purely to implicate you."

He glanced at her. "That's a shrewd observation. Any idea who would want to do a thing like that? After all, my trouble was with Webb."

She did not reply. She got to her feet. "My father used to box," she said. "Back in the old country he was considered quite good. They had a rule in boxing. I've heard him quote it. It was 'protect yourself at all times.'

"I am going back to town, but I think you should be very, very careful. And you'd better go. Foster will have about thirty riders in that posse. You'd better start moving."

"I've done nothing. I shall wait for them to come."

She went to her horse. "When you get thirty men

together," Sharon said, "you get all kinds. You have to consider their motives, Mr. McQueen."

"Kim, ride along with Miss Clarity, will you? See that she gets safely home."

"Yes, *sir!*" Kim had been tired. Suddenly he was no longer so. "But what about that posse?"

"There'll be no trouble. Take good care of Miss Clarity. She is a very bright young woman."

In Pelona, Oliver went to the Bat Cave and seated himself at the card table. The saloon was empty save for himself and the bartender, a man with whom he was not particularly friendly, but the cards were there and he gathered them up and began to shuffle. He always thought better with cards in his hands. He carefully laid out a game of solitaire, but his mind was not on the cards.

He was both puzzled and worried. For some years now he had considered himself both an astute and a wise young man. He made his living with his adept fingers and his skill at outguessing men with cards. He knew all the methods of cheating and was a skilled card mechanic but he rarely used such methods. He had a great memory for cards and the odds against filling any hand. He won consistently without resorting to questionable methods. He rarely won big. The show-off sort of thing that attracted attention he did not want. He played every day, and when he lost it was only small amounts. The sums he won were slightly larger. Sometimes he merely broke even, but over the months he was a clear and distinct winner. At a time when a cowhand was pulling down thirty to forty dollars a month, and a clerk in a store might work for as little as half that, Ren Oliver could pull down two hundred to two hundred and fifty dollars without attracting undue attention. When a professional gambler starts winning big pots he becomes suspect.

Even Hutch did not realize how well he was doing, and Hutch was providing him with a small income for rendering various services not to be discussed. Over the past year Ren Oliver had built up a nice road stake something to take with him when he left, for he was well aware that few things last, and many difficulties could be

voided by forming no lasting attachments and keeping a
fast horse.

Now Ren Oliver was disturbed. Neal Webb had been
killed. By whom was a question, but an even larger question was why.

It disturbed him that he did not know. The obvious
answer was that he had been killed by Ward McQueen,
but Oliver did not buy that, not for a minute. McQueen
might kill Webb in a gun battle but he would not shoot
him in the back.

Moreover, there had been no confrontation between
them. The other answer was that Neal had outlived his
usefulness and was killed to implicate McQueen.

But who had actually killed him?

It disturbed Oliver that he did not know. Obviously,
Hutch was behind it, but who had done the killing? One
by one he considered the various men available and could
place none of them in the right position. This worried him
for another reason. He had considered himself close to
Hutch, yet he now realized that, like Webb when he
ceased to be useful, he might be killed. He was merely a
pawn in another man's game.

For a man of Oliver's disposition and inclinations it
was not a pleasant thought. He did not mind others believing he was a pawn, but he wished to be in control so
he could use those who believed they were using him.
Now he had the uncomfortable sensation that too much
was happening of which he was not aware and that any
moment he might be sacrificed.

He had no illusions about himself. He was without
scruples. It was his attitude that human life was cheap,
and like most men engaged in crime he regarded people
as sheep to be sheared. He was cold and callous and had
always been so.

Outwardly he was friendly and ingratiating. He went
out of his way to do favors for people even while holding
them in contempt. You never knew when such people
might appear on a jury. For the same reason he had allied
himself with Hutch.

It was unsettling to realize there was someone more
cunning than he himself. He knew Hutch was hunching

over his community like a huge spider of insatiable appe
tite. Within that community he was considered to be
something of a skinflint but nothing more. Men came an
went from his store because, after all, it was the town
leading emporium, as its name implied. That all thos
people might not be buying was not considered. Olive
believed Hutch hired his killing done, but whom did h
hire?

Bine, of course, but who else? When Oliver looke
over his shoulder he wanted to know who he was lookin
for. The fact that there was an unsuspected actor in th
play worried him.

He had the uncomfortable feeling that Neal Web
had been killed not only to implicate McQueen but t
serve as a warning to him and perhaps to others. A warn
ing that nobody was indispensable.

Oliver shuffled the cards again, ran up a couple o
hands with swiftness and skill, then dealt them, takin
several off the bottom with smoothness and ease, yet h
mind was roving and alert.

Would Hutch manage it? He had never yet, so far a
Oliver knew, encountered such a man as McQueen. No
that Oliver had any great opinion of McQueen. He wa
typically a cowman, honest, tough, and hardworking. Tha
he was good with a gun was obvious, and that segundo o
his, Kim Sartain, was probably almost as good.

Did McQueen have brains? How would he fare agains
Hutch, particularly when, as Oliver believed, McQuee
did not know who his enemy was.

Hutch had planted the Webb killing squarely o
McQueen. The timing had been good and there would b
witnesses, Oliver was sure. Trust the old man for that.

He watched Sheriff Foster leave town with his posse
and knew that several of the men in that posse wer
owned by Hutch. If the slightest excuse was offered the
were to shoot to kill. He knew their instructions as if h
had heard them himself.

The door opened and a squat, powerful man entered
his hair shaggy and untrimmed. His square, granitelik
face was clean shaved. He had gimlet eyes that flickere
with a steely glint. He wore two guns, one in a holste

the other thrust into his waistband. This was Overlin, the Montana gunman.

"Where's Foster goin'?"

"After McQueen, for the Webb killing."

"Webb? Is he dead?"

Oliver nodded. "Out on the trail." Overlin could have done it. So could Hansen Bine, but so far as anyone knew Bine was with the wounded men at Dry Leggett. "There's a witness to swear he did it."

"He might have," Overlin commented, "only I don't believe it. I've heard of McQueen. Made quite a reputation along the cattle trails and in the mining camps. He's no bargain."

"He's only one man. Maybe he'll be your dish one day."

"Or yours," Overlin agreed. "Only I'd like him, myself."

Ren Oliver remembered McQueen and said, "You can have him." He could not understand such men as Overlin. The man was good with a gun, but why would he go out of his way to match skills with a man he believed might be just as good? Overlin had to be the best. He had to know he was best.

Oliver believed he was faster with a gun than either Bine or Overlin but he was a sure-thing man. He had pride in his skill but preferred to take no chances. He would enjoy killing Ward McQueen if he could do so at no risk to himself.

A horse loped into the street, the rider waving at someone out of sight. It was Sharon Clarity. Now where had *she* been? at this hour of the night?

"See you around," he said to Overlin, and went into the night.

He dug a cigar from his pocket and lighted it. Sharon Clarity's horse had been hard ridden.

Ward McQueen was working beside Baldy Jackson, building a pole corral when the sheriff and the posse rode into the ranch yard. McQueen continued to place a pole in position and lash it there with rawhide. Then he glanced around at the posse.

"Howdy, Foster. Looks like you're here on business."

"I've come for you, McQueen. There's witnesses say you shot Neal Webb, shot him in the back."

McQueen kept his hands in sight, moving carefully not to give any false impressions. His eyes caught the slight lift to the muzzle of a Winchester and he eyed the man behind it, staring at him until the man's eyes shifted and he swallowed.

"All you had to do was send for me, Sheriff. I'd have come right in. No need for all this crowd." He paused. "And you know, Sheriff, I'd never shoot any man in the back. What would be the point? Webb was never supposed to be good with a gun, and if I wanted him killed that bad all I'd have to do would be to pick a fight with him in town. Webb's temper had a short fuse, and killing him would have been no trick."

"That may be so, but you've got to come in with me and answer charges. There will have to be a trial."

"We'll see. Maybe I can prove I was elsewhere."

"By one of your own men?" The man who spoke had a sallow face and buck teeth. "We'd not be likely to believe *them!*"

"By others, then? Kim Sartain was with me, however and if you believe he's a liar why don't you tell him so?"

"We want no trouble, McQueen. Saddle a horse and come along." Foster's eyes went to the cabin. Was there somebody inside the window?

"I'll come on one condition. That I keep my guns. If can't keep 'em you'll have to take me and you'll have some empty saddles on your way back to town."

Foster was angry. "Don't give me any trouble McQueen! I said, saddle your horse!"

"Sheriff, I've no quarrel with you. You're just doing your duty and I want to cooperate, but you've some men riding with you who would like to make a target of my back. Let me keep my guns and I'll go quiet. In case you'd like to know there are two men behind you with Winchesters. They will be riding along behind us."

Sheriff Foster studied McQueen. Inwardly, he was pleased. This McQueen was a hard case but a good man. Shoot a man in the back? It was preposterous! Especially Neal Webb.

"All right," he said, "saddle up."

"My horse is ready, Foster. A little bird told me you were coming, and my horse has been ready."

It was a black he was riding this day, a good mountain horse with bottom and speed. As he mounted and settled into the saddle he glanced at the man who had lifted his rifle.

"Just so everybody will understand. Two of my boys are going to follow us into town. Either one of them could empty a Winchester into the palm of your hand at three hundred yards."

He sat solidly and well in the saddle, his black Frisco jeans tight over his thighs, his broad chest and shoulders filling the dark gray shirt. His gun belts were studded with silver. the walnut grips worn from use. "All right, Sheriff, let's go to town!"

He rode alongside of Foster, but his thoughts were riding ahead, trying to foresee what would happen in town, and asking himself the question again: why kill Neal Webb? Who wanted him dead?

He had believed Webb the ringleader, the cause of his troubles. Most ranchers wanted more range, most of them wanted water, so the attempt to seize the Firebox came as no surprise. In fact, he would have been surprised had it not been claimed. Good grass was precious, and whenever anybody moved or died there was always someone ready to move in. The difference here was that McCracken had been a shrewd man and he had purchased the land around the various water holes, as well as the trails into and out of the range he used. The claim on Firebox range by McCracken was well established.

Webb, he was beginning to suspect, had been a mere pawn in the game, and had been disposed of when his usefulness ceased to be. But Webb's dying had implicated Ward McQueen and apparently somebody had decided to have him killed, either in capturing him or in the ride to town. A posse member could shoot him, claiming McQueen had made a move to escape.

Behind this there had to be a shrewd and careful brain. If there were witnesses to something that had not happened, his supposed murder of Neal Webb, then somebody had provided them.

Who? Why?

The Firebox was valuable range. The only other large ranch was Webb's Running W, and who was Webb's heir? Or did he himself own that ranch?

The Bear Canyon crowd? It wasn't their sort of thing. They might dry-gulch him, steal his horses or cattle, or even burn him out, but the Webb killing was more involved. Anyway, Webb had left the Bear Canyon crowd alone.

Would Sharon Clarity know? She was a handsome, self-reliant girl, yet something about her disturbed him. Why had she ridden out to warn him the sheriff was coming? Had she believed he would run?

Liking for him? Dislike of somebody else? Women's thinking was not part of his expertise. He had trouble reading their brands. Did she know who plotted against him? Did she herself hope to seize the Firebox when the shooting was over?

Who now owned the Running W? This he must discover. If that unknown owner also owned the Firebox he would control all the range around Pelona and the town as well. It made a neat, compact package and a base from which one might move in any direction.

Ruth Kermitt owned the Firebox now, and Ruth had no heirs. Ward McQueen was suddenly glad his boss was not among those present.

Pelona's main street was crowded with rigs and saddle horses when they rode in. Word had spread swiftly, and the people of the range country—the few scattered small ranchers, farmers, and gardeners—had come in, eager for any kind of a show. All had known Neal Webb, at least by sight. Many had not liked him, but he was one of their own. This Ward McQueen was a stranger and, some said, a killer. The general attitude was that he was a bad man.

A few, as always, had misgivings. Their doubts increased when they saw him ride into town sitting his horse beside the sheriff. He was not in irons. He still wore his guns. Evidently Foster trusted him. Western people, accustomed to sizing up a man by his looks, decided he didn't look like somebody who needed to dry-gulch anybody. It was more likely Webb would try to dry-gulch *him!*

Some of those who came to see drifted up between the buildings into the street. Among these was Bud Fox, with his narrow-brimmed gray hat and his long, lean body, looking like an overgrown schoolboy. The pistol on his belt was man-sized, however, and so was the Winchester he carried.

Kim Sartain, young, handsome, and full of deviltry, they recognized at once. They had seen his sort before. There was something about him that always drew a smile, not of amusement but of liking. They knew the guns on his belt were not there for show, but the west had many a young man like him, good cowhands, great riders, always filled with humor. They knew his type. The guns added another dimension, but they understood those, too.

The pattern was quickly made plain. The preliminary hearing was already set and the court was waiting. McQueen glanced at the sheriff. "Looks like a railroading, Foster. Are you in this?"

"No, but I've nothing against the law movin' fast. It usually does around here."

"When who is to get the brunt of it? *Who's* the boss around town, Foster? Especially when they move so fast I have no time to find witnesses."

"You know as much as I do!" Foster was testy. "Move ahead!"

"If I'd been around as long as you have, I'd know plenty!"

The judge was a sour-faced old man whom McQueen had seen about town. Legal procedures on the frontier were inclined to be haphazard, although often they moved not only swiftly but efficiently as well. The old Spanish courts had often functioned very well indeed, but the Anglos were inclined to follow their own procedures. McQueen was surprised to find that the prosecuting attorney, or the man acting as much, was Ren Oliver, said to have practiced law back in Missouri.

Sartain sat down beside McQueen. "They've got you cornered, Ward. Want me to take us out of here?"

"It's a kangaroo court, but let's see what happens. I don't want to appeal to Judge Colt unless we have to."

The first witness was a cowhand Ward had seen riding with Webb's men. He swore he had dropped behind Webb to shoot a wild turkey. He lost the turkey in the brush and was riding to catch up when he heard a shot and saw McQueen duck into the brush. He declared McQueen had fired from behind Webb.

McQueen asked, "You sure it was me?"

"I was sworn in, wasn't I?"

"What time was it?"

"About five o'clock of the evenin'."

"Webb comes from over east of town when he comes to Pelona, doesn't he? From the Runnin' W? And you say you saw me between you an' Webb?"

"I sure did!" The cowboy was emphatic, but he glanced at Oliver, uncertainly.

"Then," McQueen was smiling, "you were lookin' right into the settin' sun when you saw somebody take a shot at Webb? And you were able to recognize me?" As the crowd in the courtroom stirred, McQueen turned to the judge. "Your Honor, I doubt if this man could recognize his own sister under those circumstances. I think he should be given a chance to do it this evenin'. It's nice an' clear like it was the other night and the sun will be settin' before long. I think his evidence should be accepted if he can distinguish four out of five men he knows under the conditions he's talkin' about."

The judge hesitated and Oliver objected.

"Seems fair enough!" A voice spoke from the crowd, and there was a murmured assent.

The judge rapped for silence. "Motion denied! Proceed!"

Behind him McQueen was aware of changing sentiment. Western courtrooms, with some exceptions, were notoriously lax in their procedure, and there were those who had an interest in keeping them so. Crowds, however, were partisan and resentful of authority. The frontier bred freedom, but with it a strong sense of fair play and an impatience with formalities. Most western men wanted to get the matter settled and get back to their work. Most of the men and women present had ridden over that road at that time of the evening, and they saw immediately the point of his argument.

There was a stir behind them, and turning they saw Flagg Werneke shoving his way through the crowd and then down the aisle.

"Judge, I'm a witness! I want to be sworn in!"

The judge's eyes flickered to Oliver, who nodded quickly. Warneke still bore the marks of McQueen's fists, and his evidence could only be damning.

Warneke was sworn in and took the stand. Kim muttered irritably but Ward waited, watching the big man.

"You have evidence to offer?" the judge asked.

"You bet I have!" Warneke stated violently. "I don't know who killed Neal Webb but I know Ward McQueen didn't do it!"

Ren Oliver's face tightened with anger. He glanced swiftly toward a far corner of the room, a glance that held appeal and something more. McQueen caught the glance and sat a little straighter. The room behind him was seething, and the judge was rapping for order.

"What do you mean by that statement?" Oliver demanded. He advanced threateningly toward Warneke. "Be careful what you say and remember, *you are under oath!*"

"I remember. McQueen whipped me that evenin', like you all know. He whipped me good but he whipped me fair. Nobody else ever done it or could do it. I was mad as a steer with a busted horn. I figured, all right, he whipped me with his hands but I'd be durned if he could do it with a six-shooter, so I follered him, watchin' my chance. I was goin' to face him, right there in the trail, an' kill him.

" 'Bout the head of Squirrel Springs Canyon I was closin' in on him when a turkey flew up. That there McQueen, he slaps leather and downs that turkey with one shot! You heah me? One shot on the wing, an' he drawed so fast I never seen his hand move!"

Flagg Warneke wiped the sweat from his brow with the back of his hand. "My ma, she never raised any foolish children! Anybody who could draw that fast and shoot that straight was too good for anybody around here, and I wanted no part of him!

"Important thing is, McQueen was never out of my sight from the time he left town headin' west an' away from where Webb was killed until he reached Squirrel Springs Canyon, and that's a rough fifteen miles, the way he rode! It was right at dusk when he shot that turkey, so he never even seen Webb let alone killed him."

Ren Oliver swore under his breath. The crowd was shifting, many were getting up to leave. He glanced again toward the corner of the room and waited while the judge pounded for order.

Oliver attached Warneke's testimony but could not shake the man. Finally, angered, he demanded, "Did McQueen pay you to tell this story?"

Warneke's face turned ugly. "*Pay* me? Nobody lives who could pay me for my oath! I've rustled a few head of stock, and so has every man of you in this courtroom if the truth be known! I'd shoot a man if he crossed me, but by the Eternal my oath ain't for sale to no man!

"I got no use for McQueen! He burned us out over in Bear Canyon, he shot friends of mine, but he shot 'em face to face when they were shootin' at him! The man I'd like to find is the one who killed Chalk! Shot him off his horse to keep him from tellin' that Webb put them up to rustlin' Firebox stock!"

Ward McQueen got to his feet. "Judge, I'd like this case to be dismisses. You've no case against me."

The judge looked at Ren Oliver, who shrugged and turned away.

"Dismissed!"

The judge arose from his bench and stepped down off the platform. Ward McQueen turned swiftly and looked toward the corner of the room where Oliver's eyes had been constantly turning. The chair was empty!

People were crowding toward the door. McQueen's eyes searched their faces. Only one turned to look back. It was Silas Hutch.

McQueen pushed his way through the crowd to Flagg

Warneke. The big man saw him coming and faced him, eyes hard.

"Warneke," McQueen said, "I'd be proud to shake the hand of an honest man!"

The giant's brow puckered and he hesitated, his eyes searching McQueen's features for some hint of a smirk or a smile. There was none. Slowly the big man put his hand out and they shook.

"What are your plans? I could use a hand on the Firebox."

"I'm a rustler, McQueen. You've heard me admit it. You'd still hire me?"

"You had every reason to lie a few minutes ago, and I think a man who values his word that much would ride for the brand if he took a job. You just tell me you'll play it straight and rustle no more cattle while you're workin' for me and you've got a job."

"You've hired a man, McQueen. And you have my word."

As the big man walked away Sartain asked, "You think he'll stand hitched?"

"He will. Warneke has one thing on which he prides himself. One thing out of his whole shabby, busted up life that means anything, and that's his word. He'll stick, and we can trust him."

Tough as Ward McQueen felt himself to be, when he rode back to the ranch, he was sagging in the saddle. For days he had little sleep and had been eating only occasionally. Now, suddenly, it was hitting him. He was tired, and he was half asleep in the saddle when they rode into the yard at the Tumbling K's Firebox.

Lights in the cabin were ablaze and a buckboard stood near the barn. Stepping down from the saddle he handed the reins to Kim. No words were necessary.

He stepped up on he low porch and opened the door.

Ruth Kermitt stood with her back to the fireplace, where a small fire blazed. Even at this time of the year, at that atltitude a fire was needed.

She was tall, with a beautifully slim but rounded body that clothes could only accentuate. Her eyes were large and dark, her hair almost black. She was completely lovely.

"Ward!" She came to him quickly. "You're back!"

"And you're here!" He was pleased but worried also. "You drove all the way from the ranch?"

"McGowan drove. Shorty rode along, too. He said it was to protect me, but I think he had an idea you were in trouble. Naturally, if that were the case Shorty would have to be here."

"Ruth," he told her, "I'm glad to have you here. Glad for me, but I don't think you should have come. There is trouble, and I'm not sure what we've gotten into."

He explained, adding, "You know as well as I do that where there's good grass there will always be somebody who wants it, and what some of them haven't grasped is that we are not moving in on range. We *own* the water holes and the sources of water."

He put his hands on her shoulders. "All that can wait." He drew her to him. His lips stopped hers and he felt her body strain toward him and her lips melt softly against his. He held her there, his lips finding their way to her cheek, her ears, and her throat. After a few minutes she drew back, breathless.

"Ward! Wait!"

He stepped back and she looked up at him. "Ward? Tell me. Has there been trouble? Baldy said you were in court, that you might have to go on trial."

"That part is settled, but there's more to come, I'm afraid."

"Who is it, Ward? What's been happening?"

"That's just the trouble." He was worried. "Ruth, I don't know who it is, and there may be a joker in the deck that I'm not even aware of."

She went to the stove for the coffeepot. "Sit down and tell me about it."

"The ranch is a good one. Excellent grass, good water supply, and if we don't try to graze too heavy we should have good grass for years. McCracken handled it well and he developed some springs, put in a few spreader dams to keep the runoff on the land, but he wanted to sell and I am beginning to understand why."

"What about the trouble? Has it been shooting trouble?"

"It has, but it started before we got here." He told her about the killing of McCracken, then his own brush with rustlers, and the fight with Flagg Warneke and the killing of Warneke's brother before he could talk. And then the killing of Neal Webb.

"Then he wasn't the one?"

"Ruth, I believe Webb had played out his usefulness to whoever is behind this, who deliberately had Webb killed, with the hope of implicating me. He'd have done it, too, but for Warneke."

"He must be a strange man."

"He's a big man. You'll see him. He's also a violent man, but at heart he's a decent fellow. His word is his pride. I think he's going to shape up into quite a man. Some men get off on the wrong foot simply because there doesn't seem any other way to go.

"Without him, I think that Bear Canyon outfit will drift out and move away. I doubt if they will try to rebuild what was destroyed."

"Ward, we've been over this before. I hate all this violence! The fighting, the killing! It's awful! My own brother was killed. But you know all that. It was you who pulled us out of that."

"I don't like it, either, but it is growing less, Ruth, less with each year. The old days are almost gone. What we have here is somebody who is utterly ruthless, someone who has no respect for human life at all. You're inclined to find good in everybody, but in some people there just isn't any.

"Whoever is behind this, and I've a hunch who it is, is someone who is prepared to kill and kill until he has all he wants. He's undoubtedly been successful in the past, which makes it worse.

"No honest man would have such men as Hansen Bine and Overlin around. They did not ride for Webb—we know that now. They ride for whomever it was Webb was fronting for.

"I've got to ride down to Dry Leggett and roust out those wounded men, but you must be careful Ruth—this man will stop at nothing."

"But I'm a woman!"

"I don't believe that would matter with this man. He's not like a western man."

"Be careful, Ward! I just couldn't stand it if anything happened to you."

"You could. You've got the heart as well as the stamina. You've come a long way, Ruth, but you're pioneer stock. There's a rough time in any country, any new, raw country like this, before it can settle down."

As they talked, they wandered out under the trees, and when they returned to the house only Baldy was awake.

"Wonder folks wouldn't eat their supper 'stead of standin' around in the dark! A body would think you two wasn't more'n sixteen!"

"Shut up, you old squaw man," Ward said cheerfully, "an' set up the grub! I'm hungry enough to eat even your food."

"Why, Ward!" Ruth protested. "How can you talk like that? You know there isn't a better cook west of the Brazos!"

Baldy perked up. "See? See there? The boss knows a good cook when she sees one! Why you an' these cowhands around here never knowed what good grub was until I came along! You et sowbelly an' half-baked beans so long you wouldn't recognize real vittles when you see 'em!"

A yell interrupted Ward's reply. "Oh, Ward? Ward McQueen!"

Badly Jackson turned impatiently and opened the door.

"What the—!"

A bullet struck him as a gun bellowed in the night, and Baldy spun half around, dropping the coffeepot. Three more shots, fast as a man could lever a rifle, punctured the stillness. The light went out as Ward extinguished it with a quick puff and dropped to the floor, pulling Ruth down with him.

As suddenly as it had begun it ended. In the stillness that followed they heard a hoarse gasping from Baldy. Outside, all was dark and silent except for the pound of hoofs receding in the distance.

As he turned to relight the lamp, there was another shot, this from down the trail where the rider had gone. Glancing out, Ward saw a flare of fire against the woods.

"Take care of Baldy!" he said, and went out fast.

He grabbed a horse from the corral, slipped on a halter, and went down the trail riding bareback. As he drew near the fire he heard pounding hoofs behind him and slowed up, lifting a hand.

Suddenly he saw a huge man standing in the center of the trail, both hands uplifted so there would be no mistakes.

"McQueen! "It's me! I got him!" the man shouted. It was Flagg Warneke.

McQueen swung down, as did Kim Sartain, who had ridden up behind him. A huge pile of grass, dry as tinder, lay in the center of the road, going up in flames. Nearby lay a rider. He was breathing, but there was blood on his shirtfront and blood on the ground.

Warneke said, "I was ridin' to begin work tomorrow and I heard this hombre yell, heard the shot, so I throwed off my bronc, grabbed an armful of this hay McCracken had cut, and throwed it into the road. As this gent came ridin' I dropped a match into the hay. He tried to shoot me, but this here ol' Spencer is quick. He took a .56 right in the chest."

It was the sallow-faced rider Ward had seen before, one of those who had ridden in the posse. "Want to talk?" he asked.

"Go to the devil! Wouldn't if I could!"

"What's that mean? Why couldn't you talk?"

The man raised himself to one elbow, coughing. "Paid me from a holler tree," he said. "I seen nobody. Webb, he told me where I'd get paid an' how I'd—how I'd get word."

The man coughed again and blood trickled over his unshaved chin.

"Maybe it was a woman," he spoke clearly, suddenly. Then his supporting arm seemed to go slack and he fell back, his head striking the ground with a thump. The man was dead.

"A woman?" Ward muttered. "Impossible!"

Warneke shook his head. "Maybe—I ain't so sure. Could be anybody."

When the sun was high over the meadows, Ward McQueen was riding beside Ruth Kermitt near a ciénaga, following a creek toward Spur Lake. They had left the ranch after daybreak and had skirted some of the finest grazing land in that part of the country. Some areas that to the uninitiated might have seemed too dry she knew would support and fatten cattle. Much seemingly dry brush was good fodder.

"By the way," Ruth inquired, "have you ever heard of a young man, a very handsome young man named Strahan? He spells it with an aitch but they call it 'Strann.'

"When I was in Holbrook there was a Pinkerton man there who was inquiring about this man. He is badly wanted, quite a large reward offered. He held up a Santa Fe train, killing a messenger and a passenger. That was about four months ago. Before that he had been seen around this part of the country, as well as in Santa Fe. Apparently he wrecked another train, killing and injuring passengers. Each time he got away he seemed headed for this part of the country."

"Never heard of him," Ward admitted, "but we're newcomers."

"The Pinkerton man said he was a dead shot with either rifle or pistol, and dangerous. They trailed him to Alma once, and lost him again on the Gila, southeast of here."

They rode on, Ward pointing out landmarks that bordered the ranch. "The Firebox has the best range around," he explained. "The Spur Lake country, all the valley of Centerfire, and over east past the Dry Lakes to Apache Creek.

"There's timber, with plenty of shade for the hot months, and most of our range has natural boundaries that prevent stock from straying."

"What about this trouble you're having, Ward? Will it be over soon or hanging over our heads for months?"

"It won't hang on. We're going to have a showdown. I'm taking some of the boys, and we're going to round up some of the troublemakers. I'm just sorry that Baldy is laid up. He knows this country better than any of us."

"You'll have trouble leaving him behind, Ward. That was only a flesh wound, even though he lost blood. It was more shock than anything else."

They turned their horses homeward. Ward looked at the wide, beautiful country beyond Centerfire as they topped the ridge. "All this is yours, Ruth. You're no wife for a cowhand now."

"Now don't start that! We've been over it before! Who made it all possible for me? If you had not come along when you did I'd have nothing! Just nothing at all! And if my brother had not been killed he could not have handled this! Not as you have! He was a fine boy, and no girl ever had a better brother, but he wasn't the cattleman you are.

"And it isn't only that, Ward. You've worked long and you've built my ranch into something worthwhile. At least twice you've protected me when I was about to do something foolish. By rights half of it should belong to you, anyway!"

"Maybe what I should do is leave and start a brand of my own. Then I could come back with something behind me."

"How long would that take, Ward?" She put her hand over his on the pommel. "Please, darling, don't even think about it! The thought of you leaving makes me turn cold all over! I have depended on you, Ward, and you've never failed me."

They rode on in silence. A wild turkey flew up and then vanished in the brush. Ahead of them two deer, feeding early, jumped off into the tall grass and disappeared along the stream.

"Don't you understand? I'm trying to see this your way. You've told me what has to be done and I'm leaving it up to you. I'm not going to interfere. I'm a woman, Ward, and I can't bear to think of you being hurt. Or any of the other boys, for that matter. I'm even more afraid of how all this killing will affect you. I couldn't stand it if you became hard and callous!"

"I know what you mean but there's no need to worry

about that now. Once, long ago, maybe. Every time I ride into trouble I hate it, but a man must live and there are those who will ride roughshod over everybody, given a chance. Unfortunately force is the only way some people understand."

When they dismounted at the cabin, she said, "Then you're riding out tomorrow?"

"Yes."

"Then good luck!" She turned quickly and went into the house.

Ward stared after her, feeling suddenly alone and lost. Yet he knew there was no need for it. This was his woman, and they both understood that. She had come with a considerable investment, but with too little practical knowledge of range or cattle. With his hands, his savvy, and his gun he had built most of what she now possessed.

Under his guidance she had bought cattle in Texas, fattened them on the trail north, sold enough in Kansas to pay back her investment, and driven the remainder further west. Now she controlled extensive range in several states. Alone she never could have done it, nor could have Kim, one of the best men with a gun whoever walked, have had the judgment to handle a ranch, and he would have been the first to sidestep the responsibility.

Kim came down now. "Tomorrow, Ward?"

"Bring plenty of ammunition, both rifle and pistol. I'll want you, Bud Fox, Shorty Jones, and—"

"Baldy? Boss, if you don't take him it'll kill him. Or you'll have to hog-tie him to his bunk, and I'm damned if I'd help you! That ol' catamount's a-rarin' to go, an' he's already scared you're plannin' to leave him behind."

"Think he can stand the ride?"

Kim snorted. "Why, that ol' devil will be sittin' a-saddle when you an' me are pushin' up daisies! He's tougher 'n rawhide an' whalebone."

Daylight came again as the sun chinned itself on the Continental Divide, peering over the heights of the Tularosas and across the Frisco River. In the bottom of the Box, still deep in shadow, rode a small cavalcade of horsemen. In the lead, his battered old hat tugged down to cover his bald spot from the sun, rode Baldy Jackson.

Behind him, with no talking, rode McQueen, Sartain, Fox, and Jones. They rode with awareness, knowing trouble might explode at any moment. Each man knew what he faced on this day, and once begun there'd be no stopping. It was war now, a war without flags or drums, a grim war to the death.

For some reason Ward found his thoughts returning time and again to Ruth's account of the Pinkerton who was trailing the handsome killer named Strahan. It was a name he could not remember having heard.

He questioned Baldy. "Strahan? Never heard of a youngster by that name, but there was some folks lived hereabouts some years back named that. A bloody mean outfit, too! Four brothers of them! One was a shorty, a slim, little man but mean as pizen. The others were big men. The oldest one got hisself shot by one o' them Lincoln County gunfighters. Jesse Evans it was, or some friend of his.

"Two of the others, or maybe it was only one of them, got themselves hung by a posse somewhere in Colorado. If this here Strahan is one o' them, watch yourselves because he'd be a bad one."

Their route kept the ridge of the Friscos on their left, and when they stopped at Baldy's uplifted hand they were on the edge of a pine-covered basin in the hills.

Ward turned in his saddle and said, "This here's Heifer Basin. It's two miles straight ahead to Dry Leggett. I figure we should take a rest, check our guns, and get set for trouble. If Hansen Bine is down there, this will be war!"

Dismounting, they led their horses into the trees. Baldy located a spring he knew and they sat down beside it. McQueen checked his guns and then slid them back into their holsters. He rarely had to think of reloading, for it was something he did automatically whenever he used a gun.

"Mighty nice up here," Kim commented. "I always did like high country."

"That's what I like about cowboyin'," Shorty Jones commented. "It's the country you do it in."

"You ever rode in west Texas when the dust was blowin'?" Bud wanted to know.

"I have, an' I liked it. I've rid nearly every kind of country you can call to mind."

"Ssh!" Ward McQueen came to his feet in one easy movement. "On your toes! Here they come!"

Into the other end of the basin rode a small group of riders. There were six men, and the last one McQueen recognized as Hansen Bine himself.

Kim Sartain moved off to the right. Baldy rolled over behind a tree trunk and slid his Spencer forward. Jones and Fox scattered in the trees to the left of the spring.

McQueen stepped out into the open. "Bine! We're takin' you in! Drop your gun belts!"

Hansen Bine spurred his horse to the front and dropped from the saddle when no more than fifty paces away. "McQueen, is it? If you're takin' me you got to do it the hard way!"

He went for his gun.

McQueen had expected it, and the flat, hard bark of his pistol was a full beat before Bine's. The bullet struck Bine as his gun was coming up, and he twisted sharply with the impact. Ward walked closer, his gun poised. Around him and behind him he heard the roar of guns, and as Bine fought to bring his gun level McQueen shot again.

Bine fell, dug his fingers into the turf, heaved himself trying to rise, and then fell and lay quiet.

Ward looked around to find only empty saddles and one man standing, his left hand high, his right in a sling.

"Your name?"

"Bemis." The man's face was pale with shock, but he was not afraid. "I did no shooting. Never was no good with my left hand."

"All right, Bemis. You've been trailing with a pack of coyotes, but if you talk you can beat a rope. Who pays you?"

"Bine paid me. Where he got it, I don't know." His eyes sought McQueen's. "You won't believe me but I been wantin' out of this ever since the McCracken shootin'. That was a game kid."

"You helped kill him." McQueen replied coldly. "Who else was in it? Who ran that show?"

"Somebody I'd not seen around before. Young, slight build, but a ring-tailed terror with a gun. He came in with Overlin. Sort of blondish. I never did see him close up. None of us did, 'cept Overlin." Bemis paused again. "Said his name was Strahan."

That name again! The Pinkerton man had been right. Such a man was in this country, hiding out or whatever. Could it be he who was behind this? That did not seem logical. Strahan by all accounts was a holdup man, gunfighter, whatever, not a cattleman or a cautious planner.

"You goin' to hang me?" Bemis demanded. "If you are, get on with it. I don't like waitin' around."

McQueen turned his eyes on Bemis, and the young cowhand stared back, boldly. He was a tough young man, but old in the hard ways of western life.

"You'll hang, all right. If not now, eventually. That's the road you've taken. But as far as I'm concerned that's up to the law. Get on your horse."

The others were mounted, and Bine was lying across a saddle. Kim looked apologetic. "He's the only one, boss. The rest of them lit out like who flung the chunk. I think we winged a couple here or there, but they left like their tails was a-fire."

Kim Sartain looked at Bemis. "Dead or gone, all but this one. Maybe on the way in—you know, boss, it's easier to pack a dead man than a live one."

Bemis looked from Sartain to McQueen and back. "Now, see here!" he said nervously. "I said I didn't know who did the payin', but I ain't blind. Bine an' Overlin, they used to see somebody, or meet somebody, in the Emporium. There or the Bat Cave. They used to go to both places."

"So do half the men in the county," McQueen said. "I've been in both places, myself." He paused. "How about Strahan?"

"Never seen him before—or since."

"Put him on a horse and tie him," McQueen said. "We'll give him to Foster."

Ward led the way toward Pelona. There trouble awaited, he knew, and secretly he hoped Foster would be out of town. He wanted no trouble with the old lawman. Foster was a good man in his own way, trying to steer a difficult course in a county where too many men were ready to shoot. Foster was a typical western sheriff, more successful in rounding up rustlers, horse thieves, and casual outlaws than in dealing with an enemy cunning as a prairie wolf and heartless as a lynx.

They rode swiftly down the S U Canyon to the Tularosa, and then across Polk Mesa to Squirrel Springs Canyon. It was hard riding, and the day was drawing to a close when they reached the plains and cut across toward Pelona. They had ridden far and fast, and both men and horses were done in when they walked their horses up the dusty street to the jail.

Foster came to the door to greet them, glancing from McQueen to Bemis.

"What's the matter with him?"

"He rode with the crowd that killed Jimmy McCracken. Jimmy gave him the bad arm. I've brought him in for trial."

"Who led 'em?" Foster demanded of Bemis.

Bemis hesitated, obviously worried. He glanced around to see who might overhear. "Strahan," he said then. "Bine was in it, too."

Foster's features seemed to age as they watched. For the first time he looked his years.

"Bring him in," Foster said. "Then I'll go after Bine."

"No need to. McQueen jerked his head. "His body's right back there. Look," he added, "we've started a clean up. We'll finish it."

"You're forgettin' something, McQueen! I'm the law. It's my job."

"Hold your horses, Sheriff. You are the law, but Bine is dead. The boys who were with him are on the run, except for Bemis, and we're turnin' him over to you. Anybody else who will come willin' we'll bring to you."

"You ain't the law," Foster replied.

"Then make us the law. Deputize us. You can't do it alone, so let us help."

"Makes me look like a quitter."

"Nothing of the kind. Every law man I know uses deputies, time to time, and I'm askin' for the job."

"All right," Foster replied reluctantly. "You brought Bemis in when you could have hung him. I guess you aim to do right."

Outside the sheriff's office, Baldy waited for McQueen. "You name it," he said, as McQueen emerged. "What's next?"

"Fox, you, an' Shorty get down to the Emporium. If Hutch comes out, one of you follow him. Let anybody go in who wants to, but watch *him!*"

He turned to Jackson. "Baldy, you get across the street. Just loaf around, but watch that other store."

"Watch that female? What d'you take me for? You tryin' to sidetrack me out of this scrap?"

"Get goin' an' do what you're told. Kim, you come with me. We're goin' to the Bat Cave."

Foster stared after them and then walked back into his office. Bemis stood inside the bars of his cell door. "I'm gettin' old, Bemis," Foster said. "Lettin' another man do my job."

He sat down in his swivel chair. He was scared—he admitted it to himself. Scared not of guns or violence but of what he might find. Slowly the fog had been clearing, and the things he had been avoiding could no longer be avoided. It was better to let McQueen handle it, much better.

"Leave it to McQueen," Bemis was saying. "McQueen was right, and he's square." He clutched the bars. "Believe me, Sheriff, I never thought I'd be glad to be in jail, but I am. Before this day is over men will die.

"Foster, you should have seen McQueen when he killed Bine! I never would have believed anybody could beat Bine so bad! Bine slapped leather and died, just like that!"

"But there's Overlin," Foster said.

"Yeah, that will be somethin' to see. McQueen an'

Overlin." Suddenly Bemis exclaimed, "Foster! I forgot to tell them about Ren Oliver!"

"Oliver? Don't tell me he's involved?"

"Involved? He might be the ring leader! the boss man! And he packs a sneak gun! A stingy gun! Whilst you're expecting him to move for the gun you can see, he kills you with the other one."

Foster was on his feet. "Thanks, Bemis. We'll remember that when you're up for trial."

As Foster went out of the door, Bemis said, "Maybe, but maybe it's too late!"

The Bat Cave was alive and sinning. It was packed at this hour, and all the tables were busy. Behind one of them, seated where he could face the door, was Ren Oliver. His hair was neatly waved back from his brow, his handsome face composed as he dealt the tricky pasteboards with easy, casual skill. Only his eyes seemed alive, missing nothing. In the stable back of the house where he lived was a saddled horse. It was just a little bit of insurance.

At the bar, drinking heavily, was Overlin. Like a huge grizzly he hulked against the bar. The more he drank, the colder and deadlier he became. Someday that might change, and he was aware of it. He thought he would know when that time came, but for the present he was a man to be left strictly alone when drinking. He had been known to go berserk. Left alone, he usually drank the evening away, speaking to no one, bothering no one until finally he went home to sleep it off.

Around him men might push and shove for places at the bar, but they avoided Overlin.

The smoke-laden atmosphere was thick, redolent of cheap perfume, alcohol, and sweaty, unwashed bodies. The night was chill, so the two stoves glowed cherry red. Two bartenders, working swiftly, tried to keep up with the demands of the customers.

Tonight was different, and the bartenders had been the first to sense it. Overlin only occasionally came in, and they were always uncomfortable until he left. It was like serving an old grizzly with a sore tooth. But Overlin was only part of the trouble. The air was tense. They could feel trouble.

The burning of Bear Canyon, the slaying of Chalk Warneke, and the gun battle in Heifer Basin were being talked about, but only in low tones. From time to time, in spite of themselves, their eyes went to Overlin. They were not speculating if he would meet McQueen, but when.

Overlin called for another drink, and the big gun-fighter ripped the bottle from the bartender's hand and put it down beside him. The bartender retreated hastily, while somebody started a tear-jerking ballad at the old piano.

The door opened and Ward McQueen stepped in, followed by Kim Sartain.

Kim, lithe as a young panther, moved swiftly to one side, his eyes sweeping the room, picking up Ren Oliver at once, and then Overlin.

Ward McQueen did not stop walking until he was at the bar six feet from Overlin. As the big gunman reached again for the bottle, McQueen knocked it from under his hand.

At the crash of the breaking bottle the room became soundless. Not even the entry of Sheriff Foster was noted, except by Sartain.

"Overlin, I'm acting as deputy sheriff. I want you out of town by noon tomorrow. Ride, keep riding, and don't come back."

"So you're McQueen? And you got Bine? Well, that must have surprised Hans. He always thought he was good. Even thought he was better'n me, but he wasn't. He never saw the day."

McQueen waited. He had not expected the man to leave. This would be a killing for one or the other, but he had to give the man a chance to make it official. Proving that he had had a hand in the murder of Jimmy McCracken would have been difficult at best.

Overline was different from Bine. It would take a lot of lead to sink that big body.

"Where's Strahan?" McQueen demanded.

Ren Oliver started and then glanced hastily toward the door. His eyes met those of Kim Sartain, and he knew that to attempt to leave would mean a shootout, and he was not ready for that.

"Strahan, is it? Even if you get by me you'll never get past him. No need to tell you where he is. He'll find you when you least expect it."

Deliberately, Overlin turned his eyes away from McQueen, reaching for his glass with his left hand. "Whiskey! Gimme some whiskey!"

"Where is he, Overlin? Where's Strahan?"

The men were ready, McQueen knew. Inside of him, Overlin was poised for the kill. McQueen wanted to startled him, to throw him off balance, to wreck his poise. He took a half step closer, "Tell me, you drunken lobo! *Tell me!*"

As he spoke he struck swiftly with his left hand and slapped Overlin across mouth!

It was a powerful slap and it shocked Overlin. Not since he was a child had anybody dared to strike him, and it shook him as nothing else could have. He uttered a cry of choking rage and went for his gun.

Men dove for cover, falling over splintering chairs, fighting to get out of range or out the door.

McQueen had already stepped back quickly, drawn his gun, and then stepped off to the left as he fired, forcing Overlin to turn toward him. McQueen's first bullet struck an instant before Overlin could fire, and the impact knocked Overlin against the bar, his shot going off into the floor as McQueen fired again.

Overlin faced around, his shirt bloody, one eye gone, and his gun blazed again. McQueen felt himself stagger, shaken as if by a blow, yet without any realization of where the blow had come from.

He fired again, and not aware of how many shots he had fired, he drew his left-hand gun and pulled a border shift, tossing the guns from hand to hand to have a fully loaded gun in his right.

Across the room behind him, another brief drama played itself out. Ren Oliver had been watching and thought he saw his chance. Under cover of the action, all attention centered on McQueen and Overlin, he would kill McQueen. His sleeve gun dropped into his hand and cut down on

McQueen, but the instant the flash of blue steel appeared in his hand two guns centered on him and fired: Sartain was at the front door and Sheriff Foster on his left rear. Struck by a triangle of lead, Oliver lunged to his feet, one hand going to his stomach. In amazement, he stared at his bloody hand and his shattered body. Then he screamed.

In that scream was all the coward's fear of the death he had brought to so many others, In shocked amazement he stared from Foster to Sartain, both holding guns ready for another shot if need be. Then his legs wilted and he fell, one hand clutching at the falling deck of cards, his blood staining them. He fell, and the table tipped, cascading chips and cards over him and into the sawdust around him.

At the bar, Overlin stood, indomitable spirit still blazing from his remaining eye. "You—! You—!"

As he started to fall, his big hand caught at the bar's rounded edge and he stared at McQueen, trying to speak. Then the fingers gave way and he fell, striking the brass rail and rolling away.

Ward McQueen turned as if from a bad dream, seeing Kim at the door and Sheriff Foster, gun in hand, inside the rear door.

Running feet pounded the boardwalk, and the door slammed open. Guns lifted, expectantly.

It was Baldy Jackson, his face white, torn with emotion. "Ward! Heaven help me! I've killed a *woman*! I've killed Sharon Clarity!"

The scattered spectators were suddenly a mob. "*What?*" They started for him.

"Hold it!" McQueen's gun came up. "Hear him out!"

Ward McQueen was thumbing shells into his gun. "All right, Baldy. Show us."

"Before my Maker, Ward, I figured her for somebody sneakin' to get a shot at me! I seen the gun, plain as day, an' I fired!"

Muttering and angry, the crowd followed. Baldy led the way to an alley behind the store, where they stopped. There lay a still figure in a riding habit. For an instant Ward looked down at that still, strangely attractive face.

Then he bent swiftly, and as several cried out in protest he seized Sharon Clarity's red gold hair and jerked!

It came free in his hand, and the head flopped back on the earth, the close-cropped head of a man!

Ward stooped, griped the neckline, and ripped it away. With the padding removed, all could see the chest of a man, lean, muscular and hairy.

"Not Sharon Clarity," he said, "but Strahan."

Kim Sartain wheeled and walked swiftly away, McQueen following. As they reached the Emporium, Bud Fox appeared.

"Nobody left here but that girl. She was in there a long time. The old man started out but he warned him back. He's inside."

Ward McQueen led the way, with Sheriff Foster behind him, then Sartain, Jackson, Fox, and Jones.

Silas Hutch sat at his battered rolltop desk. His lean jaws seemed leaner than ever. He peered at them from eyes that were mean and cruel. "Well? What's this mean? Bargin' in like this?"

"You're under arrest, Hutch, for ordering the killing of Jimmy McCracken and Neal Webb."

Hutch chuckled. "Me? Under arrest? You got a lot to learn, boy. The law here answers to me. I say who is to be arrested and who is prosecuted.

"You got no proof of anything! You got no evidence! You're talkin' up the wind, sonny!"

Baldy Jackson pushed forward. "Ward, this here's the one I told you about! This is the first time I've had a good look at him! He's Shorty Strahan, the mean one! He's an uncle, maybe, of that one out there who made such a fine-lookin' woman!"

"Hutch, you had your killings done for you. All but one. You killed Chalk Warneke."

He turned to Foster. "Figure it out for yourself, Sheriff. Remember the position Chalk was in, remember the crowd, and Warneke on a horse. There's only one place that shot could come from—*that* window! And only one man who could have fired it, *him*!"

Silas Hutch shrank back in his chair. When Foster

eached for him, he cringed. "Don't let them hang me!"
e pleaded.

"You take it from here, Foster," McQueen said. "We
·an mesure the angle of that bullet and you've got Bemis.
·Ie can testify as to the connection between Neal Webb
·nd Hutch as well as that with Chalk. He knows all about
·t."

Ward McQueen turned toward the door. He was
·ired, very tired, and all he wanted was rest. Besides, his
·ip bone was bothering him. He had been aware of it for
·ome time, but only now was it really hurting. He looked
·lown, remembering something hitting him during the
·attle with Overlin.

His gun belt was somewhat torn and two cartridges
·lented. A bullet had evidently struck and glanced off,
·unning two perfectly good cartridges and giving him a
·ad bruise on the hip bone.

"Kim," he said, let's get back to the ranch."

MCQUEEN OF THE TUMBLING K

A working cowboy seldom wore a coat. It impeded the free action of his shoulders in roping as well as in many other activities, so he settled for a vest, usually worn open. The vest pockets carried his tobacco sack and such odds and ends as he believed necessary. Later, when there were pockets in shirts, the tobacco sack was relegated to a breast pocket with the paper tag hanging out, easy to the hand.

Shirts in the earlier days were without pockets and without collars. When a man "dressed up" he wore a starched collar or one made of celluloid. Although the latter was easy to clean it had to be kept from contact with heat, particularly from cigars, cigarettes, or even warm ashes. A celluloid collar had a way of vanishing in a burst of flame, often followed by everything in the vicinity.

The bandanna, worn loosely about the neck, usually with the full part hanging in front, was not worn for decoration. It was probably the most useful item a cowboy wore. Over a hundred possible uses have been found. Usually it was pulled up to cover the nose and mouth when riding "drag" in the dust behind a moving herd of cattle or horses. It could be used as a bandage, a sling for a broken arm, to strain water for drinking, to protect the back of the neck from sun, and so on.

Bandannas were nearly always red. This was not a matter of choice, as other colors were not to be found. Later, blue bandannas with polkadots were made and sold largely to railroad men for whom blue seemed a uniform color. Occasionally, of course, a cowboy would wear a silk neckerchief, which might be of any color.

Shirt collars, whether starched or celluloid, were attached to the shirt by collar buttons, one behind and one in front. Collar buttons were one of the most refractory, obstinate, and just downright ornery objects a human ever had to deal with and probably were the cause of more profanity than anything man invented until the arrival of the Model-T Ford. Invariably, in the course of a man's struggle with a collar button it would slip from his fingers and roll into the most inaccessible place in the room. It was never possible to simply stoop down and pick up a collar button. One always had to get down on one's knees and reach under whatever piece of furniture was nearby and feel around for the missing object. It has been reliably reported that even ministers of the gospel used unseemly language on such occasions.

At first cowboys, as was the case with any working man, wore whatever old clothing they possessed. Pieces of uniforms from the Civil War were often seen, and especially the overcoats, in both gray and blue. These were warm, highly efficient garments and their presence on the frontier was obvious for at least forty years after the war's end. They were superseded in many cases by the buffalo coat. One of these was still around the house when I was a youngster, and nothing warmer ever existed, or heavier, I might add.

As cowboying became a trade it developed a costume of its own, and if easterners thought it picturesque it was not intentionally so. Cowboy clothing was designed for the job it had to do, chosen strictly for efficiency. Many of the horses cowboys rode in the beginning were only half broken, so the cowboy wanted a boot with a pointed toe that would slip easily into a stirrup, and a high heel so it would not slip too far.

Chaps were invented for riders in brush country where thorns or broken branches might rip the clothes from a man aboard a horse following a steer into thick brush. Riders in other parts of the country adopted the chaps as protective of clothing as well as of the legs themselves. The woolly chaps, rarely seen these days,

*were worn in Wyoming or Montana. These were often
made of cowhide with the hair left on or of sheepskin or
goatskin. When King Fisher was leading his boys down
near Uvalde, in Texas, he held up a circus and killed the
tiger to make himself a pair of tiger-skin chaps. But the
King liked colorful clothes, and none of the movie cowboys
could touch him in that respect.*

*As a matter of fact, many cowboys liked colorful
clothes but could rarely afford them. They went to work
wearing the most efficient garments they could acquire.
Another type of garment rarely seen anymore was the
leather cuff. They were often seen in movies of the silent
era when there were more working cowboys around.*

*The most important items to a cowboy were his hat,
his boots, and his saddle. The first well-made cowboy hats
to become known by a brand name were the Stetsons, a
name which soon became synonymous with "hat." Any hat
might be called a Stetson, just as any pistol might be
called a Colt, regardless of its manufacturer's name. In
the same way many westerners referred to any rifle as a
Winchester.*

McQueen of the Tumbling K

Ward McQueen reined in the strawberry roan and squinted his eyes against the sun. Salty sweat made his eyes smart, and he dabbed at them with the end of a bandanna. Kim Sartain was hazing a couple of rambunctious steers back into line. Bud Fox was walking his horse up the slope to where Ward waited, watching the drive.

Fox drew up alongside him and said, "Ward, d'you remember that old brindle ladino with the scarred hide? This here is his range but we haven't seen hide nor hair of him."

"That's one old mossyhorn I won't forget in a hurry. He's probably hiding back in one of the canyons. Have you cleaned them out yet?"

"Uh-huh, we surely have. Baldy an' me both worked em, and no sign of him. Makes a body mighty curious."

"Yeah, I suppose you've got a point. It ain't like him to be away from the action. He'd surely be down there makin' trouble." He paused, suddenly thoughtful. "Missed any other stock since I've been gone?"

Fox shrugged. "If there's any missin' it can't be but a few head, but you can bet if that old crowbait is gone some others went with him. He ramrods a good-sized herd all by himself."

Baldy Jackson joined them on the slope. He jerked his head to indicate a nearby canyon mouth, "Seen some mighty queer tracks over yonder," he said, "like a man afoot."

"We'll go have a look," McQueen said. "A man afoot in this country? It isn't likely."

He started the roan across the narrow valley, with Baldy and Bud following.

The canyon was narrow and high walled. Parts of it were choked with brush and fallen rock, with only the winding watercourse to offer a trail. In the spreading fan of sand where the wash emptied into the valley, Baldy drew up.

Ward looked down at the tracks Baldy indicated. "Yes, they do look odd," said Ward. "Fixed him some homemade footgear. Wonder if that's his blood or some critter?" Leading the roan he followed the tracks up the dry streambed.

After a few minutes, he halted. "He's been hurt. Look at the tracks headed this way. Fairly long, steady stride. I'd guess he's a tall man. But see here? Goin' back the steps are shorter an' he's staggerin'. He stopped twice in twenty yards, each time to lean against something."

"Reckon we'd better follow him?" Baldy looked at the jumble of boulders and crowded brush. "If he doesn't aim to be ketched he could make us a powerful lot of trouble."

"We'll follow him anyway. Baldy, you go back an help the boys. Tell Kim an' Tennessee where we're at. Bud will stay with me. Maybe we can track him down, an he should be grateful. It looks like he's hurt bad."

They moved along cautiously for another hundred yards. Bud Fox stopped, mopping his face. He doesn't figure on bein' followed. He's makin' a try at losin' his trail. Even tried to wipe out a spot of blood."

Ward McQueen paused and looked up the watercourse with keen, probing eyes. There was something wrong about all this. He had been riding this range for months now and believed he knew it well, yet he remembered no such man as this must be, and had seen no such tracks. Obviously the man was injured. Just as obviously he was trying, even in his weakened condition, to obliterate his trail. That meant that he expected to be followed and that those who followed were enemies.

Pausing to study the terrain he ran over in his mind

the possibilities from among those whom he knew. Who might the injured man be? And who did he fear?

They moved on, working out the trail in the close, hot air of the canyon. The tracks split suddenly and disappeared on a wide ledge of stone where the canyon divided into two.

"We're stuck," Fox said, "he won't leave tracks with those makeshift shoes of his, and there's nowhere he can go up the canyons."

The right-hand branch ended in a steep, rocky slide, impossible to climb without hours of struggle, and the left branch ended against the sheer face of a cliff against whose base lay a heaped-up pile of boulders and rocky debris.

"He may have doubled back or hidden in the brush," Fox added.

Ward shrugged. "Let's go back. He doesn't want to be found, but hurt like he is he's apt to die out here without care."

Deliberately, he had spoken loudly. Turning their mounts they rode back down the canyon to rejoin the herd.

Ruth Kermitt was waiting on the steps when they left the grassy bottom and rode up to the bunkhouse. With her was a slender, narrow-faced man in a black frock coat. As Ward drew up the man's all-encompassing glance took him in, then slid away.

"Ward, this is Jim Yount. He's buying cattle and wants to look at the herd you just brought in."

"Howdy," Ward said, agreeably. He glanced at Yount's horse and then at the tied-down gun.

Two more men sat on the steps of the bunkhouse. A big man in a checkered shirt and a slim redhead with a rifle across his knees.

"We're looking to buy five hundred to a thousand head," Yount commented. "We heard you had good stock."

"Beef?"

"No, breeding stock, mostly. We're stockin' a ranch. I'm locatin' the other side of Newton's place."

Ward commented, "We have some cattle. Or rather, Miss Kermitt has. I'm just the foreman."

"Oh?" Yount looked around at Ruth with a quick, flashing smile. "Miss, is it? Or are you a widow?"

"Miss. My brother and I came here together, but he was killed."

"Hard for a young woman to run a ranch alone, isn't it?" His smile was sympathetic.

"Miss Kermitt does very well," Ward replied coolly, "and she isn't exactly alone."

"Oh?" Yount glanced at McQueen, one eyebrow lifted. "No," he said after a minute, "I don't expect you could say she was alone as long as she had cattle on the place, and cowhands."

Ruth got up quickly, not liking the look on Ward's face. "Mr. Yount? Wouldn't you like some coffee? Then we can talk business."

When they had gone inside Ward McQueen turned on his heel and walked to the bunkhouse, leading his horse. He was mad an he didn't care who knew it. The thin-faced redhead looked at him as he drew near.

"What's the matter, friend? Somebody steal your girl?"

Ward McQueen halted and turned slowly. Baldy Jackson got up quickly and moved out of line. The move put him at the corner of the bunkhouse, leaving Yount's riders at the apex of a triangle of which McQueen and himself formed the two corners.

"Miss Kermitt," McQueen's tone was cold, "is my boss. She is also a lady. Don't get any funny notions."

The redhead chuckled. "Yeah, and our boss is a ladies' man! He knows how to handle 'em." Deliberately, he turned his back on Baldy. "Ever been foreman on a place like this, Dodson. Maybe you or me will have a new job."

Ward walked into the bunkhouse. Bud Fox was loitering beside the window. He, too, had been watching the pair.

"Don't seem the friendly type," Bud commented, pouring warm water into the tin washbasin. "Almost like they wanted trouble!"

"What would be the idea of that?" Ward inquired.

Bud was splashing in the basin and made no reply, but Ward wondered. Certainly their attitude was not typical. He glanced toward the house, and his lips tightened.

Jim Yount was a slick-talking sort and probably a woman would think him good-looking.

Out beyond the ranch house was a distant light, which would be Gelvin's store in Mannerhouse. Gelvin had ranched the country beyond Newton's. Suddenly, McQueen made up his mind. After chow he would ride into Mannerhouse and have a little talk with Gelvin.

Supper was served in the ranch house as always and was a quiet meal but for Ruth and Jim Yount, who laughed and talked at the head of the table.

Ward, seated opposite Yount, had little to say. Baldy, Bud, and Tennessee sat in strict silence. Only Red Lund, seated beside Pete Dodson, occasionally ventured a remark. At the foot of the table, lean, wiry Kim Sartain let his eyes rove from face to face.

When supper was over, Ward moved outside into the moonlight and Kim followed. "What goes on?" Kim whispered. "I never did see anybody so quiet."

Ward explained, adding, "Yount may be a cattle buyer, but the two riders with him are no average cowpunchers. Red Lund is a gunhand if I ever saw one, and Dodson's right off the Outlaw Trail or I miss my guess." He hitched his belt. "I'm ridin' into town. Keep an eye on things, will you?"

"I'll do that." He lowered his tone. "That Lund now? I don't cotton to him. Nor Yount," he added.

Gelvin's store was closed but McQueen knew where to find him. Swinging down from the saddle, he tied his horse and pushed through the batwing doors. Abel was polishing glasses behind the bar, and Gelvin was at a table with Dave Cormack, Logan Keane, and a tall, lean-bodied stranger. They were playing poker.

Two other strangers lounged at the bar. They turned to look at him as he came in.

"Howdy, Ward! How's things at the Tumblin' K?"

The two men at the bar turned abruptly and looked at Ward again, quick, searching glances. He had started to speak to Gelvin, but something warned him and instead he walked to the bar.

"Pretty good," he replied. "Diggin' some stuff out of

the breaks today. Tough work. All right for a brushpopper, but I like open country."

He tossed off his drink, watching the two men in the bar mirror. "They tell me there's good range beyond the Newtons. I think I'll ride over and see if there's any lyin' around loose."

Gelvin glanced up. He was a short, rather handsome man with a keen, intelligent face.

"There's plenty that you can have for the taking. That country is going back to desert as fast as it can. Sand moving in, streams drying up. You can ride a hundred miles and never find a drink. Why," he picked up the cards and began to shuffle them, ". . . old Coyote Benny Chait came in two or three weeks ago. He was heading out of the country. He got euchred out of his ranch by some slick card handler. He was laughin' at the man who won it, said he'd get enough of the country in a hurry."

The two men at the bar had turned and were listening to Gelvin. One of them started to speak and the other put a cautioning hand on his arm.

"Who was it won the ranch? Did he say?"

"Sure!" Gelvin began to deal. "Some driftin' card-sharp by the name of—"

"You talk too much!" The larger of the two men at the bar stepped toward the card table. "What d'you know about the Newton country?"

Startled by the unprovoked attack, Gelvin turned his chair. His eyes went from one to the other of the two men. Ward McQueen had picked up the bottle.

"What is this?" Gelvin asked, keeping his tone even. These men did not seem to be drunk, yet he was experienced enough to know he was in trouble, serious trouble. "What did I say? I was just commenting on the Newton country."

"You lied!" The big man's hand was near his gun. "You lied! That country ain't goin' back! It's as good as it ever was!"

Gelvin was a stubborn man. This man was trying to provoke a fight, but Gelvin had no intention of being killed over a trifle. "I did not lie," he replied coolly. "I lived in that country for ten years. I came in with the first white men, and I've talked with the Indians who were there earlier. I know of what I speak."

"Then you're sayin' I'm a liar?" The big man's hand spread over his gun.

Ward McQueen turned in one swift movement. His right hand knocked the bottle spinning toward the second man and he kept swinging around, his right hand grabbed the big man by the belt. With a heave he swung the big man off balance and whirled him, staggering, into the smaller man who had sprung back to avoid the bottle.

The big man staggered again, fell, and then came up with a grunt of fury. Reaching his feet his hand went to his gun, then froze. He was looking into a gun in Ward McQueen's hand.

"That was a private conversation," Ward said mildly. "In this town we don't interfere. Understand?"

"If you didn't have the drop on me you wouldn't be talkin' so big!"

Ward dropped his six-gun into its holster. "All right, now you've got an even break."

The two men faced him, and suddenly neither liked what they saw. This was no time for bravery, they decided. "We ain't lookin' for trouble," the smaller man said. "We just rode into town for a drink."

"Then ride out," Ward replied. "And don't butt into conversations that don't concern you."

"Hollier'n me," the big man started to speak but then suddenly stopped and started for the door.

Ward stepped back into the bar. "Thanks, Gelvin. You told me something I needed to know."

"I don't get it," Gelvin protested. "What made them mad?"

"That card shark you mentioned? His name wouldn't be Jim Yount, would it?"

"Of course! How did you know?"

The tall stranger playing cards with Gelvin glanced up and their eyes met. "You wouldn't be the Ward McQueen from down Texas way, would you?"

"That's where I'm from. Why?"

The man smiled pleasantly. "You cut a wide swath

down thataway. I heard about your run-in with the Maravillas Canyon outfit."

McQueen was cautious when he took the trail to the Tumbling K, but he saw nothing of the two men in the saloon. Hollier . . . he was the smaller one. There had been a Hollier who escaped from a lynch mob down Uvalde way a few years back. He had trailed around with a man called Packer, and the larger of these two men had a P burned on his holster with a branding iron.

What was Jim Yount's game? Obviously, the two men from the saloon were connected with him somehow. They had seemed anxious Yount's name not be spoken, and they seemed eager to quiet any talk about the range beyond the Newtons.

The available facts were few. Yount had won a ranch in a poker game. Gelvin implied the game was crooked. The ranch he won was going back to desert. In other words, he had won nothing but trouble. What came next?

The logical thing for a man of Yount's stamp was to shrug off the whole affair and go on about his business. He was not doing that, which implied some sort of a plan. Lund and Dodson would make likely companions to Packer and Hollier. Yount was talking of buying cattle, but he was not the sort to throw good money after bad. Did they plan to rustle the cattle?

One thing was sure. It was time he got back to the ranch to alert the boys for trouble. It would be coming sooner, perhaps, because of what happened tonight. But what about Ruth? Was she taken with Yount? Or simply talking busness and being polite? Did he dare express his doubts to her?

The Tumbling K foreman was riding into the ranch yard when the shot rang out. Something had struck a wicked blow on his head, and he was already falling when he heard the shot.

His head felt tight, constricted, as if a tight band had been drawn around his temples. Slowly, fighting every inch of the way, he battled his way to consciousness. His lids fluttered, then closed, too weak to force themselves open. He struggled against the heaviness and finally got his eyes open. He was lying on his back in a vague half-light. The air felt damp, cool.

Awareness came. He was in a cave or mine tunnel. Turning his head carefully, he looked around. He was lying on a crude pallet on a sandy floor. Some twenty feet away was a narrow shaft of light. Nearby, his gun belt hung on a peg driven into the wall and his rifle leaned against the wall.

The rift of light was blotted out and someone crawled into the cave. A man came up and threw down an armful of wood. Then he lighted a lantern and glanced at McQueen.

"Come out of it, did you? Man, I thought you never would!"

He was lean and old, with twinkling blue eyes and almost white hair. He was long and tall. Ward noted the footgear suddenly. This was the man they had trailed up the canyon!

"Who are you?" he demanded.

The man smiled and squatted on his heels. "Charlie Quayle's the name. Used to ride for Chait, over in the Newton's."

"You're the one we trailed up the canyon the other day. Yesterday, I believe it was."

"I'm the man, all right, but it wasn't yesterday. You've been lyin' here all of two weeks, delirious most of the time. I was beginning to believe you'd never come out of it."

"Two weeks?" McQueen struggled to sit up, but the effort was too much. He sank back. "Two weeks? They'll figure I'm dead back at the ranch. Why did you bring me here? Who shot me?"

"Hold your horses! I've got to wash up and fix some grub." He poured water in a basin and began to wash his face and hands. As he dried his hands he explained. "You was shot, and I ain't sure who done it. Two of them rustlin' hands of Yount's packed you to the canyon and dropped you into the wash. Then they caved sand over you and some brush. But they weren't about to do more than need be, so figurin' you were sure enough dead, they rode off.

"I was almighty curious to know who'd been killed, so

I pulled the brush away and dug into the pile and found you was still alive. I packed you up here, and mister, it took some packin'! You're a mighty heavy man."

"Were you trailin' them when they shot me?"

"No. To tell you the truth I was scoutin' the layout at the ranch, figurin' to steal some coffee when I heard the shot. Then I saw them carry you off, so I follered."

Quayle lighted his pipe. "There's been some changes," he added. "You friend Sartain has been fired. So have Fox and that bald-headed gent. Tennessee had a run-in with Lund, and Lund killed him. Picked a fight and then beat him to the draw. Yount is real friendly with Ruth Kermitt, and he's runnin' the ranch. One or more of those tough gunmen of his is there all the time."

Ward lay back on his pallet. Kim Sartain fired! It didn't seem reasonable. Kim had been with Ruth Kermitt longer than any of them! He had been with them when Ruth and her brother came over the trail from Montana.

Kim had been with her through all that trouble at Pilot Range when Ward himself had first joined them. Kim had always rode for the brand. Now he had been fired, run off the place!

And Tennessee killed!

What sort of girl was Ruth Kermitt? She had fired her oldest and most loyal hands and taken on a bunch of rustlers with a tinhorn gambler for boss. And to think he had been getting soft on her! He'd actually been thinking she was the girl for him, and the only reason he'd held off was because he had no money, nothing to offer a woman. Well, this showed what a fool he would have been.

"You've got a hard head," Quayle was saying, "or you'd be dead by now. That bullet hit right over your eye and skidded around your skull under the skin. Laid your scalp open. You had a concussion, too. I know the signs. And you lost blood."

"I've got to get out of here!" Ward said. "I've got to see Ruth Kermitt."

"You'd be better off to sit tight and get well. Right now she's right busy with that there Yount. Rides all over the range with him, holdin' hands more'n half the time. Everybody's seen 'em. And if she fired all the rest of her hands you can be sure she doesn't want her foreman back."

He was right, of course. What good would it do to even talk to a woman who would fire such loyal hands as she had?

"Where d' you fit into all this?"

Quayle sliced bacon into a frying pan. "Like I told you, I rode for Chait. Yount rooked him out of his ranch, but as a matter of fact, Chaitt was glad to get shut of it. When Yount found what he'd won he was sore. Me, I'd saved me nigh on a year's wages an' was fixin' to set up for myself. One of those hands of Yount's, he seen the money and trailed me down, said it was ranch money. We had us a fight and they got some lead into me. I got away an' holed up in this here canyon."

All day McQueen rested in the cave, his mind busy with the problem. But what could he do? If Ruth Kermitt had made her choice it was no longer any business of his. The best thing he could do was to get his horse and ride out of there, just drop the whole thing.

It was well after dark before Quayle returned, but he had news and was eager to talk.

"That Yount is takin' over the country! He went into Mannerhouse last night huntin' Gelvin, but Gelvin had gone off with that stranger friend of his that he plays poker with all the time.

"Yount had words with Dave Cormack and killed him. They say this Yount is greased lightning with a gun. Then Lund an' Pete Dodson pistol-whipped Logan Keane. Yount told them he was runnin' the Tumblin' K and was going to marry Ruth Kermitt, and he was fed up with the talk about him and his men. He thinks he's got that town treed, an' maybe he has. Takes some folks a long time to get riled."

Ruth to marry Jim Yount! Ward felt a sharp pang. He realized suddenly that he was in love with Ruth. Now that he realized it he knew he had been in love with her for a long time. And she was to marry Yount!

"Did you see anything of Kim Sartain?"

"No," Quayle replied, "but I heard the three of them rode over into the Newtons."

Ward McQueen was up at daybreak. He rolled out of his blankets, and although his head ached he felt better. No matter. It was time to be up and doing. His long period of illness had at least given him rest, and his strength was such that he recovered rapidly. He oiled his guns and reloaded them. Quayle watched him preparing to travel but said nothing until he pulled on his boots.

"Better wait until sundown if you're huntin' trouble," he said. "I got a hoss for you. Stashed him down in the brush."

"A horse? Good for you! I'm going to have a look at the ranch. This deal doesn't figure right to me."

"Nor me." Quayle knocked the ash from his pipe. "I seen that girl's face today. They rid past as I lay in the brush. She surely didn't look like a happy woman. Not like she was ridin' with a man she loved. Maybe she ain't willin'."

"I don't like to think she'd take up with a man like Yount. Well, tonight I ride."

"*We* ride!" Quayle insisted. "I didn't like gettin' shot up any more than you-all. I'm in this fight, too."

"I can use the help, but what I'd really like you to do is hunt down Kim Sartain and the others. I can use their help. Get them back here for a showdown. Warn them it won't be pretty."

Where Quayle had found the quick-stepping buckskin Ward neither knew nor cared. He needed a horse desperately, and the buckskin was not only a horse but a very good one.

Whatever Yount's game was he had been fast and thorough. He had moved in on the Tumbling K, had Ward McQueen dry-gulched, had Ruth Kermitt fire her old hands, replaced them with his own men, and then rode into Mannerhouse and quieted all outward opposition by killing Dave Cormack and beating another man.

If there was to have been opposition it would have been Cormack and Keane who would have led it. Tennessee, too, had been killed, but Tennessee was not known in town, and that might be passed off as a simple dispute between cowhands. Yount had proved to be fast, ruthless, and quick of decision. As he acted with the real or apparent consent of Ruth Kermitt there was nothing to be done by the townspeople in the village of Mannerhouse.

Probably, with Cormack and Keane out of the picture and Gelvin off God knew where, they were not inclined to do anything. None of them were suffering any personal loss, and nothing was to be gained by bucking a man already proved to be dangerous. Obviously, the gambler was in control. He had erred in only two things. He had failed to kill Charlie Quayle and to make sure that McQueen was dead.

The buckskin had a liking for the trail and moved out fast. Ward rode toward the Tumbling K, keeping out of sight. Quayle had ridden off earlier in the day to find Kim, Baldy, and Bud Fox. The latter two were good cowhands and trustworthy, but the slim, dark-faced youngster, Kim Sartain, was one of the fastest men with a gun Ward had ever seen.

"With him," Ward told the buckskin, "I'd tackle an army!"

He left the buckskin in a clump of willows near the stream and then crossed on stepping-stones, working his way through the brush toward the Tumbling K ranch house.

He had no plan of action, nor anything on which to base a plan. If he could find Ruth and talk to her or if he could figure out what it was that Yount was trying to accomplish, it would be a beginning.

The windows were brightly lit. For a time he lay in the brush studying the situation. An error now would be fatal, if not to him, at least to their plans.

There would be someone around, he was sure. Quayle had said one of the gunmen was always on the ranch, for the gambler was a careful man.

A cigarette glowed suddenly from the steps of the bunkhouse. Evidently the man had just turned toward him. Had he inadvertently made a sound? At least he knew that somebody was there, on guard.

Ward eased off to the left until the house was between himself and the guard. Then he crossed swiftly to the side of the house. He eased a window a little higher.

It was a warm night and the window had been open at the bottom.

Jim Yount was playing solitaire at the dining room table. Red Lund was oiling a pistol. Packer was leaning his elbows on the table and smoking, watching Yount's cards.

"I always wanted a ranch," Yount was saying, "and this is it. No use gallivanting around the country when a man can live in style. I'd have had it over in the Newtons if that damned sand bed I got from Chait had been any good. Then I saw this place. It was too good to be true."

"You worked fast," Packer said, "but you had a streak of luck when Hollier an' me got McQueen. From what I hear, he was nobody to fool around with."

Yount shrugged. "Maybe so, but all sorts of stories get started and half of them aren't true. He might be fast with a gun, but he had no brains, and it takes brains to win in this kind of game."

He glanced at Lund. "Look, that Logan Keane outfit lies south of Hosstail Creek, and it joins onto this one. Nice piece of country, thousands of acres with good water, running right up to the edge of town.

"Keane's scared now. Once me and Ruth Kermitt are married so our title to this ranch is cinched we'll go to work on Keane. We'll rustle his stock, run off his hands, and force him to sell. I figure the whole job shouldn't take more than a month, at the outside."

Red glanced up from his pistol. "You get the ranches, what do we get?"

Yount smiled. "You don't want a ranch, and I do, but I happen to know that Ruth has ten thousand dollars cached. You boys," for a moment his eyes held those of Red Lund, "can split that among you. You can work out some way of dividing it even up all around."

Lund's eyes showed his understanding, and McQueen glanced at Packer, but the big horse thief showed no sign of having seen the exchange of glances. Ward could see how the split would be made, it would be done with Red Lund's six-shooter. They would get the lead, he'd take the cash.

It had the added advantage to Jim Yount of leaving only one witness to his treachery.

Crouched below the window, Ward McQueen calculated his chances. Jim Yount was reputed to be a fast man with a gun. Red Lund had already proved his skill. Packer would also be good, even if not an artist like the others. Three to one made the odds much too long, and at the bunkhouse would be Hollier and Pete Dodson, neither a man to be trifled with.

A clatter of horse's hoofs on the hard-packed trail, and a horseman showed briefly in the door and was ushered into the room. It was the lean stranger who had played poker with Gelvin and Keane.

"You Jim Yount? Just riding by and wanted to tell you there's an express package at the station for Miss Kermitt. She can drop in tomorrow to pick it up if she likes."

"Express package? Why didn't you bring it out?"

"Wouldn't let me. Seems like its money or something like that. A package of dinero that's payment for some property in Wyoming. She's got to sign for it herself. They won't let anybody else have it."

Yount nodded. 'All right. She's asleep, I think, but come morning I'll tell her."

The rider went out and a few minutes later Ward heard his horse's hoofs on the trail.

"More money?" Packer grinned. "Not bad, Boss! She can pick it up for us and we'll split it."

Red Lund was wiping off his pistol. "I don't like it," he spoke suddenly. "Looks like a move to get us off the ranch and the girl into town."

Yount shrugged. "I doubt it, but suppose that's it? Who in town has the guts or the skill to tackle us? Personally, I believe it's the truth, but if it ain't, why worry? We'll send Packer in ahead to scout. If there's any strangers around he can warn us. I think its all right. We'll ride in tomorrow."

An hour later, and far back on a brush-covered hillside, Ward McQueen bedded down for the night. From where he lay he could see anybody who arrived at or left the ranch. One thing he knew, tomorrow was the payoff. Ruth Kermitt would not be returning to the ranch.

At daylight he was awake and watching, his buckskin saddled and ready. It had been a damp, uncomfortable night, and he stretched, trying to get the chill from his muscles. The sunshine caught reflected light from the window. Hollier emerged and began roping horses in the corral. He saddled his own, Ruth's brown mare, and Yount's big gray.

Ward McQueen tried to foresee what would happen. He was convinced, as was Red Lund, that the package was a trick. There were only nine buildings on the town's main street, scarecely more than two dozen houses scattered about.

The express and stage office was next to the saloon. Gelvin's store was across the street.

Whatever happened, Ruth would be in danger. She would be with Yount, closely surrounded by the others. To fire on them was to endanger her.

And where did that young rider stand? He had been called Rip, and he had known of McQueen's gun battle in Maravillas Canyon. Ward was sure he was not the aimless drifter he was supposed to be. His face was too keen, his eyes too sharp. If he had baited a trap with money, he had used the only bait to which these men would rise. But what was he hoping to accomplish?

There were no men in Mannerhouse who could draw a gun in the same league with Yount or Lund.

Gelvin would try, if he was there, but Gelvin had only courage, and no particular skill with a handgun, and courage alone was not enough.

It was an hour after daylight when Packer mounted his paint gelding and started for town. Ward watched him go, speculating on what must follow. He had resolved upon his own course of action. His was no elaborate plan. He intended to slip into town and at the right moment kill Jim Yount and, if possible, Red Lund.

The only law in Mannerhouse was old John Binns, a thoroughly good man of some seventy years who had been given the job largely in lieu of a pension. He had been a hardworking man who owned his home and a few acres of ground, and he had a wife only a few years younger.

Mannerhouse had never been on the route of trail drives, land booms, or mining discoveries, and in consequences the town had few disturbances or characters likely to cause them. The jail had been used but once, when the town first came into being, and few citizens could remember the occasion. John Binns's enforcement of the law usually was a quiet suggestion to be a little less noisy or to "go home and sleep it off."

Ward McQueen, a law-abiding man, found himself faced with a situation where right, justice, and the simple rules of civilized society were being pushed aside by men who did not hesitate to kill. One prominent citizen had been murdered, another pistol-whipped. Their stated intention was to do more of the same, to say nothing of Jim Yount's plan to marry Ruth, and his implication had been that it was simply a means to seize her land. Once they had won what they wished there was no reason to believe the violence would cease. Gangrene had infected the area, and the only solution open to Ward McQueen was to amputate.

Yet he was no fool. He knew something of the gun skills of the men he would face. Even if he was killed himself he must eliminate them. The townspeople could take care of such as Hollier and Packer.

If he succeeded, Kim Sartain could handle the rest of it, and would. That was Kim's way.

Mounting the buckskin he started down the trail toward Mannerhouse, only a few miles away. When he had ridden but a few hundred yards he saw from his vantage point above the ranch that three riders were also headed for town. Jim Yount, Ruth, and a few yards behind, Red Lund.

Pete Dodson, riding a sorrel horse, was also headed for town but by another route. Jim Yount was taking no chances.

The dusty main street of Mannerhouse lay warm under the morning sun. On the steps of the Express Office Rip was sunning himself. Abel, behind his bar, watched nervously both his window and his door. He was on edge and aware, aware as a wild animal is when a strange creature nears its lair. Trouble was in the wind.

Gelvin's store was closed, unusual for this time of day. Abel glanced at Rip, and his brow furrowed. Rip was wearing two tied-down guns this morning, unusual for him.

Abel finished polishing the glass and put it down, glancing nervously at Packer. Suddenly Packer downed the drink and got to his feet. Walking to the door he glanced up and down the street. All was quiet, yet the big man was worried. A man left the post office and walked along the boardwalk to the barber shop and entered. The sound of the closing door was the only sound. A hen pecked at somehting in the mouth of the alley near Gelvin's store. As he watched he saw Pete Dodson stop his horse behind Gelvin's. Pete was carrying a rifle. Packer glanced over at Rip, noting the guns.

Packer turned suddenly, glaring at Abel. "Give me that scatter-gun you got under the bar!"

"Huh?" Abel was frightened. "I ain't got—"

"Don't give me that! I want that gun!"

There was an instant when Abel considered covering Packer or even shooting him, but the big man frightened him and he put the shotgun on the bar. Packer picked it up and tiptoed to the window and put the gun down beside it. Careful to make no sound, he eased the window up a few inches. His position now covered Rip's side and back.

Abel cringed at what he had done. He liked Rip. The lean, easygoing, friendly young man might now be killed because of him. He'd been a coward. He should have refused, covered Packer, and called Rip inside. And he could have done that. If he wasn't such a coward. Now, because of him a good man might be murdered, shot in the back. What was going on, anyway? This had been such a quiet little town.

Jim Yount rode up the street with Ruth beside him. Her face was pale and strained, and her eyes seemed unnaturally large. Red Lund trailed a few yards behind. He drew up and tied his horse across the street.

From the saloon Abel could see it all. Jim Yount and Ruth Kermitt were approaching Rip from the west. North and west was Red Lund. Due north and in the shadow of Gelvin's was Pete Dodson. In the saloon was Packer. Rip was very neatly boxed, signed, and sealed. All but delivered.

Jim Keane, Logan's much older brother, was the express agent. He saw Jim Yount come, saw Red Lund across the street.

Rip got up lazily, smiling at Ruth as she came up the steps with Jim Yount.

"Come for your package, Miss Kermitt?" he asked politely. "While you're here would you mind answering some questions."

"By whose authority?" Yount demanded sharply.

Ward McQueen, crouched behind the saloon heard the reply clearly. "The State of Texas, Yount," Rip replied. "I'm a Texas Ranger."

Jim Yount's short laugh held no humor. "This ain't Texas, and she answers no questions."

Ward McQueen opened the back door of the saloon and stepped inside.

Packer, intent on the scene before him, heard the door open. Startled and angry, he whirled around. Ward McQueen, whom he had buried, was standing just inside the door. The shotgun was resting on the windowsill behind Rip. Packer went for his six-gun, but even as he reached he knew it was hopeless. He saw the stab of flame, felt the solid blow of the bullet, and felt his knees turn to butter under him. He pitched forward on his face.

Outside all hell broke loose. Ruth Kermitt, seeing Rip's situation, spurred her horse to bump Yount's, throwing him out of position. Instantly, she slid from the saddle and threw herself to the ground near the edge of the walk.

All seemed to have begun firing at once. Yount, cursing bitterly, fired at Rip. He in turn was firing at Red Lund. Ward stepped suddenly from the saloon and saw himself facing Yount, who had brought his mount under control. He fired at Yount, and a bullet from Dodson's rifle knocked splinters from the post in front of his face.

Yount's gun was coming into line and McQueen fired an instant sooner. Yount fired and they both missed. Ward's second shot hit Yount, who grabbed for the pommel. Ward walked a step forward, but something hit him and he went to his knee. Red Lund loomed from somewhere and Ward got off another shot. Lund's face was covered with blood.

There was firing from the stage station and from Gelvin's store. There was a thunder of hoofs, and a blood-red horse came charging down the street, its rider hung low like an Indian, shooting under the horse's neck.

Yount was down, crawling on his belly in the dust. He had lost hold of his six-shooter, but his right hand held a knife and he was crawling toward Ruth. McQueen's six-shooter clicked on an empty chamber. How many shots were left in his other gun? He lifted it with his left hand. Something was suddenly wrong with his right. He rarely shot with his left hand, but now—

Yount was closer now. Ruth was staring across the street, unaware. McQueen shot past Ruth, squeezing off the shot with his left hand. He saw Yount contract sharply as the bullet struck. McQueen fired again and the gambler rolled over on his side and the knife slipped from his fingers.

Abel ran from the saloon with a shotgun, and Gelvin from his store, with a rifle. Then Ruth was running toward him and he saw Kim Sartain coming back up the street, walking the red horse. He tried to rise to meet Ruth, but his knees gave way and he went over on his face, thinking how weak she must think him. He started to rise again, and blacked out.

When he could see again Ruth was beside him. Kim was squatting on his heels. "Come on, Ward!" he said. "You've only been hit twice and neither of 'em bad. Can't you handle lead any more?"

"What happened?"

"Clean sweep, looks like. Charlie Quayle got to us and we hightailed it to the ranch. Hollier wanted to give us trouble but we smoked him out. I believe there were others around, but if there were they skipped the country.

"Whilst they were cleanin' up around I took it on the run for town. Halfway there I thought I heard a shot and when I hit the street everybody in town was shootin', or that's what it looked like. Reg'lar Fourth of July celebration!

"Pete Dodson is dead, and Red Lund's dying with four bullets in him. Yount's alive, but he won't make it either. Packer's dead."

Ward's head was aching and he felt weak and sick,

but he did not want to move, even to get out of the street. He just wanted to sit, to forget all that had taken place. With fumbling fingers, from long habit, he started to reload his pistols. Oddly, he found one of them contained three live shells. Somehow he must have reloaded, but he had no memory of it.

Rip came over. "My name's Coker, Ward. I couldn't figure any way to bust up Yount's operation without getting Ruth Kermitt away from him first, so I faked that package to get them into town, hoping I could get her away from them. I didn't figure they'd gang up on me like they did."

They helped him up and into the saloon. Gelvin brought the doctor in. "Yount just died," Gelvin said, "cussing you and everybody concerned."

He sat back in a chair while the doctor patched him up. Again he had lost blood. "I've got to find a bed," he said to Kim. "There must be a hotel in town."

"You're coming back to the ranch," Ruth said. "We need you there. They told me you left me, Ward. Jim Yount said you pulled out and Kim with you. I hadn't seen him, and Yount said he'd manage the ranch until I found someone. Then he brought his own men in and fired Kim, whom I hadn't seen, and I was surrounded and scared. If you had been there, or if I'd even known you were around, I—"

"Don't worry about it." Ward leaned his head back. All he wanted was rest.

Baldy Jackson helped him into a buckboard, Bud Fox driving. "You know that old brindle longhorn who turned up missin'? Well, I found him. He's got about thirty head with him, holed up in the prettiest little valley you ever did see. Looks like he's there to stay."

"He's like me," Ward commented, "so used to his range he wouldn't be happy anywhere else."

"Then why think of anywhere else?" Ruth said. "I want you to stay."

THE ONE FOR MOHAVE KID

About a mile or so from camp lay Independence Rock, 120 feet high and over 2,000 feet long according to an estimate.* It is covered with the names of travellers. A few miles further along is Devil's Gate, where the Sweetwater passes through a cleft some 30 yards wide and 300 yards long. The rock walls tower several hundred feet, sheer rock. There was grass for our stock. We camped at a bend of the river just after sundown.

From a diary, August 19, 1849

Twelve years earlier a party of mountain men were camped here: "Immense numbers of buffalo in sight . . . here I am at a beautiful spring, a hot fire of buffalo dung, a set of good, sweet hump-ribs roasting . . . I have forgotten everything but my ribs and my sweetheart."

*Above dimensions not accurate, LL

The One for the Mohave Kid

We had finished our antelope steak and beans, and the coffee pot was back on the stove again, brewing strong, black cowpuncher coffee just like you'd make over a creosote and ironwood fire out on the range.

Red was cleaning his carbine and Doc Lander had tipped back in his chair with a pipe lighted. The stove was cherry red, the woodbox full, and our beds were warming up for the night. It was early autumn, but the nights were already cool. In a holster, hanging from the end of a bunk, was a worn-handled, single-action .44 pistol—and the holster had seen service as well as the gun.

"Whenever," Doc Lander said, "a bad man is born, there is also born a man to take him. For every Billy the Kid there is a Pat Garrett, an' for every Wes Hardin there's a John Selman."

Temple picked up a piece of pinewood and flicking open the stove door, he chucked it in. He followed it with another, and we all sat silent, watching the warm red glow of the flames. When the door was shut again, Red looked up from his rifle. "An' for every John Selman there's a Scarborough," he said, "an' for every Scarborough, a Logan."

"Exactly," Doc Lander agreed, "an' for every Mohave Kid there's a . . ."

Some men are born to evil, and such a one was the Mohave Kid. Now I'm not saying that environment doesn't have its influence, but some men are born with twisted minds, just as some are born with crooked teeth. The

Mohave Kid was born with a streak of viciousness and cruelty that no kindness could eradicate. He had begun to show it when a child, and it developed fast until the Kid had killed his first man.

It was pure, unadulterated murder. No question of fair play, although the Kid was deadly with any kind of a gun. He shot an old Mexican, stole his outfit and three horses which he sold near the border. And the Mohave Kid was fifteen years old when that happened.

By the time he was twenty-two he was wanted in four states and three territories. He had, the records said, killed eleven men. Around the saloons and livery stables they said he had killed twenty-one. Actually, he had killed twenty-nine, for the Kid had killed a few when they didn't know he was in the country, and they had been listed as murders by Indians or travelers. Of the twenty-nine men he had killed, nine of them had been killed with something like an even break.

But the Mohave Kid was as elusive as he was treacherous. And his mother had been a Holdstock. There were nine families of Holdstocks scattered through Texas, New Mexico, and Arizona, and three times that many who were kinfolk. They were a clannish lot, given to protecting their own, even as bad an apple as the Mohave Kid.

At twenty-two, the Kid was five feet seven inches tall and weighed one hundred and seventy pounds. He had a round, flat face, a bland expression, and heavy-lidded eyes. He did not look alert, but his expression belied the truth, for he was always wary, always keyed for trouble.

He killed for money, for horses, in quarrels, or for pure cruelty, and several of his killings were as senseless as they were ruthless. This very fact contributed much to the fear with which he was regarded, for there was no guessing where he might strike next. People avoided looking at him, avoided even the appearance of talking about him when he was around. Usually, they got out of a place when he came into it, but as unobtrusively as possible.

Aside from the United States marshals or the Texas Rangers in their respective bailiwicks, there was only local law. Little attention was given to arresting men for crimes committed elsewhere, which served as excuse for officers of the law who preferred to avoid the risks of trying to arrest the Mohave Kid.

Ab Kale was an exception. Ab was thirty-three when elected marshal of the cow town of Hinkley, and he owned a little spread of his own three miles out of town. He ran a few cows, raised a few horses, and made his living as marshal. For seven years he was a good one. He kept order, never made needless arrests, and was well liked around town. At thirty-four he married Amie Holdstock, a second cousin to the Mohave Kid.

As the Kid's reputation grew, Kale let it be known throughout the family that he would make no exception of the Kid, and the Kid was to stay away from Hinkley. Some of the clan agreed this was fair enough, and the Kid received word to avoid the town. Others took exception to Kale's refusal to abide by clan law where the Kid was concerned, but those few dwindled rapidly as the Kid's murderous propensities became obvious.

The Holdstock clan began to realize that in the case of the Mohave Kid they had sheltered a viper in their bosom, a wanton killer as dangerous to their well-being as to others. A few doors of the clan were closed against him, excuses were found for not giving him shelter, and the feeling began to permeate the clan that the idea was a good one.

The Mohave Kid had seemed to take no exception to the hints that he avoid making trouble for cousin Kale, yet as the months wore on, he became more sullen and morose, and the memory of Ab Kale preyed upon his mind.

In the meantime, no man is marshal of a western cow town without having some trouble. Steady and considerate as Kale was, there had been those with whom he could not reason. He had killed three men.

All were killed in fair, stand-up gunfights, all were shot cleanly and surely, and it was talked around that Kale was some hand with a gun himself. In each case he had allowed an even break and proved faster than the men he killed. All of this the Mohave Kid absorbed, and here and there he heard speculation, never in front of him, that the

Mohave Kid was avoiding Hinkley because he wanted no part of Ab Kale.

Tall, well built, and prematurely gray, Kale was a fine-appearing man. His home was small but comfortable, and he had two daughters, one his own child, one a stepdaughter of seventeen whom he loved as his own. He had no son, and this was a matter of regret.

Ab Kale was forty when he had his showdown with the Mohave Kid. But on the day when Riley McClean dropped off a freight train on the edge of Hinkley, the date of that showdown was still two years away.

If McClean ever told Kale what had happened to him before he crawled out of that empty boxcar in Hinkley, Ab never repeated it. Riley was nineteen, six feet tall, and lean as a rail. His clothes were in bad shape, and he was unshaven and badly used up, and somebody had given him a beating. What had happened to the other fellow or fellows, nobody ever knew.

Ab Kale saw McClean leave the train and called out to him. The boy stopped and stood waiting. As Kale walked toward him he saw the lines of hunger in the boy's face, saw the emaciated body, the ragged clothes, the bruises and cuts. He saw a boy who had been roughly used, but there was still courage in his eyes.

"Where you headed for, son?"

Riley McClean shrugged. "This is as good a place as any. I'm hunting a job."

"What do you do?"

"Most anything. It don't make no difference."

Now when a man says that he can do most anything, it is a safe bet he can do nothing, or at least, that he can do nothing well. If a man has a trade, he is proud of it and says so, and usually he will do a passing job of anything, else he tackles. Yet Kale reserved his opinion. And it was well that he did.

"Better come over to my office," Kale said. "You'll need to get shaved and washed up."

McClean went along, and somehow, he stayed. Nothing was ever said about leaving by either of them. McClean cleaned up, ate at the marshal's expense, and then slept the clock around. When Kale returned to the office and jail the next morning he found the place swept, mopped, and dusted, and McClean was sitting on the cot in the open cell where he slept, repairing a broken riata.

Obviously new to the West, Riley McClean seemed new to nothing else. He had slim, graceful hands and deft fingers. He cobbled shoes, repaired harnesses, built a chimney for Chalfant's new house, and generally kept busy.

After he had been two weeks in Hinkley, Ab Kale was sitting at his desk one day when Riley McClean entered. Kale opened a drawer and took out a pair of beautifully matched .44 Russians, one of the finest guns Smith & Wesson ever made. They were thrust in new holsters on a new belt studded with cartridges. "If you're going to live out here, you'd better learn to use those," Kale said briefly.

After that the two rode out of town every morning for weeks, and in a narrow canyon on the back of Kale's little ranch, Riley McClean learned how to use a six-shooter.

"Just stand naturally," Kale advised him, "and let your hand swing naturally to the gun butt. You've probably heard about a so-called gunman's crouch. There is no such thing among gunfighters who know their business. Stand any way that is easy to you. Crouching may make a smaller target of you, but it also puts a man off balance and cramps his movements. Balance is as important to a gunfighter as to a boxer. Stand easy on your feet, let your hand swing back naturally, and take the hammer spur with the inside of the thumb, cocking the gun as it is grasped, the tip of the trigger finger on the trigger."

Kale watched McClean try it. "The most important thing is a good grip. The finger on the trigger helps to align your gun properly, and after you've practiced, you'll see that your gun will line up perfectly with that grip."

He watched McClean keenly and was pleased. The boy had the same ease with a gun he seemed to have with all tools, and his coordination was natural and easy. "You'll find," he added, "in shooting from the hip that you can change your point of aim by a slight movement of your left foot. Practice until you find just the right position for your feet, and then go through the motions until it is second nature."

Finally, he left him alone to practice, tossing him a box of shells occasionally. But no day passed that Riley McClean did not take to the hills for practice.

There are men who are born to skill, whose coordination of hand, foot, and eye is natural and easy, who acquire skills almost as soon as they lift a tool or a weapon and such a man was Riley McClean. Yet he knew the value of persistence, and he practiced consistently.

It was natural that he knew about the Mohave Kid. Riley McClean listened and learned. He talked around and made friends, and he soon began to hear the speculations about the Kid and Ab Kale.

"It'll come," they all said. "It can't miss. Sooner or later him an' Kale will tangle."

As to what would happen then, there was much dispute. Of this talk Kale said nothing. When Riley McClean had been two months in Hinkley, Kale invited him home to dinner for the first time. It was an occasion to be remembered.

The two months had made a change in Riley. The marks of his beating had soon left him, but it had taken these weeks to fill out his frame. He had gained fifteen solid pounds and would gain more, but he was a rugged young man, bronzed and straight, when he walked up the gravel path to the door of the Kale home. And Ruth Kale opened the door for him. She opened the door and she fell in love. And the feeling was mutual.

Ab Kale said nothing, but he smiled behind his white mustache. Later, when they had walked back up to town Kale said, "Riley, you've been like a son to me. If anything should happen to me, I wish you would see that my family gets along all right."

Riley was startled and worried. "Nothing will happen to you," he protested. "You're a young man yet."

"No," Kale replied seriously, "I'm not. I'm an old man as a cow-town peace officer. I've lasted a long time. Longer than most."

"But you're chain lightning with a gun!" Riley protested.

"I'm fast." Kale said it simply. "And I shoot straight. I now of no man I'd be afraid to meet face to face, although know some who are faster than I. But they don't always neet you face to face."

And Riley McClean knew that Ab Kale was thinking f the Mohave Kid.

He realized then, for the first time, that the marshal vas worried about the Mohave Kid. Worried because he new the kind of killer the Kid was. Deadly enough face o face, the Kid would be just as likely to shoot from mbush. For the Kid was a killing machine, utterly devoid f moral sense or fair play.

The people of Hinkley knew that Riley McClean had aken to carrying a gun. They looked upon this tolerantly, elieving that Riley was merely copying his adopted fa- her. They knew that Kale had been teaching him to shoot, ut they had no idea what had happened during those essons. Nor had Ab Kale realized it until a few days before he payoff.

The two were riding out to look over some cattle, and Kale remarked that it would be nice to have some rabbit tew. "If we see a fat cottontail," he said, "we'll kill it."

A mile further along, he spotted one. "Rabbit!" he aid, and grabbed for his gun.

His hand slapped the walnut butt, and then there was n explosion, and for an instant he thought his own gun ad gone off accidentally. And then he saw the smoking 44 in Riley McClean's hand, and the younger man was iding over to pick up the rabbit. The distance had been hirty yards and the rabbit had lost a head.

Ab Kale was startled. He said nothing, however, and hey rode on to the ranch, looked over the cattle, and nade a deal to buy them. As they started back, Kale ommented. "That was a nice shot, Riley. Could you do it gain?"

"Yes, sir, I think so."

A few miles farther, another rabbit sprang up. The 44 barked and the rabbit died, half his head and one ear lasted away. The distance was a shade greater than before.

"You've nothing to worry about, Riley," he said

quietly, "but never use that gun unless you must, and never draw it unless you mean to kill."

Nothing more was said, but Ab Kale remembered He was fast. He knew he was fast. He knew that he rated along with the best, and yet his hand had barely slapped the butt before that rabbit died. . . .

The days went by slowly, and Riley McClean spent more and more time at the Kale home. And around town he made friends. He was quiet, friendly, and had a healthy sense of humor. He had progressed from the town handy man to opening a shop as a gunsmith, learning his trade by applying it that way. There was no other gunsmith within two hundred miles in any direction, so business was good.

He was working on the firing pin of a Walker Colt when he heard the door open. He did not look up, just said, "Be with you in a minute. What's your trouble?"

"Same thing you're workin' on I reckon. Busted firin' pin."

Riley McClean looked up into a dark, flat face and flat, black eyes. He thought he had never seen eyes so devoid of expression, never seen a face more brutal on a young man. With a shock of realization he knew he was looking into the eyes of the Mohave Kid.

He got to his feet and picked up the gun the Kid handed him. As he picked it up, he noticed that the Kid had his hand on his other gun. Riley merely glanced at him and then examined the weapon. The repair job was simple, but as he turned the gun in his hand, he thought of how many men it had killed.

"Take a while," he said. "I s'pose you're in a hurry for it?"

"You guessed it. An' be sure it's done right. I'll want to try it before I pay for it."

Riley McClean's eyes chilled a little. There were butterflies in his stomach, but the hackles on the back of his neck were rising. "You'll pay me before you get it," he said quietly. "My work is cash on the barrelhead. The job will be done right." His eyes met the flat black ones. "If you don't like the job, you can bring it back."

For an instant, their eyes held, and then the Kid
rugged, smiling a little. "Fair enough. An' if it doesn't
ork, I'll be back."

The Mohave Kid turned and walked out to the street,
opping to look both ways. Riley McClean held the gun
his hands and watched him. He felt cold, chilled.

Ab Kale had told the Kid to stay away from Hinkley,
d now he must meet him and order him from town. He
ust do that, or the Kid would know he was afraid, would
eliberately stay in town. The very fact that the Mohave
id had come to Hinkley was proof that he had come
anting trouble, that he had come to call Kale's bluff.

For a minute or two, Riley considered warning the
arshal, but that would not help. Kale would hear of it
on enough, and there was always a chance that the Kid
ould get his gun, change his mind, and leave before Kale
d know.

Sitting down, Riley went to work on the gun. The
otion of doctoring the gun so it would not fire properly
ossed his mind, but there was no use inviting trouble.
unning his fingers through his dark rusty hair, he went
work. And as he worked, an idea came to him.

Maybe he could get the Kid out of town to try the
n, and once there, warn him away from Hinkley him-
lf. That would mean a fight, and while he had no idea of
eing as good as the Kid, he did know he could shoot
raight. He might kill the Mohave Kid even if he got
lled in the process.

But he did not want to die. He was no hero, Riley
cClean told himself. He wanted to live, buy a place of
s own, and marry Ruth. In fact, they had talked about it.
nd there was a chance this would all blow over. The Kid
ight leave town before Ab Kale heard of his arrival, or
mething might happen. It is human to hope and human
 wish for the unexpected good break—and sometimes
ou are lucky.

As Riley was finishing work on the gun, Ruth came
. She was frightened. "Riley," she caught his arm, "the
ohave Kid's in town and Dad is looking for him."

"I know." He stared anxiously out the window. "The
id left his gun to be repaired. I've just finished it."

"Oh, Riley! Isn't there something we can do? H
face was white and strained, her eyes large.

He looked down at her, a wave of tenderness sweepi
over him. "I don't know, honey," he said gently. "I
afraid the thing I might do, your father wouldn't like. Y
see, this is his job. If he doesn't meet the Kid and ord
him to leave, he will never have the same prestige he
again. Everybody knows the Kid came here on purpose

Ab Kale had heard that the Mohave Kid was in tow
and in his own mind he was ready. Seated at his desk
saw with bitter clarity what he had known all along, th
sooner or later the Kid would come to town, and then
would have to kill him or leave the country. There cou
be no other choice where the Kid was concerned.

Yet he had planned well. Riley McClean was a go
man, a steady man. He would make a good husband
Ruth, and together they would see that Amie lacked f
nothing. As far as that went, Amie was well provided f
He checked his guns and got to his feet. As he did so,
saw a rider go by, racing out of town.

He stopped dead still in the doorway. Why, that rid
had been Riley McClean! Where would he be going
that speed, at this hour? Or had he heard the Kid was
town . . . ? Oh, no! The boy wasn't a coward. Ab knew
wasn't a coward.

He straightened his hat and touched his premature
white mustache. His eyes studied the street. A few loafe
in front of the livery stable, a couple more at the gene
store, a half-dozen horses at the hitch rails. One buc
board. He stepped out on the walk and started slowly
the street. The Mohave Kid would be in the Trail Drive
Saloon.

He walked slowly, with his usual measured step. O
of the loafers in front of the store got to his feet an
ducked into the saloon. All right, then. The Kid knew
was coming. If he came out in the street to meet him,
much the better.

Ruth came suddenly from Riley's shop and starte
toward him. He frowned and glanced at her. No sign
the Kid yet. He must get her off the street at once.

"Hello, Dad!" Her face was strained, but she smiled ~~ightly. "What's the hurry?"

"Don't stop me now, Ruth," he said. "I've got busi~~ss up the street."

"Nothing that won't wait!" she protested. "Come in ~~e store. I want to ask you about something."

"Not now, Ruth." There was still no sign of the Kid. ~~Not now."

"Oh, come on! If you don't," she warned, "I'll walk ~~ght up to the saloon with you."

He looked down at her, sudden panic within him. ~~though she was not his own daughter, he had always felt ~~at she was. "No!" he said sharply. "You mustn't!"

"Then come with me!" she insisted, grabbing his arm.

Still no sign of the Kid. Well, it would do no harm to ~~ait, and he could at least get Ruth out of harm's way. He ~~rned aside and went into the store with her. She had a ~~w bridle she wanted him to see, and she wanted to ~~ow if he thought the bit was right for her mare. Delib-~~ately, she stalled. Once he looked up, thinking he heard ~~lers. Then he replied to her questions. Finally, he got ~~ay.

He stepped out into the sunlight, smelling dust in the ~~r. Then he walked slowly across and up the street. As ~~ reached the center of the street, the Mohave Kid came ~~t of the Trail Driver and stepped off the walk, facing ~~m.

Thirty yards separated them. Ab Kale waited, his ~~en blue eyes steady and cold. He must make this defi-~~te, and if the Kid made the slightest move toward a gun, ~~ must kill him. The sun was very warm.

"Kid," he said, "your business in town is finished. We ~~n't want you here. Because of the family connection, I ~~t you know that you weren't welcome. I wanted to avoid ~~ showdown. Now I see you won't accept that, so I'm ~~ving you exactly one hour to leave town. If you are here ~~ter that hour, or if you ever come again, I'll kill you!"

The Mohave Kid started to speak, and then he stopped, ~~zen by a sudden movement.

From behind stores, from doorways, from alleys, ~~epped a dozen men. All held shotguns or rifles, all directed

at the Kid. He stared at them in shocked disbelief. John
Holdstock . . . Alec and Dave Holdstock . . . Jim Gra
their cousin . . . Webb Dixon, a brother-in-law . . . a
Myron Holdstock, the old bull of the herd.

Ab Kale was petrified. Then he remembered Riley
that racing horse and that today was old Myron's fortie
wedding anniversary, with half the family at the party.

The Mohave Kid stared at them, his face turning gr
and then dark with sullen fury.

"You do like the marshal says, Kid." Old Myr
Holdstock's voice rang in the streets. "We've protected
because you're one of our'n. But you don't start troub
with another or our'n. You git on your hoss an' git. Do
you ever show hide nor hair around here again."

The Mohave Kid's face was a mask of fury. He turn
deliberately and walked to his horse. No man could fa
all those guns, and being of Holdstock blood, he kne
what would come if he tried to face them down. Th
would kill him.

He swung into the saddle, cast one black, bleak lo
at Ab Kale, and then rode out of town.

Slowly, Kale turned to Holdstock, who had be
standing in the door of his shop. "You needn't have do
that," he said, "but I'm glad you did. . . ."

Three days went by slowly, and then the rains brok
It began to pour shortly before daybreak and continued
pour. The washes were running bank full by noon, and t
street was deserted. Kale left his office early and steppe
outside, buttoning his slicker. The street was running wi
water, and a stream of rain was cutting a ditch under t
corner of the office. Getting a shovel from the stable, I
began to divert the water.

Up the street at the gun shop, Riley McClean got
his feet and took off the leather apron in which he worke
He was turning toward the door when it darkened su
denly and he looked up to see the bleak, rain-wet face
the Mohave Kid.

The Kid stared at him. "I've come for my gun," I
said.

"That'll be two dollars," Riley said coolly.

"That's a lot, ain't it?"

"It's my price to you."

The Kid's flat eyes stared at him, and his shoulder seemed to hunch. Then from the tail of his eye he caught the movement of the marshal as he started to work with the shovel. Quickly, he forked out two dollars and slapped it on the counter. Then he fed five shells into the gun and stepped to the door. He took two quick steps and vanished.

Surprised, Riley started around the counter after him. But as he reached the end of the counter, he heard the Kid yell, "*Ab!*"

Kale, his slicker buttoned over his gun, looked around at the call. Frozen with surprise, he saw the Mohave Kid standing there, gun in hand. The Kid's flat face was grinning with grim triumph. And then the Kid's gun roared, and Ab Kale took a step backward and fell, face down in the mud.

The Mohave Kid laughed, suddenly, sardonically. He dropped his gun into his holster and started for the horse tied across the street.

He had taken but one step when Riley McClean spoke: "*All right, Kid, here it is!*"

The Mohave Kid whirled sharply to see the gunsmith standing in the doorway. The rain whipping against him, Riley McClean looked at the Kid. "Ab was my friend," he said. "I'm going to marry Ruth."

The Kid reached then, and in one awful, endless moment of realization, he knew what Ab Kale had known for these several months, that Riley McClean was a man born to the gun. Even as the Kid's hand slapped leather, he saw Riley's weapon clearing and coming level. The gun steadied, and for that endless instant the Kid stared into the black muzzle. Then his own iron was clear and swinging up, and Riley's gun was stabbing flame.

The bullets, three of them fired rapidly, smashed the Mohave Kid in and around the heart. He took a step back, his own gun roaring and the bullet plowing mud, and then he went to his knees as Riley walked toward him, his gun poised for another shot. As the Kid, died, his brain flared with realization, with knowledge of death, and he fell forward, sprawling on his face in the street. A rivulet, diverted by his body, curved around him, ran briefly red, and then trailed on.

People were gathering, but Riley McClean walked to Ab Kale. As he reached him, the older man stirred slightly. Dropping to his knees, Riley turned him over. The marshal's eyes flickered open. There was a cut from the hairline on the side of his head in front that ran all along his scalp. The shattered end of the shovel handle told the story. Striking the shovel handle, which had been in front of his heart at the moment of impact, the bullet had glanced upward, knocking him out and ripping a furrow in his scalp.

Ab Kale got slowly to his feet and stared up the muddy street where the crowd clustered about the Mohave Kid.

"You killed him?"

"Had to. I thought he'd killed you."

Ab nodded. "You've got a fast hand. I've known it for months. I hope you'll never have to kill another man."

"I won't," Riley said quietly. "I'm not even going to carry a gun after this."

Ab Kale glanced back up the street. "So he's dead at last. I've carried that burden a long time." He looked up, his face still white with shock. "They'll bury him. Let's go home, son. The women will be worried."

And the two men walked down the street side by side, Ab Kale and his son. . . .

THE LION HUNTER
AND THE LADY

Growing up, the boys and girls of the frontier learned to make every shot count. The girls as witness Annie Oakley hunted meat for the table also.

Ira Freeman, in his History Of Montezuma County *(Colorado) says,"Every rider carried a gun, usually a revolver or six-shooter, as it was most often called . . . almost always it was a Colt and nearly everyone wanted a .45.*

". . . Nearly every rider was skilled in the use of these fire-arms. They practiced shooting all their purse would allow, and the aim was to be quick on the draw. Often how quick a man was, was the difference between life and death."

Harry Drachman, commenting on the shooting of Jeff Milton, frontier peace office, tells of him "tossing half-dollars in the air, then drawing his six-shooter and hitting them on the fly."

The Lion Hunter
and the Lady

The mountain lion stared down at him with wild, implacable eyes and snarled deep in its chest. He was big, one of the biggest Morgan had seen in his four years of hunting them. The lion crouched on a thick limb not over eight feet above his head.

"Watch him, Cat!" Lone John Williams warned. "He's the biggest I ever seen! The biggest in these mountains, I'll bet!"

"You ever seen Lop-Ear?" Morgan queried, watching the lion. "He's half again bigger than this one!" He jumped as he spoke, caught a limb in his left hand and then swung himself up as easily as a trapeze performer.

The lion came to its feet then and crouched, growling wickedly, threatening the climbing man. But Morgan continued to mount toward the lion.

"Give me that pole," Morgan called to the older man. "I'll have this baby in another minute."

"You watch it," Williams warned. "That lion ain't foolin'!"

Never in the year he had been working with Cat Morgan had Lone John become accustomed to seeing a man go up a tree after a mountain lion. Yet in that period Morgan had captured more than fifty lions alive and had killed as many more. Morgan was not a big man as big men are counted, but he was tall, lithe, and extraordinarily strong. Agile as a cat, he climbed trees, cliffs, and rocky slopes after the big cats, for which he was named, and had made a good thing out of supplying zoo and circus animal buyers.

With a noose at the end of the pole, and only seven feet below the snarling beast, Morgan lifted the pole with great care. The lion struck viciously and then struck again, and in that instant after the second strike, Morgan put the loop around his neck and drew the noose tight. Instantly the cat became a snarling, clawing, spitting fury, but Morgan swung down from the tree, dragging the beast after him.

Before the yapping dogs could close with him, Lone John tossed his own loop, snaring the lion's hind legs. Morgan closed with the animal, got a loop around the powerful forelegs, and drew it tight. In a matter of seconds the mountain lion was neatly trussed and muzzled, with a stick thrust into its jaws between its teeth, and its jaws tied shut with rawhide.

Morgan drew a heavy sack around the animal and then tied it at the neck, leaving the lion's head outside.

Straightening, Cat Morgan took out the makin's and began to roll a smoke. "Well," he said, as he put the cigarette between his lips, "that's one more and one less."

Hard-ridden horses sounded in the woods and then a half dozen riders burst from the woods and a yell rent the air. "Got 'em, Dave! Don't move, you!" The guns the men held backed up their argument, and Cat Morgan relaxed slowly, his eyes straying from one face to another, finally settling on the big man who rode last from out of the trees.

This man was not tall, but blocky and powerful. His neck was thick and his jaw wide. He was clean-shaven, unusual in this land of beards and mustaches. His face wore a smile of unconcealed satisfaction now, and swinging down he strode toward them. "So, you finally got caught, didn't you? Now how smart do you feel?"

"Who do you think we are?" Morgan asked cooly. "I never saw you before!"

"I reckon not, but we trailed you right here. You've stole your last horse! Shake out a loop, boys! We'll string 'em up right here."

"Be careful with that talk," Lone John said. "We ain't horse thieves an' ain't been out of the hills in more'n a year. You've got the wrong men."

"That's tough," the big man said harshly, "because you hang, here and now."

"Maybe they ain't the men, Dorfman. After all, we lost the trail back yonder a couple of miles." The speaker was a slender man with black eyes and swarthy face.

Without turning Dorfman said sharply, "Shut up! When I want advice from a breed, I'll ask it!"

His hard eyes spotted the burlap sack. The back of it lay toward him, and the lion's head was faced away from him. All he saw was the lump of the filled sack. "What's this? Grub?" He kicked hard at the sack, and from it came a snarl of fury.

Dorfman jumped and staggered back, his face white with shock. Somebody laughed, and Dorfman wheeled, glaring around for the offender. An old man with gray hair and a keen, hard face looked at Morgan. "What's in that sack?" he demanded.

"A mountain lion," Cat replied calmly. "A nice, big, live lion. Make a good pet for your loudmouthed friend." He paused and then smiled tolerantly at Dorfman. "If he wouldn't be scared of him!"

Dorfman's face was livid. Furious that he had been frightened before these men, and enraged at Morgan as the cause of it, he sprang at Morgan and swung back a huge fist. Instantly, Cat Morgan stepped inside the punch, catching it on an upraised forearm. At the same instant he whipped a wicked right uppercut to Dorfman's wind. The big man gasped and paled. He looked up, and Morgan stepped in and hooked hard to the body and then the chin. Dorfman hit the ground in a lump.

Showing no sign of exertion, Morgan stepped back. He looked at the older man. "He asked for it," he said calmly. "I didn't mind, though." He glanced at Dorfman, who was regaining his breath and his senses and then his eyes swung back to the older man. "I'm Cat Morgan, a lion hunter. This is Lone John Williams, my partner. What Lone John said was true. We haven't been out of the hills in a year."

"He's telling' the truth." It was the half-breed. The man was standing beside the tree. "His hounds are tied right back here, an' from the look of this tree they just caught that cat. The wood is still wet where the bark was skimmed from the tree by his boots."

"All right, Loop." The older man's eyes came back to Morgan. "Sorry. Reckon we went off half-cocked. I've heard of you."

A wiry, yellow-haired cowhand leaned on his pommel. "You go up a tree for the cats?" he asked incredulously. "I wouldn't do it for a thousand dollars!"

Dorfman was on his feet. His lips were split and there was a cut on his cheekbone. One eye was rapidly swelling. He glared at Morgan. "I'll kill you for this!" he snarled.

Morgan looked at him. "I reckon you'll try," he said. "There ain't much man in you, just brute and beef."

The older man spoke up quickly. "Let's go, Dorf! This ain't catchin' our thief!"

As the cavalcade straggled from the clearing, the man called Loop loitered behind. "Watch yourself, Morgan," he said quietly. "He's bad, that Dorfman. He'll never rest until he kills you, now. He won't take it lyin' down."

"Thanks." Cat's gray-green eyes studied the half-breed. "What was stolen?"

Loop jerked his head. "Some of Dorfman's horses. Blooded stock, stallion, three mares, and four colts."

Morgan watched them go and then walked back down the trail for the pack animals. When they had the cat loaded, Lone John left him to take it back to camp.

Mounting his own zebra dun, Morgan now headed downcountry to prospect a new canyon for cat sign. He had promised a dealer six lions and he had four of them. With luck he could get the other two this week. Only one of the hounds was with him, a big, ugly brute that was one of the two best lion dogs he had, just a mongrel. Big Jeb was shrewd beyond average. He weighed one hundred and twenty pounds and was tawny as the lions he chased.

The plateau was pine clad, a thick growth that spilled over into the deep canyon beyond, and that canyon was a wicked jumble of wrecked ledges and broken rock. At the bottom he could hear the roar and tumble of a plunging mountain stream, although he had never seen it. That canyon should be home for a lot of lions.

There was no trail. The three of them, man, dog, and horse, sought a trail down, working their way along the rim over a thick cover of pine needles. At last Cat Morgan saw the slope fall away steeply, but at such a grade that he could walk the horse to the bottom. Slipping occasionally on the needles, they headed down.

Twice Jeb started to whine as he picked up old lion smell, but each time he was dissuaded by Cat's sharp-spoken command.

There was plenty of sign. In such a canyon as this it should take him no time at all to get his cats. He was walking his horse and rolling a smoke when he heard the sound of an ax.

It brought him up standing.

It was impossible! There could be nobody in this wild area, nobody! Not in all the days they had worked the region had they seen more than one or two men until they encountered the horse-thief hunters.

Carefully, he went on, calling Jeb close to the horse and moving on with infinite care. Whoever was in this wilderness would be somebody he would want to see before he was seen. He remembered the horse thieves whose trail had been lost. Who else could it be?

Instantly, he saw evidence of the correctness of his guess. In the dust at the mouth of the canyon were tracks of a small herd of horses!

Grimly, he eased his Colt in the holster. Horse thieves were a common enemy, and although he had no liking for Dorfman, this was his job, too.

Taller than most, Cat Morgan was slender of waist. Today he wore boots, but usually moccasins. His red flannel shirt was sun faded and patched, his black jeans were saddle polished and his face was brown from sun and wind, hollow cheeked under the keen gray-green eyes. His old hat was black and flat crowned. It showed rough usage.

Certainly, the thief had chosen well. Nobody would

ever find him back in here. The horses had turned off to
the right. Following, Cat went down, through more tum-
bled rock and boulders and then drew up on the edge of a
clearing.

It was after sundown here. The shadows were long,
but near the far wall was the black oblong of a cabin, and
light streamed through a window and the wide-open door.

Dishes rattled, the sound of a spoon scraping something from a dish, and he heard a voice singing. A woman's voice!

Amazed, he started walking his horse nearer, yet the
horse had taken no more than a step when he heard a
shrill scream, a cry odd and inhuman, a cry that brought
him up short. At the same instant, the light in the house
went out and all was silent. Softly, he spoke to his horse
and walked on toward the house.

He heard the click of a back drawn hammer, and a
cool, girl's voice said, "Stand right where you are, mister!
And if you want to get a bullet through your belt buckle,
just start something!"

"I'm not moving," Morgan said impatiently. "But this
isn't a nice way to greet visitors!"

"Who invited you?" she retorted. "What do you want,
anyway? Who are you?"

"Cat Morgan. I'm a lion hunter. As for bein' invited,
I've been a lot of places without bein' invited. Let me talk
to your dad or your husband."

"You'll talk to me. Lead your horse and start walkin'
straight ahead. My eyes are mighty good, so if you want to
get shot, just try me."

With extreme care, Morgan walked on toward the
house. When he was within a dozen paces a shrill but
harsh voice cried, "Stand where you are! Drop your guns!"

Impatiently, Morgan replied, "I'll stand where I am,
but I won't drop my guns. Light up and let's see who you
are!"

Someone moved, and later there was a light. Then
the girl spoke. "Come in, you!"

She held a double-barreled shotgun and she was well
back inside the door. A tall, slender but well-shaped girl,

she had rusty-red hair and a few scattered freckles. She wore a buckskin shirt that failed to conceal the lines of her lovely figure.

Her inspection of him was cool, careful. Then she looked at the big dog that had come in and stood alongside him. "Lion hunter? You the one who has that pack of hounds I hear nearby every day?"

He nodded. "I've been runnin' lions up on the plateau. Catchin' 'em, too."

She stared. "*Catching* them? *Alive?* Sounds to me like you have more nerve than sense. What do you want live lions for?"

"Sell 'em to some circus or zoo. They bring anywhere from three to seven hundred dollars, dependin' on size and sex. That beats punchin' cows."

She nodded. "It sure does, but I reckon punchin' cows is a lot safer."

"How about you?" he said. "What's a girl doin' up in a place like this? I didn't have any idea there was anybody back in here."

"Nor has anybody else up to now. You ain't to tell, are you? If you go out of here an' tell, I'll be in trouble. Dorfman would be down here after me in a minute."

"For stealin' horses?" Morgan asked shrewdly.

Her eyes flashed. "They are not his horses! They are mine! Every last one of them!" She lowered the gun a trifle. "Dorfman is both a bully and a thief! He stole my dad's ranch, then his horses. That stallion is mine, and so are the mares and their get!"

"Tell me about it," he suggested. Carefully, he removed his hat.

She studied him doubtfully and then lowered the gun. "I was just putting supper on. Draw up a chair."

"Let's eat!" a sharp voice yelled. Startled, Cat looked around and for the first time saw the parrot in the cage.

"That's Pancho," she explained. "He's a lot of company."

Her father had been a trader among the Nez Perce Indians, and from them he obtained the splended Appaloosa stallion and the mares from which his herd was started. When Karl Dorfman appeared, there had been trouble. Later, while she was east on a trip, her father had been killed by a fall from a horse. Returning, she found the ranch sold and the horses gone.

"They told me the stallion had thrown him. I knew better. It had been Dorfman and his partner, Ad Vetter, who found Dad. And then they brought bills against the estate and forced a quick sale of all property to satisfy them. The judge worked with them. Shortly after, the judge left and bought a ranch of his own. Dad never owed money to anyone. I believe they murdered him."

"That would be hard to prove. Did you have any evidence?"

"Only what the doctor said. He told me the blows could not have been made by the fall. He believed Dad had been struck while lying on the ground."

Cat Morgan believed her. Whether his own dislike of Dorfman influenced it, he did not know. Somehow the story rang true. He studied the problem thoughtfully.

"Did you get anything from the ranch?"

"Five hundred dollars and a ticket back east." Anger flashed in her eyes as she leaned toward him to refill his cup. "Mr. Morgan, that ranch was worth at least forty thousand dollars. Dad had been offered that much and refused it."

"So you followed them?"

"Yes. I appeared to accept the situation, but discovered where Dorfman had gone and followed him, determined to get the horses back, at least."

It was easier, he discovered two hours later, to ride to the secret valley than to escape from it. After several false starts, he succeeded in finding the spot where the lion had been captured that day, and then hit the trail for camp. As he rode, the memory of Dorfman kept returning—a brutal, hard man, accustomed to doing as he chose. They had not seen the last of him, they knew.

Coming into the trees near the camp, Cat Morgan grew increasingly worried, for he smelled no smoke and saw no fire. Speaking to the horse, he rode into the basin and drew up sharply. Before him, suspended from a tree, was a long black burden!

Clapping the spurs to the horse he crossed the clearing and grabbed the hanging figure. Grabbing his hunting knife, he slashed the rope that hung him from the tree and then lowered the old man to the ground. Loosening his clothes, he held his hand over the old man's heart. Lone John was *alive*!

Swiftly, Morgan built a fire and got water. The old man had not only been hanged, but had been shot twice through the body and once through the hand. But he was still alive.

The old man's lids fluttered, and he whispered, "Dorfman. Five of 'em! Hung me—heard somethin'—they done—took off." He breathed hoarsely for a bit. "Figured it—it was you—reckon."

"*Shhh*! Take it easy now, John. You'll be all right."

"No. I'm done for. That rope—I grabbed it—held my weight till I plumb give out."

The wiry old hand gripping his own suddenly eased its grip, and the old man was dead.

Grimly, Cat got to his feet. Carefully, he packed what gear had not been destroyed. The cats had been tied off a few yards from the camp and had not been found. He scattered meat to them, put water within their reach, and returned to his horse. A moment only, he hesitated. His eyes wide open to what lay ahead, he lifted the old man across the saddle of a horse and then mounted his own. The trail he took led to Seven Pines.

It was the gray hour before the dawn when he rode into the town. Up the street was the sheriff's office. He knocked a long time before there was a reply. Then a hard-faced man with blue and cold eyes opened the door. "What's the matter? What's up?"

"My partner's been murdered. Shot down, then hung."

"*Hung?*" The sheriff stared at him, no friendly light in his eyes. "Who hung him?"

"Dorfman. There were five in the outfit."

The sheriff's face altered perceptibly at the name. He walked out and untied the old man's body, lowering it to the stoop before the office. He scowled. "I reckon," he said dryly, "if Dorfman done it he had good reason. You better light out if you want to stay in one piece."

Unbelieving, Morgan stared at him. "You're the sheriff?" he demanded. "I'm chargin' Dorfman with murder. I want him arrested."

"*You* want?" The sheriff glared. "Who the devil are you? If Dorfman hung this man he had good reason. He's lost horses. I reckon he figured this hombre was one of the thieves. Now you slope it afore I lock you up."

Cat Morgan drew back three steps, his eyes on the sheriff. "I see. Lock me up, eh? Sheriff, you'd have a mighty hard job lockin' me up. What did you say your name was?"

"Vetter, if it makes any difference."

"Vetter, eh? Ad Vetter?" Morgan was watching the sheriff like a cat.

Sheriff Vetter looked at him sharply. "Yes, Ad Vetter. What about it?"

Cat Morgan took another step back toward his horses, his eyes cold now. "Ad Vetter—a familiar name in the Nez Perce country."

Vetter started as if struck. "What do you mean by that?"

Morgan smiled. "Don't you know," he said, chancing a long shot, "that you and Dorfman are wanted up there for murderin' old man Madison?"

"You're a liar!" Sheriff Vetter's face was white as death. He drew back suddenly, and Morgan could almost see the thought in the man's mind and knew that his accusation had marked him for death. "If Dorfman finds you here, he'll hang you, too."

Cat Morgan backed away slowly, watching Vetter. The town was coming awake now, and he wracked his brain for a solution to the problem. Obviously, Dorfman was a man with influence here, and Ad Vetter was sheriff. Whatever Morgan did or claimed was sure to put him in the wrong. And then he remembered the half-breed, Loop, and the older man who had cautioned Dorfman the previous afternoon.

A man was sweeping the steps before the saloon, and Morgan stopped beside him. "Know a man named Loop? A breed?"

"Sure do." The sweeper straightened and measured Morgan. "Huntin' him?"

"Yeah, and another hombre. Older feller, gray hair, pleasant face but frosty eyes. The kind that could be mighty bad if pushed too hard. I think I heard him called Dave."

"That'll be Allen. Dave Allen. He owns the D over A, west of town. Loop lives right on the edge of town in a shack. He can show you where Dave lives."

Turning abruptly, Morgan swung into the saddle and started out of town. As he rounded the curve toward the bridge, he glanced back. Sheriff Vetter was talking to the sweeper. Cat reflected grimly that it would do him but little good, for unless he had talked with Dorfman the previous night, and he did not seem to have, he would not understand Morgan's reason for visiting the old rancher. And Cat knew that he might be wasting his time.

He recognized Loop's shack by the horse in the corral and drew up before it. The breed appeared in the door, wiping an ear with a towel. He was surprised when he saw Cat Morgan, but he listened as Morgan told him quickly about the hanging of Lone John Williams and Vetter's remarks.

"No need to ride after Allen," Loop said. "He's comin' down the road now. Him and Tex Norris. They was due in town this mornin'."

At Loop's hail, the two riders turned abruptly toward the cabin. Dave Allen listened in silence while Cat repeated his story, only now he told all, not that he had seen the girl or knew where she was, but that he had learned why the horses were stolen, and then about the strange death of old man Madison. Dave Allen sat his horse in silence and listened. Tex spat once, but made no other comment until the end. "That's Dorfman, Boss! I never did cotton to him!"

"Wait." Allen's eyes rested thoughtfully on Cat. "Why tell me? What do you want me to do?"

Cat Morgan smiled suddenly, and when Tex saw that smile he found himself pleased that it was Dorfman this man wanted and not him. "Why, Allen, I don't want you to do anythin'! Only, I'm not an outlaw. I don't aim to become one for a no-account like Dorfman, nor another like this here Vetter. You're a big man hereabouts, so I figured to tell you my story and let you see my side of this before the trouble starts."

"You aim to go after him?"

Morgan shook his head. "I'm a stranger here, Allen. He's named me for a horse thief, and the law's against me, too. I aim to let them come to me, right in the middle of town!"

Loop walked back into his cabin, and when he came out he had a Spencer .56, and mounting, he fell in beside Morgan. "You'll get a fair break," he said quietly, his eyes cold and steady. "I aim to see it. No man who wasn't all right would come out like that and state his case. Besides, you know, that old man Williams struck me like a mighty fine old gent."

Dorfman was standing on the steps as they rode up. One eye was barely open, the other swollen. The marks of the beating were upon him. That he had been talking to Vetter was obvious by his manner, although the sheriff was nowhere in sight. Several hard-case cowhands loitered about, the presence creating no puzzle to Cat Morgan.

Karl Dorfman glared at Allen. "You're keepin' strange company, Dave."

The old man's eyes chilled. "You aimin' to tell me who I should travel with, Dorfman? If you are, save your breath. We're goin' to settle more than one thing here today."

"You sidin' with this here horse thief?" Dorfman demanded.

"I'm sidin' nobody. Last night you hanged a man. You're going to produce evidence here today as to why you believed him guilty. If that evidence isn't good, you'll be tried for murder."

Dorfman's face turned ugly. "Why, you old fool! You can't get away with that! Vetter's sheriff, not you! Besides," he sneered, "you've only got one man with you."

"Two," Loop said quietly, "I'm sidin' Allen—and Cat Morgan, too."

Hatred blazed in Dorfman's eyes. "I never seen no good come out of a breed yet!" he flared. "You'll answer for this!"

Dave Allen dismounted, keeping his horse between himself and Dorfman. By that time a good-sized crowd had gathered about. Tex Norris wore his gun well to the front, and he kept his eyes roving from one to the other of Dorfman's riders. Cat Morgan watched but said nothing.

Four men had accompanied Dorfman, but there were others here who appeared to belong to his group. With Allen and himself there were only Tex and Loop, and yet, looking at them he felt suddenly happy. There were no better men than these, Tex with his boyish smile and careful eyes, Loop with his long, serious face. These men would stick. He stepped then into the van, seeing Vetter approach.

Outside their own circle were the townspeople. These, in the last analysis, would be the judges, and now they were saying nothing. Beside him he felt a gentle pressure against his leg, and looking down saw Jeb standing there. The big dog had never left him. Morgan's heart was suddenly warm and his mind was cool and ready.

"Dorfman!" His voice rang in the street. "Last night you hung my ridin' partner! Hung him for a horse thief, without evidence or reason! I charge you with murder!

"The trail you had followed you lost, as Dave Allen and Loop will testify! Then you took it upon yourself to hang an old man simply because he happened to be in the vicinity!"

His voice was loud in the street, and not a person in the crowd but could hear every syllable. Dorfman shifted his feet, his face ugly with anger, yet worried, too. Why didn't Vetter stop him? Arrest him?

"Moreover, the horses you were searching for were stolen by you from Laurie Madison, in Montana! They were taken from the ranch after that ranch had been illegally sold, and after you and Vetter had murdered her father."

"That's a lie!" Dorfman shouted. He was frightened now. There was no telling how far such talk might carry. Once branded, a man would have a lot of explaining to do.

Suppose what Morgan had told Vetter was true? That they were wanted in Montana? Suppose something had been uncovered?

He looked beyond Morgan at Allen, Loop, and Tex. They worried him, for he knew their breed. Dave Allen was an Indian fighter, known and respected. Tex had killed a rustler only a few months ago in a gun battle. Loop was cool, careful, and a dead shot.

"That's a lie," he repeated. "Madison owed me money. I had papers agin' him!"

"Forged papers! We're reopenin' the case, Dorfman, and this time there won't be any fixed judge to side you!"

Dorfman felt trapped. Twice Cat Morgan had refused to draw when he had named him a liar, but Dorfman knew it was simply because he had not yet had his say. Of many things he was uncertain, but of one he was positive. Cat Morgan was not yellow.

Before he spoke again, Sheriff Ad Vetter suddenly walked into sight. "I been investigatin' your claim," he said to Morgan, "and she won't hold water. The evidence shows you strung up the old man yourself."

Cat Morgan shrugged. "Figured somethin' like that from you, Vetter. What evidence?"

"Nobody else been near the place. That story about a gal is all cock and bull. You had some idea of an alibi when you dragged that in here."

"Why would he murder his partner?" Allen asked quietly. "That ain't sense, Ad."

"They got four lions up there. Them lions are worth money. He wanted it all for himself."

Cat Morgan smiled, and slowly lifting his left hand, he tilted his hat slightly. "Vetter," he said, "You got a lot to learn. Lone John was my partner only in the campin' and ridin'. He was workin' for me. I catch my own cats. I got a contract with Lone John. Got my copy here in my pocket. He's goin' to be a hard man to replace because he'd learned how to handle cats. I went up the trees after 'em. Lone John was mighty slick with a rope, and when a lion hit ground he dapped a rope on 'em fast. I liked that old man, Sheriff, and I'm chargin' Dorfman with murder like I said. I want him put in jail—now."

Vetter's face darkened. "You givin' orders now?"

"If you've got any more evidence against Morgan," Allen interrupted, "trot it out. Remember, I rode with Dorfman on that first posse. I know how he felt about this. He was frettin' to hang somebody, and the beatin' he took didn't set well. He figured Lone John's hangin' would scare Morgan out of the country."

Vetter hesitated, glancing almost apologetically at Dorfman. "Come on, Dorf," he said. "We'll clear you. Come along."

An instant only the rancher hesitated, his eyes ugly. His glance went from Allen back to Cat Morgan, and then he turned abruptly. The two men walked away together. Dave Allen looked worried and he turned to Morgan. "You'd better get some evidence, Cat," he said. "No jury would hang him on this, or even hold him for trial."

It was late evening in the cabin and Laurie filled Cat's cup once more. Outside, the chained big cats prowled restlessly, for Morgan had brought them down to the girl's valley to take better care of them, much to the disgust of Pancho, who stared at them from his perch and scolded wickedly.

"What do you think will happen?" Laurie asked. "Will they come to trial?"

"Not they—just Dorfman. Yes, I've got enough now so that I can prove a fair case against him. I've found a man who will testify that he saw him leave town with four riders and head for the hills, and that was after Allen and that crowd had returned. I've checked that rope they used, and it is Dorfman's. He used a hair rope, and most everybody around here uses rawhide riatas. Several folks will swear to that rope."

"Horse thief," Pancho said huskily. "Durned horse thief!"

"Be still, Laurie said, turning on the parrot. "You be still!"

Jeb lifted his heavy head and stared curiously, his head cocked, at the parrot, who looked upon Jeb with almost as much disfavor as the cats.

"These witnesses are all afraid of Dorfman, but if he is brought to trial, they will testify."

Suddenly, Pancho screamed, and Laurie came to her feet, her face pale. From the door there was a dry chuckle. "Don't scream, lady. It's too late for that!" It was Ad Vetter's voice!

Cat Morgan sat very still. His back was toward the door, his eyes on Laurie's face. He was thinking desperately.

"Looks like this is the showdown." That was Dorfman's voice. He stepped through the door and shoved the girl. She stumbled back and sat down hard on her chair. "You little fool! You wouldn't take that ticket and money and let well enough alone! You had to butt into trouble! Now you'll die for it, and so will this lion-huntin' friend of yours."

The night was very still. Jeb lay on the floor, his head flattened on his paws, his eyes watching Dorfman. Neither man had seemed to notice the parrot. "Allen will be askin' why you let Dorfman out," Morgan suggested, keeping his voice calm.

"He don't know it," Vetter said smuggly. "Dorf'll be back in jail afore mornin', and in a few days when you don't show up as a witness against him, he'll be freed. Your witnesses won't talk unless you get Dorf on trial. They are scared. As for Dave Allen, we'll handle him later, and that breed, too."

"Too bad it won't work," Morgan said, yet even as he spoke he thought desperately that this was the end. He didn't have a chance. Nobody knew of this place, and the two of them could be murdered here, buried, and probably it would be years before the valley was found. Yet it was Laurie of whom he was thinking now. It would be nothing so easy as murder for her, not to begin with. And knowing the kind of men Dorfman and Vetter were, he could imagine few things worse for any girl than to be left to their mercy.

He made up his mind then. There was no use waiting. No use at all. They would be killed; the time to act was now. He might get one or both of them before they got him. As it was he was doing nothing, helping none at all.

"You two," he said, "will find yourselves lookin' through cottonwood leaves at the end of a rope!"

"*Horse thief!*" Pancho screamed. "Durned horse thief!"

Both men wheeled, startled by the unexpected voice, and Cat left his chair with a lunge. His big shoulder caught Dorfman in the small of the back and knocked him sprawling against the pile of wood beside the stove. Vetter whirled and fired as he turned, but the shot missed, and Morgan caught him with a glancing swing that knocked him sprawling against the far wall. Cat Morgan went after him with a lunge, just as Dorfman scrambled from the wood pile and grabbed for a gun. He heard a fierce growl and whirled just as Jeb hurtled through the air, big jaws agape.

The gun blasted, but the shot was high and Jeb seized the arm in his huge jaws and then man and dog went rolling over and over on the floor. Vetter threw Morgan off and came to his feet, but Morgan lashed out with a left that knocked him back through the door. Dorfman managed to get away from the dog and sprang through the door just as Ad Vetter came to his feet, grabbing for his gun.

Cat Morgan skidded to a stop, realizing even as his gun flashed up that he was outlined against the lighted door. He felt the gun buck in his hand, heard the thud of Vetter's bullet in the wall beside him, and saw Ad Vetter turn half around and fall on his face. At the same moment a hoarse scream rang out behind the house, and darting around, Morgan saw a dark figure rolling over and over on the ground among the chained lions!

Grabbing a whip, he sprang among them, and in the space of a couple of breaths had driven the lions back. Then he caught Dorfman and dragged him free of the beasts. Apparently blinded by the sudden rush from light into darkness, and mad to escape from Jeb, the rancher had rushed right into the middle of the lions. Laurie bent over Morgan. "Is—is he *dead*?"

"No. Get some water on, fast. He's living, but he's badly bitten and clawed." Picking up the wounded man he carried him into the house and placed him on the bed.

Quickly, he cut away the torn coat and shirt. Dorfman was unconscious but moaning.

"I'd better go for the doctor," he said.

"There's somebody coming now, Cat. Riders."

Catching up his rifle, Morgan turned to the door. Then he saw Dave Allen, Tex, and Loop with a half dozen other riders. One of the men in a dark coat was bending over the body of Ad Vetter.

"The man who needs you is in here," Morgan said. "Dorfman ran into my lions in the dark."

Dave Allen came to the door. "This clears you, Morgan," he said, "and I reckon a full investigation will get this lady back her ranch, or what money's left, anyway. And full title to her horses.

"Loop," he added, "was suspicious. He watched Vetter and saw him slip out with Dorfman and then got us and we followed them. They stumbled onto your trail here, and we came right after, but we laid back to see what they had in mind."

"Thanks." Cat Morgan glanced over at Laurie, and their eyes met. She moved quickly to him. "I reckon, Allen, we'll file a claim on this valley, both of us are sort of attached to it."

'Don't blame you. Nice place to build a home."

"That," Morgan agreed, "is what I've been thinkin'."

And they were tough!

Virgil Earp, ambushed on the streets of Tombstone, was shot in the back with a charge of buckshot, exposing a part of his backbone. A second charge shattered his left arm. Virgil crossed the street to the Oriental Saloon to inform his brother Wyatt of what had happened, then went to his room in the Cosmopolitan Hotel where he was attended by Drs. Matthews and Goodfellow.

The condition of his arm was immediately obvious but the wound in his back was not discovered until his shirt had been removed. Dr. Goodfellow removed considerable buckshot from the elbow as well as several inches of bone. Virgil assured his wife he still had one good arm with which to hug her.

The details are recounted in the diaries of George Parsons, as well as in the columns of the Tombstone Epitaph.

A Gun for Kilkenny

Nobody had ever said that Montana Croft was an honest man. To those who knew him best he was a gunman of considerable skill, a horse and cow thief of first rank, and an outlaw who missed greatness simply because he was lazy.

Montana Croft was a tall, young, and not unhandsome man. Although he had killed four men in gun battles, and at least one of them a known and dangerous gunman, he was no fool. Others might overrate his ability, but Montana's judgment was unaffected.

He had seen John Wesley Hardin, Clay Allison, and Wyatt Earp in action. This was sufficient to indicate to him that he rated a very poor hand indeed. Naturally, Montana Croft kept this fact to himself. Yet he knew a good thing when he saw it, and the good thing began with the killing of Johnny Wilder.

Now Wilder himself was regarded as a handy youngster with a gun. He had killed a few men and had acquired the reputation of being dangerous. At nineteen he was beginning to sneer at Billy the Kid and to speak with a patronizing manner of Hardin. And then the stranger on the black horse rode into town, and Johnny took in too much territory.

Not that Johnny was slow—in fact, his gun was out and his first shot in the air before Croft's gun cleared leather. But Johnny was young, inexperienced, and impatient. He missed his first shot and his second. Montana Croft fired coolly and with care—and he fired only once.

Spectators closed in, looking down upon the remains. The bullet had clipped the corner of Johnny Wilder's breast pocket, and Johnny was very, very dead.

Even then, it might have ended there but for Fats Runyon. Fats, who was inclined to view with alarm and accept with enthusiasm, looked up and said, "Only one man shoots like that! Only one, I tell you! *That's Kilkenny!*"

The words were magic, and all eyes turned toward Croft. And Montana, who might have disclaimed the name, did nothing of the kind. Suddenly he was basking in greater fame than he had ever known. He was Kilkenny, the mysterious gunfighter whose reputation was a campfire story wherever men gathered. He could have disclaimed the name, but he merely smiled and walked into the saloon.

Fats followed him, reassured by Croft's acceptance of the name. "Knowed you right off, Mr. Kilkenny! Only one man shoots like that! And then that there black hat, them black chaps—it couldn't be nobody else. Sam, set up a drink for Kilkenny!"

Other drinks followed . . . and the restaurant refused to accept his money. Girls looked at him with wide, admiring eyes. Montana Croft submitted gracefully, and instead of riding on through Boquilla, he remained.

In this alone he broke tradition, for it was Kilkenny's reputation that when he killed, he immediately left the country, which was the reason for his being unknown. Montana Croft found himself enjoying free meals, free drinks, and no bill at the livery stable, so he stayed on. If anyone noticed the break in tradition they said nothing. Civic pride made it understandable that a man would not quickly ride on.

Yet when a week had passed, Montana noticed that his welcome was visibly wearing thin. Free drinks ceased to come, and at the restaurant there had been a noticeable coolness when he walked out without paying. Montana considered riding on. He started for the stable, but then he stopped, rolling a cigarette.

Why leave? This was perfect, the most beautiful setup he had ever walked into. Kilkenny himself was far away; maybe he was dead. In any event, there wasn't one chance in a thousand he would show up in the border jumping-off place on the Rio Grande. So why not make the most of it?

Who could stop him? Wilder had been the town's toughest and fastest gun.

Abruptly, Croft turned on his heel and walked into the hardware store. Hammet was wrapping a package of shells for a rancher, and when the man was gone, Croft looked at the storekeeper. "Hammet," he said, and his voice was low and cold, "I need fifty dollars."

John Hammet started to speak, but something in the cool, hard-eyed man warned him to hold his tongue. This man was Kilkenny, and he himself had seen him down Johnny Wilder. Hammet swallowed, "Fifty dollars?" he said.

"That's right, Hammet."

Slowly, the older man turned to his cash drawer and took out the bill. "Never minded loaning a good man money," he said, his voice shaking a little.

Croft took the money and looked at Hammet. "Thanks, and between the two of us, I ain't anxious for folks to know I'm short. Nobody does know but you. So I'd know where to come if it was talked around. Get me?" With that, he walked out.

Montana Croft knew a good thing when he saw it. His first round of the town netted him four hundred dollars. A few ranchers here and there boosted the ante. Nobody challenged his claim. All assumed the demands were for loans. It was not until Croft made his second round, two weeks later, that it began to dawn on some of them that they had acquired a burden.

Yet Croft was quiet. He lived on the fat of the land, yet he drank but sparingly. He troubled no one. He minded his own affairs, and he proceeded to milk the town as a farmer milks a cow.

Nor would he permit any others to trespass upon his territory. Beak and Jesse Kennedy discovered that, to their sorrow. Two hard cases from the north, they drifted into town and after a drink or two, proceeded to hold up the bank.

Montana Croft, watching from the moment they rode in, was ready for them. As they emerged from the bank he stepped from the shadow of the hardware store with a shotgun. Beak never knew what hit him. He sprawled face

down in the dust, gold spilling out of his sack into the
street. Jesse Kennedy whirled and fired, and took Croft's
second barrel in the chest.

Montana walked coolly over and gathered up the
money. He carried the sacks inside and handed them back
to Jim Street. He grinned a little and then shoved a hand
down into one of the sacks and took out a fistful of gold.
"Thanks," he said, and walked out.

Boquilla was of two minds about their uninvited guest.
Some wished he would move on about his business, but
didn't say it; others said it was a blessing he was there to
protect the town. And somehow the news began to get
around of what was happening.

And then Montana Croft saw Margery Furman.

Margery was the daughter of old Black Jack Furman,
Indian fighter and rancher, and Margery was a thing of
beauty and a joy forever—or so Montana thought.

He met her first on the occasion of his second decision to leave town. He had been sitting in the saloon
drinking and felt an uneasy twinge of warning. It was time
to go. It was time now, to leave. This had been good, too
good to be true, and it was much too good to last. Take
them for all he could get, but leave before they began to
get sore. And they were beginning to get sore now. It was
time to go.

He strode to the door, turned right, and started for
the livery stable. And then he saw Margery Furman getting out of a buckboard. He stared, slowed, stopped, shoved
his hat back on his head—and became a man of indecision.

She came toward him, walking swiftly. He stepped
before her. "Hi," he said, "I haven't seen you before."

Margery Furman knew all about the man called
Kilkenny. She had known his name and fame for several
years, and she had heard that he was in Boquilla. Now she
saw him for the first time and confessed herself disap-
pointed. Not that he was not a big and fine-looking man,
but there was something, some vague thing she had expected to find, lacking.

"Look," he said, "I'd like to see you again. I'd like to
see more of you."

"If you're still standing here when I come back," she old him, "you can see me leave town."

With that she walked on by and into the post office.

Croft stood still. He was shaken. He was smitten. He vas worried. Leaving town was forgotten. The twinge of varning from the gods of the lawless had been forgotten. Ie waited.

On her return, Margery Furman brushed past him and efused to stop. Suddenly, he was angered. He got quickly o his feet. "Now look here," he said, "you—!"

Whatever he had been about to say went unsaid. A ider was walking a horse down the street. The horse was . long-legged buckskin; the man was tall and wore a lat-brimmed, flat-crowned black hat. He wore two guns, ung low and tied down.

Suddenly, Montana Croft felt very sick. His mouth vas dry. Margery Furman had walked onto her buck->oard, but now she looked back. She saw him standing here, flat-footed, his face white. She followed his eyes.

The tall newcomer sat his buckskin negligently. He ooked at Croft through cold green eyes from a face burned lark by the sun and wind. And he did not speak. For a ong, full minute, the two stared. Then Croft's eyes dropped .nd he started toward the buckboard, but then turned oward the livery stable.

He heard a saddle creak as the stranger dismounted. Ie reached the stable door and then turned and looked ack. Margery Furman was in her buckboard, but she was itting there, holding the reins.

The stranger was fifty yards from Montana Croft now, ut his voice carried. It was suddenly loud in the street. Heard there was a gent in town who called himself Kilkenny. Are you the one?"

As if by magic, the doors and windows were filled vith faces, the faces of the people he had robbed again .nd again. His lips tried to shape words of courage, but hey would not come. He tried to swallow, but gulp as he vould, he could not. Sweat trickled into his eyes and marted, but he dared not move a hand to wipe it away.

"I always heard Kilkenny was an honest man, a man vho set store by his reputation. Are you an honest man?"

Croft tried to speak but could not.

"Take your time," the stranger's voice was cold, "take your time, then tell these people you're not Kilkenny. Tell them you're a liar and a thief."

He should draw . . . he should go for his gun now . . . he should kill this stranger . . . kill him or die.

And that was the trouble. He was not ready to die and die he would if he reached for a gun.

"Speak up! These folks are waitin'! Tell them!"

Miraculously, Croft found his voice. "I'm not Kilkenny," he said.

"The rest of it." There was no mercy in this man.

Montana Croft suddenly saw the truth staring him brutally in the face. A man could only die once if he died by the gun, but if he refused his chance now he would die many deaths . . .

"All right, damn you!" he shouted the words. "I'm not Kilkenny! I'm a liar an I'm a thief, but I'll be damned if I'm a yellowbellied coward!"

His hands dropped, and suddenly, with a shock of pure realization, he knew he was making the fastest draw he had ever made. Triumph leaped within him and burst in his breast. He'd show them! His guns sprang up . . . and then he saw the blossoming rose of flame at the stranger's gun muzzle and he felt the thud of the bullet as it struck him.

His head spun queerly and he saw a fountain of earth spring from the ground before him, his own bullet kicking the dust. He went down, losing his gun, catching himself on one hand. Then that arm gave way and he rolled over, eyes to the sun.

The man stood over him. Montana Croft stared up. "You're Kilkenny?"

"I'm Kilkenny." The tall man's face was suddenly soft. "You made a nice try."

"Thanks . . ."

Montana Croft died there in the street of Boquilla, without a name that anyone knew.

Margery Furman's eyes were wide. "You . . . you're Kilkenny?" For this time it was there, that something she

ad looked for in the face of the other man. It was there,
he kindliness, the purpose, the strength.

"Yes," he said. And then he fulfilled the tradition. He
ode out of town.

About Louis L'Amour

I think of myself in the oral tradition—as a troubadour, a village tale-ller, the man in the shadows of the campfire. That's the way I'd like to e remembered—as a storyteller. A good storyteller."

is doubtful that any author could be as at home in the world re-cre-ted in his novels as Louis Dearborn L'Amour. Not only could he hysically fill the boots of the rugged characters he wrote about, but he terally "walked the land my characters walk." His personal experi-aces as well as his lifelong devotion to historical research combined to ve Mr. L'Amour the unique knowledge and understanding of people, vents, and the challenge of the American frontier that became the hall-aarks of his popularity.

Of French-Irish descent, Mr. L'Amour could trace his own family in orth America back to the early 1600s and follow their steady progres-on westward, "always on the frontier." As a boy growing up in amestown, North Dakota, he absorbed all he could about his family's ontier heritage, including the story of his great-grandfather who was alped by Sioux warriors.

Spurred by an eager curiosity and desire to broaden his horizons, Ir. L'Amour left home at the age of fifteen and enjoyed a wide variety f jobs including seaman, lumberjack, elephant handler, skinner of dead attle, miner, and an officer in the transportation corps during World Iar II. During his "yondering" days he also circled the world on a eighter, sailed a dhow on the Red Sea, was shipwrecked in the West dies and stranded in the Mojave Desert. He won fifty-one of fifty-nine ghts as a professional boxer and worked as a journalist and lecturer. e was a voracious reader and collector of rare books. His personal orary contained 17,000 volumes.

Mr. L'Amour "wanted to write almost from the time I could talk." fter developing a widespread following for his many frontier and lventure stories written for fiction magazines, Mr. L'Amour published s first full-length novel, *Hondo,* in the United States in 1953. Every te of his more than 100 books is in print; there are nearly 260 million opies of his books in print worldwide, making him one of the best-lling authors in modern literary history. His books have been trans-ted into twenty languages, and more than forty-five of his novels d stories have been made into feature films and television movies.

His hardcover bestsellers include *The Lonesome Gods, The Walking rum* (his twelfth-century historical novel), *Jubal Sackett, Last of the reed,* and *The Haunted Mesa.* His memoir, *Education of a Wandering an,* was a leading bestseller in 1989. Audio dramatizations and adap-tions of many L'Amour stories are available on cassette tapes from antam Audio publishing.

The recipient of many great honors and awards, in 1983 Mr. Amour became the first novelist ever to be awarded the Congressional old Medal by the United States Congress in honor of his life's work. 1984 he was also awarded the Medal of Freedom by President eagan.

Louis L'Amour died on June 10, 1988. His wife, Kathy, and their vo children, Beau and Angelique, carry the L'Amour tradition forward ith new books written by the author during his lifetime to be published Bantam.

LOUIS L'AMOUR

AMERICA'S FAVORITE FRONTIER WRITER

Be sure to read all of the titles in the Sackett series: follow them
from the Tennessee mountains as they head west to ride the trails,
pan the gold, work the ranches, and make the laws.